AMERICAN BLASPHEMER

AMERICAN BLASPHEMER

a novel

John Matthew Gillen

Epigraph Books
Rhinebeck, New York

Paperback ISBN 978-1-951937-12-6
eBook ISBN 978-1-951937-13-3

Library of Congress Control Number: 2020903573

Book design by Colin Rolfe

Cover photo by Berenice Abbot, 1937, courtesy of the New York Public Library

Epigraph Books
22 East Market Street, Suite 304
Rhinebeck, New York 12572
(845) 876-4861
epigraphps.com

Contents

a friend of mine told me he's taken a new job
he's going to be a big shot

he also mentioned
that last weekend
he'd spent
at the beach
with *her*
making love
making plans
and making love again
I shook his hand
and smiled
and something died

I walked home
past the Museum of Sex
with its clean windows
full of pretty young women
handling huge synthetic penises
and laughing

further down the street
I saw two feral dogs
breeding
in a Manhattan alley

The Clumsy Panting of Drooling Mouths
The Amorous Frenzy of Ravenous Lust
The Graceless Spasms of Imbecile Flesh

and
for the first time
I felt myself
briefly make peace
with atheism

I've read many scriptures
many times
but there is
no gospel
no apologetic
no philosophy
against
The Humid Fornication of the Feral Dogs of Suicide

it is this gospel
which
I
intend
to
write

Christmas in Wonderland

Last Christmas my brother David ate a headful of acid then we went to church in tailored suits and put five thousand dollars cash in the collection plate. Jesus said the woman with the two mites had given more than all the rich men with their bags of coins. What about our torn envelope of filthy dollars? What would Jesus say about that? He doesn't say much about anything these days. The guy with the collection plate sure as all hell didn't say anything about it. Not one Goddamn word. Not even "Merry Christmas."

Down the Rabbit Hole

It started with the drive down. Donny and I were both in New York and we had to drive home to Virginia for Christmas. When the engine turned over in Donny's truck, the red beeping light told us we needed an oil change. Mr. Goodlube was closed. We decided to just go.

Fuck it.

My younger brother Donny is what they put into the bombs that won World War II. He's started three companies, outrun the police half a dozen times, and is the only person I know who is just as comfortable in a Fortune 100 boardroom as he is at an EDM festival. He's sharp, and thin, and he looks like Clint Eastwood. Whenever I see him, he asks me to do psychedelic drugs.

I Am the Walrus

"Dude, do you still not do drugs?"

Jesus Christ, here we go again.

"No, Donny."

"John, I'm telling you, man—you gotta do fuckin' drugs."

"Okay, thanks," I said, trying to get him to drop it, but my noncombatant attitude only made him dial up the intensity.

"No, now look. You know I love you and I respect you and your rules and shit, but I've been doing a lot of weed, acid, and shrooms lately—and I'm fucking telling you—you gotta do fuckin' drugs."

"Donny, we've been over this."

"I have talked to God. Do you understand what I'm saying to you?"

"Just drive the car," I said pointing at the road. He kept his eyes on me.

"Like I know what you think God is, and I'm telling you—I know what that *really is* and that I've experienced it."

"Okay."

"Don't just say okay. Do it."

"No, Donny."

"Why not?"

"Because that doesn't help, alright? It's like using a cheat code. I mean, okay, maybe you've experienced God. Fine. I can't question that. I don't even know what that means, but I can tell you that it's not something that can be communicated or reliably reproduced for someone else."

"So, the fuck what?"

"So, that makes it useless. How am I supposed to help anyone with that? If you can't explain it, or write it down, or paint it, or sing it, or make it a fucking movie or something—then it's like it never happened. It's just vanity. It's masturbation. It's immoral. I'm not sure how, but I just know it is. So, before I dive into all of that I want to try things my way first."

"Whaddya mean—like with words and shit?"

"I don't know, maybe."

"Well, you're never gonna find it if you don't take DMT. That's all I'm sayin'," Donny tightened his grip on the wheel.

"No, that's fuckin' bullshit. That's the whole point of life and art, man. Finding the absolute in the relative. The timeless in the temporal. The fuckin' spiritual in the—the fuckin'—I mean William Blake had it all down—and Schopenhauer and stuff. It's fuckin' Mahayana man. Samsara and Nirvana are one." I knew he didn't understand what I meant by that, but it sounded good.

Donny shook his head. "What the fuck are you—Dude, why do you always make everything so—okay—have you ever seen *Alice in Wonderland*?"

Right away I spouted off, "The time has come, the walrus said, to talk of other things. Of shoes, and ships, and sealing wax. Of cabbages and kings. And why the sea is boiling hot. And whether pigs have wings."

He gave me a blank stare. "John, what the fuck are you talking about?"

"What? The walrus—it's from the book."

He shook his head again. "You're so fuckin' weird."

Fuck it.

A Long-Expected Mad Tea Party

We got to our parent's house at about one in the morning. Our headlights pushed back the winter night to reveal our oldest brother, David, standing out in the middle of the yard. There were two years between each of us, and even though I was in the middle, I'd always sort of been the big brother of the family.

David was barefoot and wearing a red silk robe that hung open to reveal a leopard-print thong. He squinted at us through yellow-tinted Ray-Ban shooters, just like the ones Hunter S. Thompson used to wear. The portable speaker cradled in his arms was blasting Captain Beefheart, and upon his head, with a regal tilt, sat his custom-fitted, oversized Mad Hatter's hat.

"Ah, fuck he's already high," Donny said as he parked and turned off the truck. David came walking out of the darkness like he was ready for a reckoning.

"Hi, David," I said.

"Our father has been three inches tall his entire life," David said through gritted teeth.

"Okay, David—let's get you inside." I touched his arm. He was shivering. I could tell he'd already taken a self-destructive dose of Val Kilmer and God knows what else. That's part of the code we use. I'd tell you what that means, but that defeats the purpose of having the code. We all went to David's room and talked. It was good to be home with my brothers again. None of the old wars, just love. Then Donny went to see a woman, and David and I started watching movies.

Traditions of Men

There are weird holiday traditions in every family. For Christmas, most people put up a tree, or go caroling, or do whatever the fuck these fucking Walmart Christians do. I don't know. Fuck that shit. In my family we don't put out cookies for Santa, buy festive sweaters, or hang stockings— and we don't give gifts anymore either. Every Christmas Eve, David eats eight hits of pure white LSD 25, and he and I watch *The Lord of The Rings* trilogy all the way through. A lot of people can't understand this, but that's part of our religion. I'd tell you what that means, but that defeats the purpose of having the Goddamned religion.

Since I was a boy, I've always been able to watch movies in enormous quantities without losing focus. David is the only person I've ever known who can movie as hard as I can, but even he gets tired sometimes. After the third or fourth feature film it starts to hurt. If this happens, David takes a big whiff of isobutyl nitrate. Poppers.

He sticks a little black bottle of the highly volatile liquid up one nostril and inhales like he's been underwater for too long. Then he holds his breath until he turns red as a lobster and falls on the floor stamping and writhing and doesn't let go until he breaks a sweat. That lights him up enough to stay awake and fight through the pain. I stay up just as long as he does, but I do it sober as a hanging judge. Not that it doesn't hurt me just as badly, it's just that I've given up trying to escape from pain. That's part of my religion too. I just watch the movies.

Breakfast

After *Return of The King* we put on *Elvis: Aloha from Hawaii* first thing on Christmas morning. My parents get up very early, but they know not to come wake us on this or any other morning. I'm not sure what they think is going on—we've never discussed it—but it doesn't matter. They have their breakfast, we have ours, and Elvis Presley is the best thing in the world for an acid comedown after a night of foul monsters and crazy debauchery. Elvis is the Great American Answer to all of God's little prisons. And so, it has become tradition that every Christmas morning finds David and I thanking God for Elvis Presley.

When the concert is over and my father has had his coffee, we come out to eat. The fighting starts as soon as my parents and brothers are all gathered around the kitchen table again. Usual shit. Go to church, shave, don't use bad words, why don't you work harder, drink your milk, and so on.

Donny wanted to bring his girlfriend over for dinner to meet our parents. They said no. Called him a failure, and a fornicator, and a bunch of other cruel things. Told me I was throwing my life away. Said I was never going to make it as an artist in New York and told me to just give up and come home. I don't remember most of this. You have to tune out noise like that at some point.

The Slaughter of the Holy Innocents

My brothers are drug people, and drug people get a lot of shit, but I'll say one thing for 'em—I've never seen a person who had a serious drug situation quibble with someone over petty bullshit. Once you've seen your body melting into the carpet while little green men are fucking your earlobes, you stop giving a shit if someone moves your laundry hamper.

After a steady stream of ridicule from Dad, David said he wanted to kill himself. Mom said she didn't care, as long as he didn't make a big bloody mess on her white carpets—which is a heavy thing to lay on a wild bastard who's been up for days, twisted on drugs, killing Orcs in Middle Earth—especially if it's coming from his mother. I mean—Jesus Christ, he's just a boy, for God's sake.

Fucking savages.

David smashed something, and the three of us went back into his room. We huddled in the corner while my father pounded on the locked door. I held David in my arms while he screamed about wanting to die. Hot tears dripped onto my chest. He kept saying how much he loved me. Donny took pulls from a bottle of Jack and talked about how much he loved David and how much he didn't want him to die.

They were both crying and howling and talking about love. David cried till he threw up. I was laughing my guts out. It was all so absurd. I've never known anyone like my brothers—these magnificent Quasimodo souls afflicted with deep passion trying to make peace. It was the first time in years we'd all been together on Christmas.

Puke and hot tears.

Dinner

Come time for dinner we couldn't figure out plans. Dad was mad, Mom was indifferent, Donny was off somewhere with a woman again, and David was scared to go out in public because he'd taken too much of the Jimi Hendrix. He didn't say this to our parents, of course. He's suicidal, but he's not stupid.

I got us a reservation at an upscale restaurant downtown. When I told David, the horror seized him immediately. He said it was impossible. He simply could not go outside while the spirit was still on him. I started singing the lyrics to Dylan's *Rainy Day Women #12 & 35* about how everybody must get stoned. Most people think that song is about drugs, but Dylan said he had the book of Acts in mind. The part where they stoned Stephen while the Apostle Paul held their coats.

David was dressed and ready to go before I finished the second verse.

Fuck it.

An hour later, I was sitting in an elegant family restaurant listening to Nat King Cole with David and our parents. Two well dressed, Republican, *Leave It to Beaver*, evangelical Christians—and a degenerate, militant, hedonist with his consciousness caught in a rainbow typhoon of weapons-grade LSD.

The waiter had just taken my appetizer order when I saw Donny come into the restaurant with his phone to his ear. He was calling me. I answered.

"Hey, I'm here, where are you?" Donny said.

"I'm waving," I said with my hand in the air.

"Okay, I see you, Dude. I brought Cassie."

"Who's Cassie?"

"This chick I've been banging out, the amateur porn star I told you about."

"What?"

"This is gonna be awesome. They have no idea."

"Donny you brought a —" I looked at my Mother and stopped myself,

"—you brought a *model* to dinner?"

He laughed hard at the euphemism. "Yeah, she's nineteen and she makes a living masturbating online. You fucking believe that? She pays her rent with a set of dildos and a web-cam. It's funny as shit, dude. Hey, hey—did you get spareribs? Tell that fuck I want spareribs."

"Yeah, I got 'em."

"Okay good. Dude, last night I fucked her till my eyes dried out. My cock's sore and my nuts still hurt."

"I'm very happy to hear that, now come sit down."

Go Ask Alice

That dinner was the most pleasant family meal we'd had in over a decade. David was too stoned to fight with anyone, Donny was finger blasting Cassie under the table, and my parents were on their best behavior because a stranger was among them. I ordered the porterhouse, and nobody fucked with me. Peace on Earth.

I talked to Cassie while Donny was in the bathroom. She's been drawing and painting all her life. Loves flowers. Cassie told me her real name is Pachysandra. She and her father used to garden together before her parents got divorced. She has a bookcase in her apartment with five hundred notebooks she's filled with sketches of flowers and plants and growing things. Doesn't show them to anyone, not even Donny, and she hasn't gardened since her father left.

Donny had his fingers back inside of her before I could ask her anything else. These days Cassie spends most of her time getting stoned and cumming in front of strangers online.

Sweet girl.

When *White Rabbit* Peaks

That night David and I watched *Labyrinth*, *Watership Down*, *Inherent Vice*, *The Rum Diary*, and *Alice in Wonderland*.

David kept taking things—Terence McKenna, Johnny Cash, God knows what else. I guess maybe you'll say I should have been watching him. Maybe you'll say that being sleep-deprived and lost in the movies is no excuse. Not when your brother's life is at stake. Maybe you'll say I'm supposed to be my brother's keeper. Maybe you'll say that's how Jesus wanted it. Well, he's not your fucking brother, he's mine. And Jesus never said anything about him. Not one Goddamn word. I know David sure as all hell didn't say anything about it. Right up until Alice met the hookah-smoking caterpillar.

David started to grunt and squirm. He lifted his hat and dragged a greasy paw through tangled black hair over and over with tweaky obsession. His fingers began plucking hairs out of his scalp. Carefully. One at a time. Like he'd found a foreign malignancy and was making a needed removal. I didn't take special notice of this as he was known to do a lot of strange things after receiving the elements, but as the ostentatious caterpillar blew his multicolored smoke, David's murmurs grew louder. Poor Alice was still small.

"I should like to be a little larger sir."

"Why?"

"Well after all, three inches is such a wretched height and—"

"I am exactly three inches high, and it is a very good height, indeed!"

(The Caterpillar got mad and turned into a butterfly.)

"One side will make you grow taller," the butterfly said.

"One side of *what?*"

"And the other side will make you grow shorter."

"The other side of *what?*"

David screamed the butterfly's reply so loudly and so violently that we both fell on the floor.

"THE MUSHROOM, OF COURSE!"

His screaming face landed on top of me. He was naked, twisted, and red.

"THE MUSHROOM, OF COURSE!"

"THE MUSHROOM, OF COURSE!"

"GAHHH!"

I was pinned to the ground.

"THREE INCHES!"

"THREE INCHES YOU FUCK!"

His hat fell off, and he put it back on.

"OUR FATHER HAS BEEN THREE INCHES HIS ENTIRE LIFE!"

"I'M TEN THOUSAND FEET TALL!"

"AND HE WANTS ME!"

"TO BE!"

"THREE!"

"FUCKING!"

"INCHES!"

"GAHHH!"

He screamed himself out and went limp.

I paused the movie.

Then I carried him to the bathroom.

For the next hour David alternated between vomiting and diarrhea, which was impressive, considering he'd been fasting for more than a day. All prophets fast, but David is the only one who pukes. He knelt when he puked, and sat when he shat, like a good Catholic at Mass. Most people don't involve God in Christmas because he tends to spoil their plans, but David demanded divine participation. David didn't want a Norman Rockwell Christmas—he wanted a showdown with the Almighty.

And he got it.

I suppose you'll say I should have taken him to a hospital, and I guess I would agree with that, but no doctor could fix what was wrong with David, and he'd already taken plenty of medicine. So, I put Lou Reed's *Waves of Fear* on the portable speaker and sat beside him on the bathroom floor. David lifted his head from the bowl and looked at me through raw, salty eyes. A long string of saliva and vomit clung to his lip. We were in there for a couple of hours and in all that time he could only push one sentence through the honey-thick glaze of sleepless drug-induced stupor that hung over him. Each word left a slime trail across the electric guitar riffs that filled the air.

"There's only one way to stop a mad watch," David said as he fixed his hat.

To Rule Them All

I convinced David to join me for church with Mom and Dad on Christmas morning. On the way out, Dad reminded us to pay tithes. David had a few remarks about this request.

"He thinks that makes him a good person—all his fucking money. He spent his whole life on that. His entire life he's just been cutting the lawn, and going to work, and paying his fucking tithes, and for what? Huh? What the fuck does all that even mean? Does that make him a Holy Man or something?"

"I couldn't say," I said.

"Why is he imposing his dick on me!? Why do I have to do whatever the fuck he says? Giving them that fucking money isn't going to change anything. Not one Goddamn thing."

"I'm not telling you to do anything, David," I told him.

"Good, 'cause I'm not. Fuck 'em, you understand me? Fuck 'em. They're all hypocrites and pharisees. If Jesus Christ set foot in that place, he'd fucking puke. They're a bunch of stuck-up fake fuckers and they can all go fuck themselves."

"Alright, calm down." David never calms down.

"I don't need some car salesman with an outdated rule book telling me who I can fuck, and what I can eat, and how to hold my cock when I piss. My third eye is wide fucking open. I've seen Baphomet masturbating in the dark—do you understand that? I don't have to put up with some cunt in dockers telling *me* about God."

"I know, David."

"Fucking money. Fucking money. That's all they want is the fucking Christ-fuck money!"

David went to his room and pulled a crinkled envelope wrapped in rubber bands out of his wall safe, then stomped back to the kitchen and flung it across the table. "Help me count this. Help me count their Goddamn money."

I counted three thousand dollars.

"Good. There's three grand for those fuckers. Do you think that's enough to make Jesus love me? Merry fucking un-birthday, Jesus—here's three thousand pieces of love. Please let the Orioles win next year."

I discreetly added my twenty, crisp, hundred-dollar bills to the envelope. David grabbed it and we went to church.

When the ushers came down the aisle to receive the offering, they found David and I sitting next to our parents in tailored suits completely out of our minds with Christmas cheer. We smiled and put five thousand dollars of illicit monies into the collection plate.

And nobody said a Goddamn word.

The Queen of Hearts

Donny and Cassie broke up after that dinner. He drove her to her apartment—they smoked, fucked, fought, and that was it. I haven't seen her since, but I know where to look if I ever want to, because she sent me a link with VIP access.

Advent of The Bodhisattva

When David finally stopped puking and shitting, his naked body collapsed onto the cold tile. Neither of us had slept in days, and he hadn't eaten anything since I'd been home except the sacraments. He looked thin, like butter scraped over too much bread. His words crawled out from under labored breath.

"I'm too orange for this entire situation."

"I know, David."

"I'm ten thousand feet tall."

"I know, David."

"There's only one way to stop a mad watch."

"I know, David."

He lifted his head and looked at me.

"John?"

"Yeah?"

"The Rabbi is busy."

"I know, David."

He smiled and laid his head back down.

"Feed my sheep," he said.

"I love you too, David."

His eyes closed and he began to dissolve.

"Feed my sheep."

Once he was gone, I put him to bed.

Still with his hat on.

A Very Merry Un-Birthday

When Christmas was over, David put on a suit and went back to work, Samwise went back to The Shire, Alice returned to London Town, and I crawled back to Manhattan.

Mom and Dad called and said they'd had a great time.

Donny called and said the same.

David told me to take DMT rectally.

Jesus Christ could not be reached for comment.

But there's always next year.

Baked Beans

When I was five years old my father nearly choked me to death with baked beans. Mom cooked rice and beans for dinner one night, and when I tasted them, I declined to eat them. So did David and Donny. My father rubbed a fistful of beans in David's face and Donny screamed in his highchair as I fled the table. My father chased me with a plate of the dreadful beans. I could hear him yelling and making threats as I scrambled up the stairs to the second floor of our suburban home. At the time, David and I shared a bedroom, which was where I usually sought sanctuary—but, before I could hide, I was snatched off the floor and thrown onto David's bed.

My father pinned me down and held my nose while he forced a spoonful of pungent beans into my mouth. I gagged. Hard. His giant hand clamped over my mouth. I couldn't spit, chew, or breathe. My whole body clenched. I vomited. But with his hand pressed over my face, there was nowhere for it to go. I felt the slime packing into my ears. Then, realizing I was going to die if I didn't clear my windpipe, I choked down the ghastly discharge like a python swallowing a pig. It was over fifteen years before I could eat baked beans again without violently gagging. They used to make fun of me for it in Scouts.

After I finished my dinner, I went limp, and my father left me alone. I laid on David's bed looking up at the ceiling and went into one of the first, great, emotional crises of my life. There were several such times in my childhood. Hours passed with angry tears, wishing to unmake the universe because I could see no virtue in it.

On some level, I have never forgiven my family for the abuses of my childhood. My mother wasn't responsible. She is a good woman, but she had been taught helplessness and lived for thirty years as though ignoring problems would make them go away. My brothers were not responsible either. They were bad kids, but bad kids are, at least in part, the responsibility of their parents. A father is the God of a child's universe. He's supposed to be benevolent and righteous. When he repeatedly fails to protect his child, or to do something that the child knows to be morally right, it destroys the child's basic faith in the idea of justice and leaves the child with a sense that the world is evil.

I lay on my older brother's bed with the revolting beans clogging my sinus passage and raged for about an hour. As upset and I was about what had just happened, I was more upset about what I knew would happen next.

Later that night, our father came into our bedroom in his bathrobe and tenderly told David and I how much he loved us and how sorry he was that he had lost his temper. I didn't plead with him not to do it again, and I wasn't moved by his tearful apology, as I had been in the past. By this time, my five-year-old brain had detected a pattern that would be a daily source of suffering for my family for the rest of our lives.

Rage addiction. An endless cycle of manic abuse with no beginning or end. My father must have put this system in place a long time ago in order to cope with his own existence—a self-defense mechanism he established in response to circumstances beyond his control. Even though my instinct told me to be angry with him, he wasn't responsible either. He'd simply been forced to rely on a bad system, a system which meant that I was going to have to tolerate a lot of abuse in my life, especially because my brothers adopted this behavior as well.

I learned many lessons of darkness as a young man, but I learned other things too. Once, during a church service when I was about thirteen, a little girl stepped out of the pew and started walking up the aisle. She stopped and vomited all over the carpeted sanctuary floor. Her mother took her hand and led her out, leaving the mess behind. Without hesitation, my father went out and got some cleaning supplies from the janitor's closet. He got down on his knees in his two-thousand-dollar suit and cleaned up the vomit. It wasn't his job. Nobody asked him to— he just saw a problem and helped. I've never forgotten that simple act of service. Love—Christian charity—is sacrifice.

The lessons sons learn from their fathers are often the ones that decide what kind of man they will become. I learned that there are no good men, that love is sacrifice, and that the world is full of evil. I learned that the easy path is usually the wrong one and that everyone must survive on their own. I learned that anger and violence do not solve problems, and I learned that baked beans taste better with rice.

Heartbreak, Prostitution, and the International House of Pancakes

The winter after college graduation was one of the worst times of my life. I had fallen in love with a woman with whom I had no right to be in love. I had tried to commit to her and to God and ended up sinning against them both. It was all very complicated. She finally decided to end it. We had brunch one morning, and she told me she didn't want to be dating anyone anymore.

And so, at the beginning of winter after college graduation I lost my God and the woman I loved. For a long time, I didn't know who I was or why I was living. I lost fifteen pounds and slept two hours in the first three days after that brunch. The panic attacks were nearly constant. My behavior was erratic, my moods shifted between numb and suicidal. There was no color. No flavor. No meaning. Weeks passed in a painful blur.

Stacey

Between 2:00 and 5:00 a.m. on a weeknight in December or February, I was sitting in an IHOP ordering food from a waitress named Stacey. I was the only one in the restaurant. Stacey sat down to keep me company. I don't remember much of that winter, other than the pain, but I remember Stacey very well. She was a sixty-four-year-old great-grandmother who had never been married and who worked as a waitress on the graveyard shift at an IHOP in Northern Virginia. She used to be a child psychologist and guidance counselor at a school in Tennessee, but there were budget cuts, and Stacey lost her job. She started working as a waitress at an IHOP in Memphis.

One day, her manager found out she'd been fucking the busboy. This wouldn't have been such a big problem, except that the busboy, who had sworn he was eighteen, turned out to be a sixteen-year-old illegal immigrant. The manager told Stacey he wouldn't turn her over to the cops, but he had to fire both of them.

She went home and told her boyfriend. He was upset, but not because she had been fucking the underaged busboy, he was upset because she had been fired. Stacey and her boyfriend were quite fond of meth, and losing her job meant they wouldn't be able to afford it anymore. So Stacey's boyfriend did what he usually did when he was upset.

He beat the shit out of her.

Among other things, he broke several of her ribs with a baseball bat. She waited until he drank himself to sleep, as he did almost every night, then she quickly packed and drove away. Even though she had a huge family of bastard children, she knew that none of them could afford to take her in, so she found a place far away from her boyfriend where she could get a job quick.

After changing her name, "Stacey" became a waitress on the graveyard shift at an IHOP in Northern Virginia. But waitresses live off tips, and waitresses on the graveyard shift at IHOPs in Northern Virginia in the dead of winter don't get a lot of tips. At this point, Stacey had less than one hundred dollars to her name. So, in her spare time Stacey returned to a vocation that she hadn't pursued since she was very young. Back then it had just been a fun way for a sexy southern girl to make extra money and party the way she wanted, but the parties were over now. Fifty-five years of drug addiction, abusive men, six bastard children, God knows how many grandchildren, and at least four great-grandchildren had worn away all the fun. Now someone's sweet innocent daughter was just a flat-broke, meth-addicted, cock-sucking whore named Stacey.

And sometime between 2:00 and 5:00 a.m. on a cold Goddamned winter night in December or February, she saw a young man with a scraggly beard sitting alone in her section with a look on his face darker than the night he had walked out of.

She had seen that look before.

He looked like a customer.

She asked if I could use some company and sat with me while I struggled to eat. She told me about some of the Johns she'd been with and their strange fetishes—all the sick, depraved things she'd had to do so she wouldn't starve on the street. She laughed about it, but you could hear something behind her laugh that said part of her soul had died.

As she talked, I thought about Rahab the Harlot.

Rahab and Bertha

In the book of Joshua, Joshua leads the nation of Israel to the promised land, but they are blocked by the walled city called Jericho. Joshua sends two spies to scout the city, and they are almost caught and killed, but this woman named Rahab hides Joshua's spies and helps them escape. In return, God spares her life when the walls come down. She had a few great-grandchildren too, among them King David and Jesus Christ.

I always found it annoying that Rahab is referred to as "Rahab the Harlot." She helped save Israel, and the only thing we remember about her is that, for part of her life, she was a whore. As if that makes her different from other people.

I also thought about the movie *Boxcar Bertha* where Martin Scorsese plays a John who has just had sex with Bertha, paid, and is about to leave—but instead turns to her and says, "If I pay you fifteen dollars, can I sleep here? I don't want to be alone tonight."

Bertha silently nods, and they go back to bed.

Ribs

Stacey and I had a lot of things in common. She loved meth, and I felt like getting stoned too. Personally, I'd prefer cocaine, but it makes no difference. It's all just artificial love for people who can't get the real thing.

Stacey had fucked hundreds of men and women. I wanted to have sex with the woman I loved, but instead I chose, as Paul says, to "abstain from fornication." I'm still wrestling with that decision. Even though I can't change my answer anymore. Maybe Stacey was right. Maybe I was wrong. But I think most likely we were both wrong.

We both had just been through bad breakups.

And then there were the ribs.

When I was about eight, I got hit in the chest with a baseball bat while trying to break up a fight. To this day, I have a dent in the left side of my torso just below my heart. I have often wondered what would have happened if I'd been hit a couple of inches higher and the bones had punctured my heart. Anyway, the point is Stacey and I had both had our ribs broken, in almost the same place, by angry men with baseball bats.

After thinking over everything we had in common, I realized how little difference there was between us. When you come right down to it, the only differences were our age, sex, and faith in Jesus Christ. But time is an illusion, so age is meaningless. A person's sex doesn't define them, and faith is something that can be lost or found in a matter of seconds. The only real difference between us was our choices—the choices we had made and the choices we had yet to make.

A Generous Man

Then suddenly she said, "I like spending time with handsome, strong, young men like you. As long as they are generous, of course. You are a generous man, aren't you John?"

"Yes," said the lonely man with the punctured heart, "yes, I am."

I waited until her shift ended and then took her back to her grimy, extended-stay motel. We talked for a while, but she'd had enough conversation.

"So, what can I do for you, John?" She offered me everything. Everything except what I wanted. I wanted to not be alone, but there was only one woman who could make me feel that way, and it wasn't Stacey. What I really wanted was Love, because only Love drives out loneliness. I tried to explain, but Stacey couldn't understand why I didn't want to have sex with her. Not that it matters, but for the record, I did want sex and I do want sex as badly as any man or woman does, I suppose. But I read somewhere that, "You can't fuck your way out of a lonely heart." That's not in the Bible, but it's still the Gospel according to John. Stacey was convinced that I wanted something so kinky I was embarrassed to ask for it, so she kept pressing me. Finally, I said, "If I pay you fifty dollars, can I sleep here? I don't want to be alone tonight."

Stacey silently nodded, and we went to bed.

Lullaby

Panic attacks are periods of sudden, intense fear accompanied by symptoms like heart palpitations, dizziness, shortness of breath, or feelings of unreality. If I think too long about that woman who broke up with me, I panic. Heavy breathing, strong muscle spasms—I even had heart palpitations for a couple of weeks. Panic attacks feel like you're being dragged to hell in a hurricane. I started getting them in college, but when I was with *her*, they stopped.

In *Avengers: Age of Ultron*, when they need to turn Hulk back into Bruce Banner, Black Widow touches his hand and looks into his eyes, and he has peace. They call it a lullaby. I know what that's like. But when I lost her the panic attacks came back. And this time, there were no lullabies. I would wake up sweating and screaming at 3:00 a.m. Out of breath. Always dreaming. But with Stacey asleep on my chest, I was able to relax a little and just breathe easily for an hour or two before I went back to work. I didn't sleep, just rested.

Maybe.

Maybe not.

Maybe that wasn't the choice I made.

Maybe Stacey said, "I like spending time with handsome, strong, young men like you. As long as they are generous, of course. You are a generous man, aren't you John?"

And maybe I was lonely, so she gave me one of the key cards to her room and I agreed to wait for her there.

Son of a Bitch

There is an organization called The Gideons that places a free Bible in every hotel room. I took Gideon's Bible out of Stacey's nightstand and opened it to the Gospel according to John, which is the Gospel written by Jesus's best friend, a man referred to as "the disciple whom Jesus loved."

I wrote, "Jesus loves you, Stacey" on the grimy, extended-stay motel stationery and placed the note on the open

Bible. I know that is a terrible cliché that has lost all meaning, but I like that.

The meaninglessness is holy.

I went downstairs and spoke to Emmanuel at the front desk. I made arrangements for Stacey to keep her room for as long as she needed it. Emmanuel asked me why I was doing this. I think he knew about Stacey's side job. Maybe he was a customer too—maybe even a regular. I told him I was her son. He knew I was lying, but I didn't care. The movie *Mean Streets* begins with Martin Scorsese speaking in voice-over narration saying, "You don't make up for your sins in church. You do it in the streets, you do it at home. The rest is bullshit and you know it."

That's not in the Bible either, but it's still the Gospel according to John.

While Emmanuel processed the payment, I asked if he'd ever seen *Mean Streets*.

He hadn't.

Emmanuel means "God with us."

I walked out of the motel into the cold Goddamn morning and drove home.

Tip Your Waitresses

Maybe.

Or maybe that's a lie too.

Maybe that's not the choice I made either.

Maybe what really happened is Stacey said, "I like spending time with handsome, strong, young men like you. As long as they are generous, of course. You are a generous man, aren't you John?"

And maybe I said I had to go home and get some rest. Maybe I ate my breakfast, tipped her twenty percent, and went home to bed like a good, innocent, Christian boy.

Or maybe she said, "I like spending time with handsome, strong, young men like you. As long as they are generous, of course. You are a generous man, aren't you John?"

And I was so lonely I took her back to her grimy extended-stay motel and spent over three hours fucking her in every hole she had and every position she knew. Just to make sure I wasn't missing out on anything. I could tell her body had been well-used, but she knew what she was doing. I came five times, showered, dressed, paid her six-hundred-and-fifty dollars I got out of an ATM downstairs, ate the extra omelet I'd brought back from IHOP, and drove to work with my heart beating a little slower and not thinking about God, or Jesus, or Martin Scorsese, or the girl I loved and the lost paradise of her lullaby eyes.

Maybe.

Maybe not.

Maybe I made some of these choices, maybe I didn't.

Maybe I made the whole thing up.

Maybe what happened is none of your Goddamned business.

Maybe what really happened doesn't matter.

Because there are millions of Staceys and millions of Johns and the point is not what happened to this particular Stacey and John, the point is the next time you find yourself on either side of this situation, what will you do? What choices will you make? Because all of us have suffered, and all of us have opportunities to take advantage of the suffering of others. And the only thing that makes us different, the only thing that matters, is the choices that we have made and the choices we have yet to make.

Man of Constant Sorrow

Matthew writes about John the Baptist and the beginning of Jesus's ministry. "In those days came John the Baptist, preaching in the wilderness of Judaea, And saying, repent ye: for the kingdom of heaven is at hand. For this is he that was spoken of by the prophet Esaias, saying, The voice of one crying in the wilderness, Prepare ye the way of the Lord, make his paths straight."

Jesus is baptized by John, then goes into the wilderness to be tempted by the Devil. While Jesus is gone, King Herod throws John the Baptist in jail.

"Now when Jesus had heard that John was cast into prison, he departed into Galilee; And leaving Nazareth, he came and dwelt in Capernaum …. From that time Jesus began to preach, and to say, Repent: for the kingdom of heaven is at hand."

This is the first time Jesus preaches, and he begins his ministry where John the Baptist left off by saying "repent," but there is no mention of temples. John the Baptist and Jesus of Nazareth were out in the wilderness, wandering city streets, preaching repentance to sinners. Because, like it says in *Mean Streets* and the Gospel according to John, you don't make up for your sins in church, you do it in the streets, you do it at home. The rest is bullshit and you know it.

The ending of this story is something you must daily choose for yourself, but as far as how to live, and what choices to make, I cannot advise you. I cannot recommend the choices that Stacey made, nor can I recommend my own fucked up life of sin or my Goddamn lonely love.

I cannot tell you what to do about the needs you have that go unmet.

I cannot tell you how to stop the panic attacks.

I cannot tell you how to ease a troubled mind or comfort a lonely heart.

I cannot advise you.

Isaiah, writing of the Messiah, said, "He is a man of sorrows, and well acquainted with grief." This man once said to love thy neighbor as thyself. He said to bless those who curse you and do good to them which despitefully use you. He said do unto others as you would have them do unto you. I believe this man of constant sorrow who wasted his time on sinners and whores was right. Even though everyone knows that no good Christian would ever associate with a sixty-four-year-old, poor, filthy, meth-addicted, cock-sucking whore who waits tables on the graveyard shift at an IHOP in Northern Virginia.

I guess Jesus wouldn't make a very good Christian.

The Gospel According to John

Maybe I'm wrong, though. I'm not sure of anything any-more, to be honest with you. I know I just got all preachy, but honest to God, I don't have any answers. I want to do the right thing, but it's impossible to know what the right thing is.

What was the right thing to do when I first met that woman I fell in love with?

What was the right thing to do when I met Stacey?

What would you have done?

What would Jesus have done?

What if sometimes there is no right thing to do?

What should I do now?

I don't know. And so, like everyone, I have sinned many sins. So, live your life and make your choices, and God help us all. Maybe Jesus is right, but maybe he is just as full of shit as I am.

I mean, what did Jesus know, anyway?

He was just another one of God's lonely men.

A man of sorrows and well-acquainted with grief.

Just another son of some whore.

Right?

Robotripping

Donny's Prescription for Heartbreak

Alright listen I'll tell ya what ya do
Ya go down to CVS
Get yourself a bottle of Robitussin
The regular shit, not extended release
DO. NOT. BUY. Extended release

Ya drink the bastard
Pray to God Jesus, lil' baby Jesus God, you don't throw up
That's no fun for anybody
Ya got this red mentholated puke shit all over
Burns like hell
It's awful

But if ya don't throw up
You sit the fuck down and chill out
Preferably, you watch a Disney movie, *Fantasia*, some bullshit
I watched *Pocahontas*
That—
That was like being born for a second time

Holy Christ, that was a great fuckin' movie

But look I'm just saying, if you're eighty-seven, you break your leg
At that point it's just like—fuck it
You know
You fuckin' do heroin
Fuck your brains out
Fuck it

Because we're all fucked anyway
More or less, you know
We're all guilty

But CVS
Ten bucks

Turn your couch into God

The Divine Comedy Isn't Funny

The National Headquarters of the United States Postal Service is the heart of darkness of American bureaucracy. I discovered this when I worked there one summer with four hundred other semiconscious parasites in a beige cubicle bay. These people relied on protocol for everything. They had policy for what to wear, what to say, what to think, and damn near everything else. They'd given up something. No one was steering their boats—they were just floating down the river.

Purgatory

My boss hated me. She was middle-aged and out-of-shape with a hundred thousand pictures of the same drooling mutt. We rarely spoke. I found out later she thought I was lazy. Although it's true I did a terrible job, in fairness, there wasn't much of a job to do. The whole operation had the personality of a pair of khakis and moved slower than a sloth in tar.

Of course, there were a few absurdities that gave the experience novelty. One guy at the office kept about fifty flavors of hot sauce on his desk and a couple dozen kinds of gum in his steel cabinet. He had a certificate over his cubicle that said: Best Collection. He was very proud of all this. I don't know why. We never spoke.

My favorite coworker was Flucker. That was his real, God-given name. I spent several hours on that. Flucker, Fluck you, Fluck me, Fluck that, go Fluck yourself, mother-Flucker, I don't give a flying Fluck, Fluck the Flucking Fluckers.

You get it.

Flucker was his last name too, which meant somewhere there was a whole flock of Fluckers. Generations of them. Flucked up from being tormented in elementary school. I never spoke to Flucker either, but I loved him dearly.

The guy who sat next to me was the one I hated the most. "Torrez" insisted that everyone call him by his last name and had been officially reprimanded about his body odor twice.

Officially.

By the United States Postal Service.

Twice.

Torrez wore a black, gestapo-style, leather overcoat in the humid summer swamp of Washington. His greasy, rattail hair went down to his ass, and he wore the worst bitch-fedora I've ever seen. Surprisingly, his officially fetid body odor and his sadomasochistic fashion crimes weren't the worst things about him. The worst thing about Torrez was his ringtone. This man had an overacted dramatic reading of *The Raven* by Edgar Allen Poe as the ringtone on his iPhone.

Imagine, if you will, sitting in this silent monochromatic workplace with four hundred strangers. No one speaks to you all day. You get a couple of emails, but you spend most of your time waiting for death and zooming in and out on blank spreadsheets. Then, "SUDDENLY THERE CAME A TAPPING AS OF SOMEONE GENTLY RAPPING, RAPPING AT MY CHAMBER DOOR!"

This happened several times a day. I hated Torrez and his stupid Warcraft guild.

Each day I rode the Metro an hour to work and an hour back. The Metro in the morning is Hell. Everyone looks dead, or like they'd rather be dead. It's always too crowded to sit, so you must stand there and breathe their death into you—feeling all of them wanting to die and touching you with their deaths. Helpless against the anonymous horde of death. Thousands of faces with a unique shade of suicidal depression riding along in subterranean steel coffins. A mass grave that's always behind schedule. A publicly funded hot box of death throttling through the long dark surrounded by the demonic shrieking of scraping metal and blue sparks. Hellscape by committee.

But one morning on the Metro a girl in a pink dress smiled at me. She did it again. We caught eyes once more and this time she laughed. I went over and asked for her number. She said she didn't give out her number, but she would take mine. Her cheeks were flushed and she was biting her lip. Her name was Deborah. We met for coffee the next morning.

Meet Me in Hell

Debbie wasn't especially attractive. Just another insecure twenty-something. College underclassman, you know the kind. She had a summer internship at the Smithsonian one stop from my office. She was an easy laugh, so I went for funny, and it worked. I knew it wouldn't go anywhere, and to be honest, I didn't want it to, but *you* try spending twelve hours a day riding the Metro and working in the National Headquarters of the United States Postal Service with no one to talk to—and see how you feel.

It was a question of sanity.

So, a few times a week for about two months, I swam out of the cubicle bay, walked two blocks down to the Smithsonian Castle, and had lunch with Debbie. It seemed a shame to squander our free access to the museums, so we started exploring. Our favorite was the Hirshhorn because it was packed with a lot of weird modern art. In one of the rooms upstairs was a big amorphous blob hanging from the ceiling. The fat sack of tiny white balls filled a huge room. I said it looked like a mind. Debbie laughed.

There was a uniformed guard in that room. His job was to guard the big sack of tiny white balls stapled to the ceiling of a windowless room on the National Mall. I thought about that a lot. Did he just stare at that ball sack all day? What if I pulled out my keys and tore a hole in the big sack? What would he do? Would he arrest me? Would I stand trial for tearing the Smithsonian's Ball Sack?

The basement of the Hirshhorn was red and black and covered floor-to-ceiling with white block print letters. It felt like God was screaming at you.

BELIEF + DOUBT = SANITY

WHO DIES FIRST? WHO LAUGHS LAST?

WHEN WAS THE LAST TIME YOU LAUGHED?

WHOSE POWER?

WHOSE VALUES?

WHO PRAYS THE LOUDEST?

WHO IS BEYOND THE LAW? WHO IS FREE TO CHOOSE?

WHO SPEAKS? WHO IS SILENT?

A RICH MAN'S JOKES ARE ALWAYS FUNNY

A toddler was having a tantrum on top of all these questions. Taking off his clothes and screaming through his tears. I said I guess he got frustrated trying to answer them all. Debbie didn't think that was funny. She said she wanted to leave. I followed her up the escalator. There was a small note—the only thing in the room that hadn't been written on the wall with the finger of God.

The materials for this project have been generously donated by [a very large corporation].

After seeing the little boy cry, Debbie didn't want to go the Hirshhorn anymore.

Debbie's office was somewhere in the basement of the Smithsonian African Art Museum. That summer their display was *The Divine Comedy: Heaven, Purgatory, and Hell Revisited by Contemporary African Artists.*

I never figured out the layout of that building. It was hexagonal with crisscrossing staircases. Everything looked the same. I couldn't track it. The walls were covered with red banners and quotes from Dante, like "The path to paradise begins in hell." and other cryptic shit like that.

I asked her if she thought *The Divine Comedy* was funny or not.

She laughed. I said I was serious. She said she hadn't read it.

She used to text me, "Meet me in Hell," when she was ready for me to come over for lunch. She thought that was funny. Hell was full of art. We went to Purgatory too. I assume we went to Paradise, but I don't remember it. Every time we came to the atrium, I looked for it, and I could see it up there. But when we walked up the stairs, we always seemed to end up at the exit. Once we tried the elevator. We got off and turned the corner and went down some stairs, but then we were back at the same spot at the elevators. Hopeless.

The Smithsonian Castle itself was very regal, but they had a crypt right by the front door, which I thought was odd. The remains of James Smithson were kept there in this ancient stone urn. He'd never been to America when he was alive, and I don't understand why he's here now. He died in Italy and was buried there. Then, about seventy-five years later, they dug him up and brought him to America. I'm not sure why they felt it was important to plant his ass right by the front door, but at least they gave him his own security guard.

My favorite exhibit was the movie theater. In one of the museums, there was a screening room that played the same short over and over all day. It was about five minutes long. There was a shot of a desert and a cracked road. A truck comes out of the desert and drives along the road toward the camera. Then there was a fade-out/fade-in to a reverse-angle shot, and the truck drove away and disappeared back into the desert. Fade to black. The only sounds were the wind and the truck. There were words on the screen, but I don't remember what they said. Some poem, I think. Egyptian filmmakers. I don't know, I just loved the movie. The theater only had two seats, but they were the most comfortable seats in the entire Smithsonian, so we sat there a lot. She'd kiss me, and I'd feel her up. She did that excited nervous breathing young women do when they really want it. I've never heard that from an older woman. I think they sort of get used to it and then that breathing goes away. I was always watching the movie over her shoulder.

About a week before her internship ended, Debbie was mad at me about something. I don't remember what. I was a real bastard, I guess. I regret that, but I'd lost track of my sins by this point. I smoothed it over easily enough and she ended up laughing. The summer was over, and it was time for her to go back to college. Her roommate wasn't coming until later and she wanted me to come to stay with her in her dorm for a few days while she was alone. She said she just wanted someone to fuck her ex out of her system. That idea made me feel tired all over. I said I was flattered but I wasn't going to come. Debbie got up off the bench and I never saw her again.

A month and a half later a miracle happened. My project wasn't being continued into the next fiscal year. There wasn't enough left in the budget to keep me there any longer. I'd paid my time. I was leaving. No more cubicle bay. No more Metro. No more "quoth the raven" evermore or nevermore— or go fuck yourself, Torrez.

Divine intervention.

The Temple of Heaven

On my last day at the National Headquarters of the United States Postal Service, I decided to walk the two blocks down to the Smithsonian Castle and have lunch there one more time. I was idly wandering through the gardens and listening to music on my phone when I noticed a little walkway. It wasn't hidden, just out of the way. I must've passed it at least twice every time I'd come to see Debbie, but I'd never seen before. I followed it around a curved hedge, and it led me to something called the Moongate Garden. The plaque said that the garden had been modeled after a much larger one in China called the Temple of Heaven Garden. Ming Dynasty. Over a thousand years old.

In the middle of the garden, sunk into the ground, was a square divided into fourths. The square had a path leading from each of the four sides to an island at the center of the square. The island and the four paths were all made of pink granite. The spaces between the four walkways inside the square were pools of black water. At two opposite corners of the garden, there stood round granite structures called "moongates." They were like vertical half pipes that faced each other. Not exactly, but kind of like that, and you could walk between them. It was all made of pink granite.

None of this could be seen from outside because the Moongate Garden was enclosed by hedges and trees. My eyes traced every leaf and stone in the strange formations as my feet carried me around the square. There was a recessed area in the back with three benches. I sat down, closed my eyes, and listened peacefully to my music for a while. When I opened my eyes, a tiny, white-haired woman was sitting on the bench to my left. She was dressed in white linen, even her shoes. I figured she was about seventy years old, but her body retained the poise of a much younger woman. Her blue eyes were staring at me. I wasn't sure if she had been there when I came in, or if she had come in while my eyes were closed, but I felt as if I was intruding, so I started to leave. As soon as I moved, she jumped off her bench and ran to me. I was so surprised that I recoiled back down onto my bench. She grabbed my head with both hands and screamed in my face, "THERE ARE FOUR NOBLE TRUTHS AND AN EIGHTFOLD PATH! THE KINGDOM OF GOD IS WITHIN MAN! PREPARE YE THE WAY OF THE LORD!"

She kissed me hard, then dashed to the center of Heaven, knelt on the pink granite disc, made a few quick motions and some kind of prayer, then left through the far exit. The garden was still. I was stunned. Finally, I got up and reverently moved to the center of the island where she had prayed. I looked around empty Eden. The hedges. The square. The four paths and the black pools. The eight stones that surrounded the holy circle. I looked up at the blue sky and down at the pink granite, searching for the answer.

"Sympathy for the Devil" came into my headphones.

My wailing laughter filled the garden. Everything was so Goddamn funny.

I quit my job before they could reassign me. I didn't have a plan. I just had to get out. It was time to leave this city, my family, and all the heartbreak. It was time to find another way. By October I had an apartment in New York City. I left Hell, Purgatory, and the Moongate Garden of Heaven that day, and I haven't been back to the Smithsonian since. But for a long minute in that secret garden under the summer sun, I laughed at the divine comedy. When I couldn't stand it anymore, I laid down like the little boy in the basement of the Hirshhorn. My tears made dark spots on the hot stones.

John Can't Hang Baby

I was throwing out my jizz rags from Saturday night's fuckfest and waiting for my morning dose of Johnny Cash pills to kick in, when two black sedans pulled up to the front of my house and six Republicans got out.

Well-dressed, Sunday-morning, white people.

I was barefoot and naked except for an old pair of blue gym shorts and an aromatic medley of bodily fluids and personal lubricants. I had just brought the trash cans to the curb when these authoritarian populist radicals approached me. Big smiles and handshakes. I was outnumbered and strung out like a ball of yarn. The fanatical bastards could pull anything now.

I was on my guard.

"Excuse me, sir, is this your residence?"

"Yeah," I said in a terse grunt.

"I see, and your name, sir?"

"Who wants to know?"

"Well, sir, we're from the Republican Party of Virginia, and we're going around to speak with all registered Republicans in our district to ask if you've given any thought to who you'll be voting for this November."

"Oh, sure," I lied.

"Yes sir, so may I ask your name just to confirm for our records?"

"My name's David." I'd already said too much.

"Great, and may I ask who you'll be voting for?"

"Oh, Trump, sure." I'm an evil man.

"Right on, brother." "Good to hear that." "I'm glad you're one of the good ones."

"Yeah, sure, of course."

"This is the one that counts, you know."

"Right," I said, nodding.

"Well is there anyone else here that we can speak to?"

"No." The house was empty—I was sure of it.

"What about Albert and Brenda, do they live here? They're the homeowners, right?"

"They're at church."

"Oh, I see, and Todd? Is he here?"

"They put him in a home." My grandfather pays eight thousand a month to die under apathetic supervision—The American Dream.

"Donald?"

"You mean Donny?"

"Right, yes, Donny. Is he here?"

"No, he moved away."

"Do you know where?"

"Nope, no idea." Of course, I know where he is, he's my brother.

"He's your brother, right?"

"Yeah."

"You don't know where your brother is?"

"No." I'm not telling you—you pig-fucking Nazis. You're liable to put the fucking leeches on him.

"What about John?"

"What about him?"

"Is he here?"

"No."

"I mean, does he live here? He's your brother too, right?"

This one had beady little reptilian eyes. He must be their leader. "Yeah, he's my brother. He used to live here, but he fucked off to New York."

"Does he need an absentee ballot?"

"No."

"Oh, so he's registered up there now?"

"No, I don't think so." The weasels were closing in.

"Wait, I don't understand, why not?"

"I don't think he's voting."

"He's not voting?! But this is the one that counts! He's not voting for Hillary, is he? That would be a disaster!"

"No. He's not voting." Neither am I, but I'm not telling you that.

"May I ask why not?"

"Oh, you know, he can't hang baby." Goddamn it, where am I going to hide all their bodies if this turns ugly? The trash cans are already full.

"He can't hang—?" "He has to vote—this is the one that

counts!" "What does that mean—*he can't hang*—what does that mean?"

"It means he can't hang—John—he can't hang." I was clearly too hip for the room.

"I don't understand."

"Man, say he can't hang," I repeated.

"What does that mean?" "This is the one that counts!"

"John can't hang baby. That's it. That's all he said. When he left, he said that, if anybody asks why he isn't around or why he did or didn't do something, to just say 'Oh, you know he can't hang baby.' That was it. That was all he said. John can't hang baby."

They looked at me in silence as the drugs began to take hold.

Halloween in the Chelsea Hotel

I'm writing this in the lobby of the Hotel Chelsea. The radiator is hissing. The clerk is laughing at old, soft-core horror-porn and snacking behind the desk. The furniture consists of four dirty, worn-out, red velvet armchairs. The hotel is closed for renovations. It's Halloween, and I just walked here through the Village. If you know what it's like on Halloween in the Village, that's good, because now I've got carte blanche. I could tell you any wild crazy story I wanted, and if anyone called me a liar, I'd just say, "Well it was Halloween in the Village."

But I don't have a wild, crazy story. I didn't wear a costume or go to any parties. I went to the Film Forum on West Houston. They had scaffolding up around the whole block. I bought my ticket and sat down in the dirty, worn-out theater. The seats were uncomfortable, and the screen was tiny. The Film Forum hasn't been renovated in years. The seat in front of me had a plaque with the name "Martin Scorsese" on it. I guess he donated some money or something, so they put his name on the furniture.

I've been living in New York for about two weeks. I've already been to the library and the Café Wha? Yesterday I went over to see Saint Patrick's Old Cathedral. Scorsese was an altar boy there once. The cathedral is being renovated now. Scaffolding. Muddy newspapers. Concrete dust. Paint splashes. Tape. Tarp. There was a red emergency alarm hanging down from the roof held up by a single electrical cable. Just swinging in the wind. They shot some scenes from *Mean Streets* and *The Godfather* at that Cathedral. It's being renovated because the pope declared that it's a basilica now. I don't know what that means. It's one of the oldest cathedrals in America. Looks like hell now.

The Film Forum is playing *The Apu Trilogy*. There's just been a restoration of it. I watched the whole thing, around six hours. Terrific films. There were about a dozen people in the theater. When I came out there was a sign in the lobby. "The Film Forum will be closing for renovations." I left and walked through the Village.

There was a huge Halloween parade. I think it was the forty-second annual huge Halloween parade. The streets and sidewalks were jammed with costumed bodies. People of every kind, color, and cosplay. I heard French, German, Russian, Spanish, a few Asian tongues, and English twisted into at least six of its beautiful American bastardizations. The crowds got worse. I decided to get off the street for a while, so I went into a crooked bookshop that boasted to have over thirty-five different books on Bob Dylan. The guy at the register had long grey hair under a cowboy hat. I browsed while he stood at the register humming along to "Farewell Angelina" and "Desolation Row."

I'd thumbed over a few books until I found one that was the damnedest thing. It was a series of poems Dylan had written sometime back in the sixties in response to a collection of pictures. Someone had found these things and published the poems and the pictures together in this book. Aging movie stars and Hollywood funerals. That kind of thing. The words were amazing, some of the best stuff Dylan has ever written. The lines described with uncanny clairvoyance the dark decay behind all the phony exteriors and painted masks of Hollywood—and America itself. There was a one-page interview with Dylan. They asked him questions about the poems.

He said he didn't remember writing them.

At all.

Not the pictures.

Not the poems.

Nothing.

But he said first off it was obvious that he had seen the pictures because the poems were clearly based on the images.

And secondly,

well,

he couldn't think of anything secondly.

I put down the books and left. I've been trying to figure out who Bob Dylan is for years, and it's like trying to nail ayahuasca smoke to a rainbow waterfall.

Like putting God in a box.

I walked up Seventh Avenue.

The press of bodies on the pavement moved me uptown. Ten million footed Mannahatta all dressed up with fake blood, dyed hair, and black lipstick. I passed by Superman and all the Avengers. Two lesbian vampires stood kissing out-side a bar. One of them ground her lit cigarette into the oth-er's wrist. Psychics were doing theatrical palm readings right in the middle of the sidewalk. Terrific showmanship. Great costumes. I saw a woman by the cosmetics section of a CVS. A sign in the window above her said "BEAUTY" in big, red, block letters. I thought she was in costume until she yawned and stretched out on the pavement under a cardboard blanket.

There were princesses and drag queens. Jokers and Batmen. I saw a report about Heidi Klum's seventeenth annual Halloween party somewhere in the city. She'd spent a month preparing her Jessica Rabbit costume. Hired a whole team to work on it. Fake hips, lips, boobs, ass, big red wig, and a mask molded to fit her face. It took her staff nine hours to put the whole thing on her for the party. I'm sure you can find pic-tures of it somewhere. They took lots of pictures.

I turned off Seventh onto West Twenty-third and came down here to see the old place. More scaffolding. Signs. Dirt. I actually walked past it the first time. I just didn't recognize it. They say it's closed for renovation, but that ain't the truth. The truth is—it's gone. It's been here since 1884, but it's gone now. Lots of artists have lived here. Some tenants used to pay rent with artwork instead of money, but that was back in the old days. Now they have to pay with something real.

I read all the plaques on the front of the building. William S. Burroughs, Thomas Wolfe, Arthur Miller, Dylan Thomas, Mark Twain, Pink Floyd, Sam Shepard, Tennessee Williams, Dennis Hopper, Eugene O'Neil, Hendrix, Madonna, Bukowski, Ginsberg.

Stanley Kubrick and Arthur C. Clarke wrote *2001: A Space Odyssey* here. Sid Vicious collapsed in this lobby once. That was before he stabbed Nancy Spungen to death. Anyway, they think Sid killed her, but he died of a heroin overdose a couple of months later, and the cops never investigated too much. Nobody really gave a shit.

Andy Warhol and his "superstars" filmed a movie here. Edie Sedgwick was the star. They say, "Like a Rolling Stone" is about her, or maybe it was "Just like a Woman." Maybe not, I don't know. I do know that Valerie Solanas was jealous because Andy preferred Edie, so Valerie shot him dead in his office one day. Edie set her room on fire not long after that. I'm not sure why.

Janis Joplin sucked Leonard Cohen's dick here. Not that there's anything particularly special about that. A lot of dicks get sucked in every hotel.

Gore Vidal fucked Jack Kerouac here. Or Jack fucked Gore. Or both I suppose. Not in the lobby, though. Of course, most of this isn't on the plaques out front.

Just then, Wonder Woman walked by with the Teenage Mutant Ninja Turtles.

"Is this a museum?" Michelangelo asked.

"Sort of," Wonder Woman said.

I went inside.

Patti Smith wrote a book about this place. She said she was sitting in this lobby one day, in this very room, and there was a young man sitting next to her scribbling in a notebook. The man was Robert Zimmerman, the thin Hibbing vagabond who discovered Bob Dylan. Dylan wrote "Blonde on Blonde" and a lot of other things here. Maybe this is where he wrote that book of poems and pictures. Maybe not. It wouldn't make any difference either way. I don't know why I came here tonight, but I think it has something to do with that. Like maybe I thought—well, not thought—but maybe I *hoped* that if I came here and waited long enough, Dylan would show up. That he'd just sort of shuffle through the smudgy glass doors, slump down in the dirty, worn-out, red velvet armchair next to mine, and—

Well that's just it, I don't know.

Save the world or something.

I guess that sounds crazy.

But it was Halloween in the Village and anything could happen.

So, I sat down.

The clerk asked, "Ah, you waiting someone?"

"Sort of," I said. "Not really. I guess I'm just waiting. Is that alright?"

"Oh, well, okay, but in few minute we gon start purging the hotel."

"What?"

His laughter echoed off the stone.

"Just kidding, just kidding. Yeah, you can wait. Is okay."

He went back to his softcore horror-porn and snacks.

I waited.

This is where I'd like to tell you that wild, crazy story. I'd like to say that in some special magic hour of the night, when I was waiting all alone in the lobby of the Hotel Chelsea, the great American Poet-Prophet dragged himself in off West Twenty-third Street and sat down next to me. And I'd like to tell you that he explained everything. That he gave me all the answers to all the questions and all the solutions to all the problems. That he told me how to feed all hungers, pacify all wars, and turn lead into gold. That he explained every note and word of his songs and, just because he had the time, even taught me to play his guitar.

Then he stood up and said something like, "If you need me, I'll be out there on the American Road, singin' and playin' God's salvation for all the sinners. And if you're ever on your own, a complete unknown, with no direction home, just remember kid—" He walked to the door, opened it—then looked back and said, "the answer is blowin' in the wind."

Then he winked a baby-blue eye, tipped his hat, and was gone.

But obviously that didn't happen.

Of course, Bob Dylan never came.

What happened is I sat there alone and looked at the dilapidated lobby. All the artwork has been removed. The plaster on the ceiling is cracked. The mealy yellow paint is infected. The marble floors are streaked and filthy. There are wires and pipes sticking out all over the place. The bent chandelier is missing lots of bulbs. The fireplace is empty except for a wad of pink insulation that's been stuffed into the flue. It's just a rundown dump, not the holy of holies from Solomon's temple.

But still, I watched the streets through the glass doors for hours. As the night wore on, the superheroes began to disappear. Soon they were gone altogether. The streets were empty except for the bums. The radiator sputtered, loudly clanged half a dozen times, then shut off.

There is no Messiah here.

All the Wounded Dogs

"You had your fucking cock in her, you sick fuck!"

That was the way she talked. She moved like a porn star and swore like a bitch.

I liked her right away.

"Sarah, fuck, I'm—Jesus Christ, I'm fucking sorry, okay? She doesn't mean anything, it's just it's—"

Daniel was chasing Sarah out of a club in Chelsea and trying to tuck his dick back into his pants. I just happened to be passing by on my way home.

"What, Daniel? What? Is it too much to ask for you not to fuck every slut that rubs your cock on the dance floor? I can't fucking believe you, you piece of shit!"

I took out my headphones.

"It's not like that, okay? Fuck. It's just—I was—"

Daniel was slurring his stammers.

"Oh, I'm sorry, what? What? Were you just going to fuck this one slut?"

"Sarah, no, I'm not—I didn't—"

"In front of everyone?"

They were coming toward me.

"Look, she came on to me. I was just—"

"Of *course*, she came on to you, you fucking idiot. Rachel fucking hates me, that's why she fucked you. She doesn't give a shit about you. She just wants to hurt me. Fuck, Daniel. Why don't you ever fucking listen?"

She was just over five feet and barely a hundred pounds, but she filled the entire block.

"Babe, I—"

"DON'T FUCKING CALL ME BABE, YOU PIECE OF SHIT!"

She *really* didn't like that. I stopped walking and pretended not to watch.

"Sarah, please I—"

"Fuck you, Daniel! Fuck—you. You said you were just going to stay home and smoke and then Rachel texts me and says you and your fuck boys are all out without me, and I come and find you with your cock up her ass in front of half the school!?"

God, she was pretty. She took off her heels and stepped into Eighth Avenue like she owned it.

"I can't fucking believe you!"

"Sarah, get out of the street—please, I—"

"Who fucks on the dance floor anyway? What is this— middle school?"

"Sarah!"

"I'm surprised you could even get your pathetic little dick in her trashy cunt at all."

Oh shit, macho time.

"Well what the fuck difference does it make!? You don't even fucking go there anymore, you crazy bitch. And anyway, I can't keep track of you. First, we're in love, then we're done, then you get thrown out of school and you won't text me for a week. I don't even know if you and Rachel are friends or enemies."

Calm down, Danny.

"Fuck you, Daniel."

"Whatever. You know what? Fuck you, Sarah. Ezra's right. You're hot, but you're a fucking, crazy, psycho bitch!"

Sarah wheeled around and kicked Danny boy right in the schmeckle.

Fuck.

Danny tucked and covered. She gave him a kidney shot, and he rolled onto his back.

Fuck.

She pounced and went in for a ground and pound.

Fuck me, I don't want to do this right now.

Danny screamed.

Fuck it.

"Let him go, or I'll call the police." It'd been a long time since I'd said that.

She whipped her mane of red hair around and looked me in the eye.

"What!?"

I was standing behind her and hoping I wouldn't have to pull her off him.

"I said let him go, or I'll call the cops."

Why do I always do this?

"Fuck off."

She turned back to Danny, but I hooked her arm to stop the blow. She spun back around.

"What the fuck!?"

"Stop. Please, you have to stop."

She tried to get out of my grasp. "Fuck *you*."

I let her go. She stood up and squared off. She kicked me damn hard, but I hooked my arm around her knee, then lifted her up by her leg and dropped her down on her perfect ass. She flipped her hair and looked at me, stunned.

Danny was already down the block.

"It doesn't matter what he's done, you can't attack people like that."

Her black dress was pulled up enough to show most of a red lace thong. She didn't try to cover up. The look in her eyes changed. She looked like she wanted to fuck me to death. I backed away.

"Hey," said a voice like a drooling tiger.

I looked back.

* * *

The view from my apartment at night is spellbinding. Wide windows thirty-seven stories above midtown Manhattan. She didn't even glance at it. She grabbed my chin and pulled my head around.

"When are you going to make your move?"

No response.

She rolled her ravenous eyes with a frustrated grunt. I

got a sharp slap, then she jumped up and wrapped her legs around my waist. She kissed me hard, and I let her.

"I want you to fuck me like you hate me."

* * *

"It's like a dog chasing cars," I said.

"What?" She was lying naked in my bed as I tried to explain.

"It's like a dog chasing cars. He does it because it's part of his nature—a hardwired survival instinct. He sees a car, he chases it. But if he catches the car, he realizes immediately it isn't what he really wanted, and he doesn't know what to do with it. It's the same with me. I have an innate urge to pursue women. That natural sex drive and desire for release, so I—"

"Release?"

"Yeah—yes, okay? Release. Sexual release. I'm a healthy young man—sometimes I want to cum." I should probably mention that I was naked too.

"Honey, I can give you release." Her fingertips slid across her bare breasts.

"No, you can't." I said low.

"Yeah, I can. I can make you cum so fucking hard you'll pass out."

My chest tightened. "That's not what I'm talking about. That doesn't mean anything. It doesn't lead anywhere."

"It leads to a great orgasm."

"It's not just about cumming."

"Yeah, it is."

"No, it's not, Sarah. Sex isn't just about cumming hard or

doing kinky shit. It's not just a competition of conquest and pleasure."

"Yes, it is, dude."

"No, it's fucking not."

"Well what the fuck do you know about it anyway? If you've never had sex, how the fuck would you know?"

"What makes you think I haven't had sex?"

"Have you?"

"That's irrelevant."

"Tell me."

"No."

"You must have had sex with someone, you're like, twenty-three."

"I'm twenty-four."

She sat up.

"You're twenty-four and you've never had sex? I just turned nineteen and I've had sex with, like, hundreds of guys."

"I didn't say—wait, what? *Hundreds*?"

"How did you make it halfway through your twenties without having sex? I'd fucking kill myself."

"No wait, what did you just say? Hundreds of guys? You've had sex with hundreds of guys?"

"Yeah. Probably more, I don't know."

"You don't *know*? Sarah, why are you having sex with hundreds of guys?"

"Because I like it? Duh. Sex is awesome."

"Yeah. Well, I like chocolate cake, but I don't eat it for every meal."

"What?"

"I'm just saying that seems excessive."

"Don't change the subject."

"I'm not changing the subject. I'm concerned about you."

"Oh, yeah—I'm sure you really give a shit."

"I'm just trying to—"

"Will you just shut the fuck up and come fuck me already?"

"No."

"Why the fuck not!?"

"Because that's so vacant. There's no human dignity in it. It'd be worse than masturbation."

"Dude. Whoa. No. It's way better than masturbation. You have no idea what you're missing."

"That's not what I meant."

"No, seriously, you have to trust me. You're missing out big time. Sex is fucking amazing. You seriously have to try it."

"Sarah, I'm not going to fuck you tonight." I admit I felt a little ridiculous standing naked in my bedroom saying this to the bombshell between my sheets.

"Oh, my God, are you serious, right now? Why the fuck not? I'm here. You're here. We're both horny. I have condoms and I'm on the pill. Your roommate's gone. Look if you're worried or nervous or whatever, I promise I'll teach you everything and I won't laugh at you at all or anything. We can do anal, oral, anything you want. I'll even eat your ass if you want me to."

Goddamn woman.

"Jesus Christ, Sarah."

"Well, don't you want to fuck me?"

"Of course, I want to fuck you, you're gorgeous. But that's not—"

"Then what's the fucking problem? I mean—I'm naked, shaved, and plucked—laying in your bed, begging you to fuck me. What else do you fucking want?"

"I want—"

"What? What is it? Whatever it is I promise I won't be grossed out—no matter how fucked up it is. Just tell me."

"I want a wife!"

I tore open the door and went into the hallway looking back at her through the open portal. I wanted to tear my flesh into atoms and dissolve my soul. Sarah stared at me while I stood there shaking. It was a long time before I broke the silence.

"I want a woman who annoys me because she wants my attention and pushes me to be a better man. I want a woman who fights with me and jumps on the bed and brags about me to her friends. I want a woman who knows her beauty doesn't come off the shelf at Victoria's Secret. I want a woman who makes art, even if no one gives a shit. I want a woman who asks me questions I can't answer and answers questions I don't know how to ask. I want a woman who will still be there when I make her breakfast in the morning. I want her to say, 'I love you,' not just 'I want you.' I want a woman. I want my wife."

Long silence.

"I used to masturbate more when I was younger. For a long time I didn't masturbate at all, but once I started, it was easier to just keep going. At first it was exciting. All the fantasy and discovery and everything, but over the years it turned hollow. It put ideas in my head that I didn't like. Robbed me of time and energy, started to change who I was and who I was becoming. I've been in love before, with women I still care about deeply. One of the ways I knew I was falling in love was that I didn't want to masturbate anymore. I still had the same appetites, but jerking off wasn't satisfying. I lived on her smile, and her laugh. The way my heart beat faster when she said my name or looked at me. That's what it's there for. That need that men have. To make us love a woman and have children with her and protect and provide for them. It may not be politically correct anymore, but I felt that machinery— that instinct—turning in me like an engine in a car. There is something inside of a man that tells him that when he falls in love and has an orgasm, that things are supposed to be a certain way. And if they aren't that way, then he feels wrong somewhere in his spirit.

"But it didn't work out. It never works out. I can't fucking do it. All the women I've ever loved have left me and cut off contact. They all have happy lives with other men. And some-how that just stripped my gears. But after trying both being in love and having a lot of meaningless orgasms, I know the difference. I still masturbate sometimes. I'm not a monk, but it makes me feel sick—like I'm dying inside. After all the heart-break and years of getting my hopes up, I'm just too fucking tired in my soul anymore. I still pursue women. I can't help that. I know it's not going to lead to anything, but it's hardwired into my biology. But somehow, I just don't have the stomach for all this casual, empty, fucking. All this swipe right, hook-up shit. Using women like Kleenexes. Maybe this doesn't make sense to a young woman, but I feel like—if I did that—if I went around fucking every woman who would let me fuck her—I'd rot from the inside until my heart stopped beating.

"I don't want you to think I'm some kind of holy, righteous fucker or whatever the fuck you're thinking about me, 'cause I'm not. I don't think I'm better than everyone or anything like that either. I'm not gay. I'm not stupid. I'm not a saint or a priest, I'm not any of that shit. I'm just an injured dog chasing cars."

I didn't know what else to say, so I stopped talking.

"You're fucking crazy, dude."

I sank and dropped my weight against the wall.

"Yeah, I know."

"Jesus Christ, man, I hope you figure out a way to deal with all of your bullshit and get off your high horse and just be a normal person."

"Alright, yeah, thanks."

She leaned forward and started in.

"I mean holy shit—I've heard some fucked-up shit in my life—but Goddamn, dude, you need help."

"Sarah, please—"

"I bet you've got like some weird, dark, painful shit in your past that's just fucked you up so badly you can't get hard anymore or something."

"You were just grabbing my hard cock ten minutes ago."

"That doesn't prove anything."

I started to get annoyed.

"Alright. Don't do that, okay? Don't act like I'm the only one with weird problems."

"What's that supposed to mean?"

"I mean everyone is dealing with a lot of shit."

"Yeah maybe, but not like you, dude. You're fucking crazy."

"I recognize that."

"Like you're bad fucked-up. I mean if you're straight and you can't fuck women you're attracted to, then you should see a doctor or something because that's seriously fucked-up."

"It's not that I *can't*—"

"That makes it worse!"

"Well what about you?"

"What about me?"

"I mean what about all that shit you pulled out there on the street?"

"Fuck you. That's none of your business."

"Well, I don't know about that. I mean we're both naked in my apartment at 4:00 a.m., so it kind of is a little bit my business."

"You don't know anything about my life, alright? So go fuck yourself."

"Does Daniel know how many guys you've fucked?"

"Fuck you." She crossed her arms and pushed back into the pillows.

"Is that how this started? He found out about your little hobby and was trying to catch up?"

"Oh, my God. Can you please stop all this bullshit and come back to bed?"

"No, no—I think we're finally making some real progress here. Also, why do you want me to fuck you so badly anyway?"

"Look it's not some big mystery, okay? What you did was

really hot, so I wanted to fuck you. How was I supposed to know you were some crazy fucking psycho?"

"How was I supposed to know you were the biggest slut in New York?"

That was cruel. I admit that. But at the time I wanted to get a rise out of her. Her fists pounded into the comforter as she sat up straight, dropping her chin and flaring her nostrils. I'd touched a nerve.

"I mean, do you really think getting fucked one more time is going to solve anything? What do you think you're going to suck out of my dick that's going to help you so Goddamn much?"

She picked up the glass on my nightstand and threw it at me. I ducked and it shattered on the wall.

"WHAT THE FUCK, SARAH!"

She grabbed something else off the nightstand and stood up in bed. She flicked her wrist and I heard the click of a blade locking into place and I knew instantly what it was. Sarah was holding a black, four-inch folding pocketknife.

"Oh, fuck."

I ran back to the windows in the living room.

She leaped off the bed after me and stepped on the glass.

"Ow! Fuck!"

I grabbed the big blue blanket off my couch and spun around to face her with my hands spread so the blanket came taut between my fists.

She lunged at me with the knife. "You fucking asshole!"

I wrapped her arm up in the blanket and twisted hard until I heard the knife hit the hardwood, then I kicked it skittering into the far wall. I picked her up by the waist and threw her onto the couch. I could have stopped there. I should have stopped there. She had been trying to scare me more than anything, but I have a bad history with knives, and getting stabbed hurts like you wouldn't believe. I get very uptight about people threatening me with knives. It doesn't happen often, but when it does, my reaction tends to be extreme.

"You crazy fucking bitch!"

"Get the fuck off me!"

She kicked me in the stomach. I grabbed her leg and pulled her up off the couch upside down, swung her around, and threw her on the floor. I ended up on top of her with my hands clamped tight around her pretty neck. She clawed at my chest and spit on me. I realized what I was doing and let her go. As soon as I took my hands away, she grabbed my hips and tried to pull my cock toward her open mouth.

I pushed her away. "What the fuck are you doing?!"

She tried again. I couldn't believe it. It scared me. Something was wrong.

"Fucking stop it."

"Will you please just fuck me?"

"You're fucking crazy, Sarah."

She desperately looked from one of my eyes to the other. Searching for something that just wasn't there.

Then she started crying. And, I mean, like fucking wailing, crying. Not pretty, gentle crying—but like slobbering, shoulder-heaving, animal-groans crying.

An awareness of how much damage had been done to this woman tonight came into my mind like a needle through a nerve. Hundreds of men had hurt her before, but tonight had been especially bad. First it was Danny, and now it was me. Sarah had changed from a sexy, unconquerable Amazon into a delicate, abused little girl. I felt like I'd just run over a puppy. I wrapped the blanket around her and hugged her close. We leaned against the wall. The salt of her tears stung the fresh scratches in my chest as I stared at the city outside the window. The sound of her weeping filled my dark, empty apartment. I rubbed her back and whispered small, deep-voiced sympathies. The woman that spoke to me now was different than the one I'd met on the street a couple hours ago.

Bloody shards of broken glass.

"My uncle used to make me do things. Isn't that pathetic? It's such a fucking cliché. What I hated the most was how he would always act so gentle and tender about it. How he'd touch my cheek and call me 'babe.' Fucking creep. I finally got the courage to tell my parents, and my dad said I was a liar. He said his brother would never do something like that, and I was just repeating something I'd seen on TV to get attention. Can you fucking believe that? I was fucking thirteen. *God*.

"And my mom was always too afraid to say anything. She just follows the rules because she doesn't want to be an outcast, so I just had to fucking take it. Until one day I couldn't anymore, and I stabbed him in his fucking leg right in the middle of a family dinner. Motherfucker. After that, everyone hated me. They all thought I was a wicked bitch, so my dad sent me to this super-strict orthodox school, 'cause apparently *I* was the fucking problem. The Rabbi told my father that God was on his side, and my mom didn't say a fucking word.

"I could never learn all their fucking rules, but by then I didn't care. My teachers punished me, so I fought back. None of them ever gave a shit about me, all they cared about was control. I got kicked out of that school and a couple others. Then, last Friday I was late for orchestra rehearsal, so I bought a slice of pizza on the street and that fucking bitch Rachel told on me. I didn't even notice there was pepperoni on it until the Rabbi pointed it out. I'm never going to be welcome in any orthodox Jewish community ever again because apparently God hates pork more than he loves me. My parents avoid seeing me as much as legally possible. They keep my brothers and sisters away from me, too.

"Anyway, Rachel texted me and said she was sorry, and invited me out, so I get dressed and come out, and then I find her fucking my boyfriend on the dance floor in front of all our friends—and I just fucking lost it. It's whatever, though, I haven't cared about any guy since my first boyfriend Isaac. Even though he won't talk to me anymore. He needs a good Jewish girl, and I'm definitely not fucking that. He's been dating someone else for a while. He still loves me, but he has to marry her, or his family will disown him. Ever since Isaac and I broke up, I've just been fucking any guy I can find because it makes me feel good, and I like being wanted. My pussy is the only thing anybody seems to care about, so if I have to be a fucking slut to not feel like a piece of shit for a couple of hours, then that's what I'm going to do, and anyone who doesn't like it can go fuck themselves."

Long silence.

I picked up the knife and started picking the glass out of her feet.

She didn't flinch.

"God bless you, Sarah." I don't know why I said that.

"Fuck God. There is no God. If there was a God, he would have fucking helped me when I needed him."

I kept pulling out the glass as I talked.

"I heard a story once about a nun. A long time ago, this bridge collapsed down in South America and killed a bunch of people. For years afterward people tried to make sense of it. Why it happened. Why it happened. What could have been done to stop it. There was one friar who spent his entire life trying to prove that it was God's will for all those people to die on that bridge. This one nun who happened to be passing when the bridge collapsed saw all their mangled, helpless bodies and said in that moment—looking at all that senseless carnage—she felt herself doubt that any loving God could exist if such a thing could happen. But then she thought—so what? At a time like that God doesn't matter. You must still love and care for suffering people. So she got to work and just kept right on trying to help. She spent her entire life caring for the blind, the insane, and the dying—and maybe that's all anybody can do. God knows we're never going to make sense of anything. We're never going to stop the bleeding, but we have to try anyway."

I finished checking her feet, and she crawled to the bedroom.

"In the end, it didn't matter, though. All those people on the bridge still died."

71

I closed the pocketknife and set it on the floor.

"But at least someone tried."

Outside the window there were wide columns of white steam pouring from the rooftops.

Rising.

And getting lost in the night.

I looked up and saw her fully dressed, heading for the door.

"Sarah, wait!"

I chased her.

But it was dark.

And I stepped on the glass.

I yelled and stumbled, still reaching out for her.

"Sarah, wait, please."

She got to the door and stopped. I struggled to my feet pressing my hands against both walls of the narrow hallway for support.

Still naked.

Still bleeding.

Still chasing *her*.

"You know something? I don't believe in God, but I would go to your church."

"Please don't go, Sarah. Please. Please don't leave me. Please."

A shade of empathy bent her lips. She stepped forward and kissed me the way a woman kisses a man she's always loved. Our lips parted and she opened her eyes without moving away. There was a long moment of intimate silence as we shared the same breaths.

Then she gently whispered, "Goodbye, you crazy faggot."

I sighed,

and in tender reply said,
"Suck a dick, you slutty bitch."
The door closed.
And I was alone.

* * *

I was sitting naked on the floor of my living room, picking glass out of my feet with a black, four-inch folding pocket-knife and reading the book of Isaiah when I felt warm light on my back.

I never saw Sarah again.
But I cleaned up the glass.
And the blood.
And—
eventually—
we both died.

Upaya Sunyata

There are a lot of reasons that New Yorkers hate Times
Square. First, it's too crowded. New Yorkers are used to tol-
erating crowds, but Times Square is ridiculous. The streets
are clogged with mindless hoards gawking at bright shiny
advertisements. They stand in huge groups watching street
performers and line up to pay twenty bucks for a selfie with
a sweaty stranger in a dirty Minnie Mouse costume. Beneath
all the neon flavored street food is the thing that New Yorkers
hate the most, nothing.

There's nothing in Times Square but the empty promises
of overpriced souvenirs and glow-in-the-dark restaurants.
It's the most vulgar, festering, capitalist abortion on Earth,
and it's all fifty percent off this week only. Tourists love it.
And the reasons tourists love it are mostly the same reasons
New Yorkers hate it. I've always found that interesting, how
people can love and hate the same thing, and the only difference is the familiarity. Like, the closer you look, the more you
see—and the more you see, the less you like.

Times Square is the place where Broadway hits Seventh

Avenue. There's a grim statue of Francis Duffy right in the middle of it. Duffy was an Irish-Catholic priest who served in World War I and used to follow medics into the thick of battle to pray for the dying soldiers—most decorated chaplain in US history. He came back to New York and started a church full of poor Mick Catholics on Forty-second Street. They put up the statue of him sometime after he died. Times Square is still full of filth and sin, and Duffy is still in the thick of it. Solemn eyes staring out of a bald head at the carnage all around him with a giant granite cross backing his stand.

Anyway, New Yorkers hate this place.

One day I was stopped at a crosswalk in Times Square, and a man dressed as a Buddhist monk approached me. He was wearing a toga like the ones they wore in Scorsese's Dalai Lama movie. The monk's head was shaved, and his wrist was covered in prayer beads. He bowed his head with folded hands and said, "Blessings. Joy to you. Blessings. Divine peace. Joy to you." Heavy accent. Then he reached down and put one of the prayer bead bracelets around my wrist while saying, "You are loved. Blessings to you. You are loved."

He did it with gentle respect and genuine kindness. I was moved. It felt like a profound divine encounter. I didn't know what to do, so I said thank you, and I meant it. He asked for my name to write on his prayer list, and I gave it to him. Then he said, "Can you make donation today? Help to buy for rice?"

I didn't have any cash on me. "I'm sorry man, not today. Thank you so much, though. God bless you."

"You don't have nothing? Two dollar? You don't have two dollar?"

"I'm sorry sir, not today, but thank you so much."

His face turned to anger. "Stupid!"

He reached out and yanked the beads off my wrist then scratched out my name. He gave the bracelet to someone else and got his two dollars. He bowed again and walked away to wait for the next orange hand on the crosswalk sign to bring a new crop of customers. He produced a huge roll of bills from his pocket and added the two dollars to it, then he put the roll away and lit a cigarette while he played Candy Crush on an iPhone. I looked down at his shoes. Nikes.

In the midst of this bitter winter, I began to boil. I wanted to yell, "Look! Everyone, look! He's a fake!" I wanted to see him drawn and quartered by a gang of vigilantes. I would lead them if no one else would. We could use the prayer beads to make a rope and lynch the deceitful fuck right there on Duffy's statue.

Before I could unleash my wrath, the light changed and everyone walked away.

I stood there staring at him, burning in the New York City winter.

He noticed me looking and returned a defiant stare.

It was hopeless. There were a hundred others just like him. I gave up and mingled back into the anonymous cold.

If you're ever in New York City, be sure to visit Times Square.

You'll love it.

Presence and Substance

If you've never been to an open mic night at a dive bar on the Lower East Side, I can tell you it's one hell of a show. The people are the real spectacle, especially with a two-drink minimum. There are the Broadway washouts who were hot shit in high school theater but didn't amount to much on the big city audition circuit, singers and songwriters who never got a record deal, and poets who couldn't fit the rhyme scheme.

The opening act was a woman who said they ought to burn all the Christian schools like the one she went to, then she proceeded to scream and slash at a cello. Black lipstick. Hot Topic. Suburban angst with a bachelor's degree. There were rappers too. One was a mentally handicapped rapper. One was a forty-year-old, timid, white rapper. One guy called himself the Ancient Mariner. He's something of a local celebrity, used to be in the navy, has a book coming out. The *New York Times* did a write-up on him. Mustache. Tattoos. Over seventy. Repeat offender. Very nice guy. Wears a hat. He wrote a lot about flirting with women at open mic nights in New York City dive bars. Big Jim was there almost every night. Big Jim was an aging metalhead with long, white hair. He wrote slam poetry, about heroin and heroin addicts. Huge guy. Huge voice.

Then there were the people in their early thirties trying to make it. Acoustic guitars, keyboards, beat tracks. They played and sang and reeked of existential dread from squandering their twenties on hookups and PBR. "Please give me a chance" was always just below the surface. Even for the good ones. Desperation and self-loathing.

My favorite was Joe.

Joe Goldman did eight minutes of unscripted free-verse poetry every night. Everybody loved Joe. He was also over seventy. Short grey hair. Grandpa sweater. Big glasses. He always sat in the same chair, ordered the same drink, and patiently waited his turn. He had a sweet, old-man voice, sort of like a Jewish piglet. People talked and clinked glasses all night, but when Joe got up to speak, the whole world listened.

Poetry is weird. When it's bad, which happens a lot, it's like throwing up during a blowjob. But when it's good—when it's really poetry—it has a strange transcendent power unlike any other art form.

And Joe was a poet.

Even the misfits knew it.

Wisdom without judgment. Hope without deception. Love without pretense.

I went back the next week and sang some songs I'd written. Just to try it. When I finished, the room was quiet. I walked to the back and sat down at the end of the bar in the corner, unsure of what to make of their reaction.

The next performer went on.

Joe stood up from his usual spot and walked over to where I was sitting. He shook my hand and asked if he could sit down.

"That was great," he said.

"Really? You think so?"

"Oh, yeah. You've got presence and substance kid, and substance counts for a lot these days."

"Thanks, Joe. That means a lot coming from you." I was touched.

"How did you come to write songs like that?" he asked.

I stammered a little then said, "Well I don't know, you know, I just—I don't know. I just do it. How do you write your stuff?"

Joe smiled a little, then sipped his drink.

We sat in silence for a couple acts.

Finally, I said, "I do it whenever I hear the songs, I guess. I usually get it all at once or not at all. I just hear some music and words to go with it, and sort of keep going until I feel like it's done. Sometimes. Sometimes it happens other ways."

Joe nodded.

"I don't know how you do what you do, though. I mean to keep going like that—for eight minutes without a mistake, or losing your rhythm, or anything like that—is an incredible skill. I could never perform without preparing first. Don't you feel—I don't know—self-conscious, or something?"

Joe laughed. "Oh, no. Up there is the only time I feel at home. It's the rest of the time I feel lost."

Goddamn.

"What do you do, Joe? I mean, what do you do for a living?" I asked.

"Well I'm retired now, but I was a cinematographer and cameraman for thirty-five years," he said.

"*Really?!*"

"Sure."

"Well, look, I love movies. Did you work on anything I would know?"

His face scrunched. "No, nothing special. Just some PBS stuff, documentaries, things like that."

"How come you're not still working?"

He shrugged and looked at his drink. "Ah, well, they don't need me anymore. I'm a dinosaur. Camera work has all changed. Used to have to get the light just right, have the right lens, and develop and cut the film and everything. It was a very complex and sensitive art. Now they just point and shoot."

"Then in post they get whatever they want out of the computer, not the camera," I said.

"Exactly, and I don't know how any of that stuff works. They don't even use film anymore." He downed his drink. It was his turn.

Joe went up to the mic and spoke a poem about a time years ago when he had shot a concert with David Bowie and Lou Reed. It just so happened that, yesterday, Bowie had died a few blocks away in his Soho apartment. Liver cancer. Joe said that while he was filming this concert, he had turned his camera on Lou during part of the show. When Bowie saw the footage, he stopped the screening and asked who had shot it. Joe said he had. David Bowie looked at him and said, "Don't you ever do that again."

Bowie didn't want to be upstaged. Ziggy Stardust was insecure. The Goblin King, himself. And so was I—so was everyone—but not Joe. He finished with some lines about a beautiful bird that never spread its wings for fear of the sky. Staying in the nest from when it hatched until it died. His eight minutes were up, and nobody said a word. He stepped off the stage and came back to his spot. I watched as he pulled on his poofy grandpa coat and snuggled on his gloves and earmuffs. He looked at me through thick glasses.

"Substance counts for a lot these days," I said.

Joe smiled.

"So long, kid."

"Next week?"

"Always."

But Joe wasn't there next week.

Or the week after.

Finally, I asked about him.

Turns out Joe Goldman died in his sleep three days after we'd met.

I stopped going to open mic nights.

Manslaughter at Fight Club

There exists, for everyone, a sentence—a series of words—
that has the power to destroy you.
—Philip K. Dick

Patrice O'Neil said that *Fight Club* was the *Scarface* of lame white guys. The hip-hop version of the American Dream, like *The Autobiography of Ben Franklin*, or a Horatio Alger novel. Except, in De Palma's version the self-made man is a drug-dealing, murdering gangster. But that fantasy is too unrealistic now. I'm not sure what happened, but at some point American men gave up on that dream. They don't believe they can be Rockefeller or Tony Montana. Their testosterone is so low they can't even jerk off without imported, jasmine-scented, moisturizing, hand lotions and ultrasoft, cool-touch, antiviral tissues. I won't speculate about how, but it happened. Mass emasculation.

America is full of these culturally castrated men, and that's a big problem. Men have a biologically innate urge to kill, and win, and fuck—at the same time, if possible. And this urge has been dangerously suppressed. *Fight Club* is a fantasy for just this type of man. The guy who wants his balls back. The one who wishes he could murder his micromanaging boss instead of kissing his ass. The guy who wants to rape the blonde goddess who won't talk to him instead of going home to his tissues again and who wants to eat three greasy, bloody hamburgers—not nibble a kale and tofu salad.

Now, you may say these are the twisted perversions of toxic masculinity rather than natural urges—and that's as may be—but right or wrong, these appetites exist, and hunger is no respecter of morality. *Fight Club* fed these hungers. It provided a generation of men with relief from their masculine constipations, but it was still just a fantasy. For all their wild talk about being jungle beasts starving in nine-to-five prisons, most of them could never be like Tyler Durden. When you came right down to it, they were scared. Fear held them back with a tight grip.

The worst they would do is say mean things to each other.

* * *

I was dancing with a woman named Julie at a club in the West Village very early on a Saturday morning. Her roommate Amy owed me a favor. Some guy had been offering Amy drinks and kept grabbing her ass, so Amy asked me to take care of it. I went into the women's bathroom and picked out one of the women who was too shitfaced to live. I told the other ladies that she was my girlfriend and that I needed to get her home. They didn't ask any questions. I pulled the drunk woman's arm around my neck and carried her to security. I told them the guy bothering Amy had roofied my girlfriend. They took care of her and got rid of him, fast.

Amy was very impressed. She said she owed me a favor. "I'm gonna get you laid tonight. Pick any girl you want. I'll make it happen," she said as if it was already done.

I pointed at Julie.

"That's my roommate," Amy said.

"I know," I told her.

In hindsight, I think Amy was hoping that I would pick her, but soon I was dancing with Julie. Early twenties. Hourglass body. She had galactically deep, insatiable eyes of desperate hedonism. Katy Perry lipstick and skin-tight black leather. A red G-string accentuated an ass you could eat till you starved to death. In clubs, songs don't start or stop, they just fade into each other, and during one of these changes, I spun Julie around and pulled her close. I took an ice cube from her drink and pressed it to her lips. My fingers slid it across her cheek, down her neck, and delicately zigzagged over her breasts. Slowing down as I went. Feeling the electric goosebumps rise. Savoring the tension. She gave a little gasp as her eyes filled with desire.

I had one hand in her shirt and one on her ass when something slammed into my head. The old familiar pain. Hands grabbed me off the floor and threw me through the air. I landed hard and slumped up against a wall. I looked around and recognized nothing. Just lights and bodies. Julie and Amy were gone. I heard laughter.

"Hey!"

Laughter.

"Hey man, you okay?"

Ringing pain.

"Hey, come here, man—come here with us. Any moth-afucka take a punch like that can sit at my table anytime. Give'm a napkin. Here, gimme the ice bucket."

Soon I was sitting in spilled drinks at a table with strangers. Napkin-wrapped ice cubes pressed against my face. Everything felt surreal.

"I never seen anybody get cold-cocked like that."

"What happened?" I asked, still not sure of anything.

"What happened!? I'll tell you what happened, man. Three big-dick thugs fucked you up and took yo bitch—that's what happened."

Laughter.

"Why? What the hell did I do?" I asked.

"Hell if I know, they ain't gimme a list of grievances. Looked like had somethin' to do with that fine bitch you's grindin' on. Maybe his girl or some shit."

"Goddamn it, Amy," I said.

Laughter.

"I tell you man, I seen me some wild shit in my time but I ain't *never* seen nobody get thrown off a dance floor like that."

Laughter. I didn't speak. It was too loud to breathe. Surging pain.

"Hey listen, man, you got somebody you want me to call?"

"No. I'm alone," I answered.

"Well, you gotta be with somebody."

"Not anymore."

"You want me to call an ambulance or something? You ought to go to Beth Israel and get checked out 'cause I know one thing—your ass definitely got a concussion. I know that shit right now."

"No, no, look I'll just—no, thank you. I'm going home."

"You sure ain't nobody I can—"

"I'll take care of myself. Thanks for the ice. Goodnight."

Standing up felt like coming out of orbit, but I couldn't stand their laughter anymore. All my senses were in agony. I found the stairs.

As I walked down, I realized someone was following me. I sat down on a bench by coat check and he sat next to me. Neither of us spoke. I closed my eyes and rubbed my head. When I opened them, he was offering me another napkin ice pack.

"Thanks," I said, looking him over and trying to remember if I'd seen him before. I hadn't. He said nothing, so after several seconds I asked, "Who are you?"

"Just some guy." He spoke in a quiet, secretive way. I turned and looked at him, worried that I was hallucinating. I'd been awake for over twenty-four hours and had just suffered head trauma. Anything was possible.

"Some guy?"

"A friend."

"Who's friend?"

"Maybe."

I stared for a moment, then sighed hard and bowed over. "Look dude, I don't know who the fuck you are, but I'm tired, angry, and in serious pain. So I'm gonna need a straight answer out of you." I sat up again and asked, "who the fuck are you, man?"

"My name is Robert Paulson," he said with a meaningful stare.

I looked from one eye to the other, and back again. "What?"

"My name is Robert Paulson, and I know a place for men like you. A place where men who are tired, angry, and in serious pain can go to deal with their problems the healthy way, the natural way."

I was more confused. I didn't know what to make of that statement. He could have been asking me to come to a gay bar, or group therapy, or the Church of Scientology for all I knew. "Alright look, Bob, I'm not sure what you're talking about—so thanks for the ice, but I'm going to have to ask you to kindly fuck off."

"Of course, the first rule is you aren't allowed to talk about it. Which unfortunately makes it a little difficult to explain to a potential new member."

I looked at him again.

"But I think if you've seen the film, or read the book, and you're interested, you'll know exactly what I'm talking about." He stopped talking but held the stare. "My name is Robert Paulson," he said again.

I paused to think. I was in no condition to think, but I did it anyway.

Fuck it.

"Yes. Yes, I can see that .... I think I understand, Bob," I said.

His eyes lit up. "Would you like to come?"

"Yeah, I think I would."

"Excellent. Fortieth and Park on the steps outside the Kalikow building. Tomorrow night, 2:00 a.m. Come alone."

He got up and disappeared.

At 1:45 a.m. the next evening, I sat in my apartment listing all the reasons why I shouldn't go. I could end up in the hospital, or in jail, or in the East River. I didn't know anything about this guy, or exactly what I was going to be attending, or who else would be there. For all I knew, I could end up raped, or murdered, or abducted, or all three. It was dangerous and indefensibly reckless.

I went.

At 2:00 a.m. I was standing on the corner of Fortieth and Park. Robert Paulson came up on foot from Grand Central.

"Hi, Bob," I said.

"You ready?" He asked.

"I am Jack's raging bile duct."

He smiled and took a blanket out of his backpack. "Take this and sit up there. They won't know you're here. Just watch for tonight. The way we do it is a little different than the book, but it accomplishes the same thing. If you're still interested, I'll introduce you next week. It's set for three. I'll be back around then."

He handed me the blanket and walked away. I didn't know this before, but a lot of homeless people sleep on the steps outside the Kalikow building. The steps are dry, clean, and they have exterior power outlets. I laid down on the spot on the landing that Bob had pointed out and pulled the blanket around me. It was February. I was almost numb when the first one showed up.

Then another.

Then a few more.

By 3:00 a.m. there were eight of them. Including Robert Paulson.

Eight anonymous men in a little circle outside of a Park Avenue office building at 3:00 a.m. in the dead of winter. There was something low about them. Stooped shoulders. Eyes on the street. Slow feet. Desperate losers with impotent rage. They all had their reasons for being there and most of the reasons were obvious. One guy was little, one guy was fat, one guy was Muslim, and one guy was black. There was one guy who just seemed like an average twenty-something. Class ring. J. Crew clothes. Trendy haircut. A little out of place. When the last one arrived, they all turned and faced each other. The sudden, purposeful movement caught my attention, and I sat up to get a better look. The fat guy moved to the center of the circle. He turned to face the black guy and received a tirade from him.

"Fat fat fatty fat fat fat."

I can't remember what Black Guy said, but that was the gist. Fatty only faced him long enough for a few words, then he turned to the next guy. A few more seconds, a few more words, then he turned to the next guy. When Fatty had completed the circle, he stepped back into his position. The next man moved to the center and began his turn. They went on like this, each man taking his turn in the center, tearing each other apart with their words, really biting into the low-hanging fruit. However, since they'd all been hit in those places countless times before, they'd all grown armor over the obvious. No matter how bad the abuse got, nobody cracked.

At first, I struggled to hold back laughter. Out of all the

things they could have chosen to do with their time, these eight ridiculous idiots were hurling hatred at each other in the middle of a winter's night on a New York City street. I watched for over an hour. They just kept going. Fast, too. As the morning came on, I started to feel uneasy. The tone was changing. There was something menacing in it. It kept building with every turn of the wheel. Faster and fouler. Spittle and red screams. Intense malice and loathing venom. It wasn't funny anymore. The night was fading. The meeting was almost over.

Twenty-Something took his last turn and came to face Pock Marks. Pock Marks paused and smiled like a gloating victor. I'll never know for sure, but I think he must have planned this. It had to have been premeditated. Pock Marks wasn't satisfied with the effect his attacks were having, so he'd picked a target and done some research. He'd found the open wound that no one else could see—the place where the blade would sink deepest. He came here with his weapon already in hand, but he didn't strike right away. He waited until the very end of the battle when his opponent was tired and he knew the blow would land hardest. Pock Marks stepped forward and with pointed force said, "Katy doesn't love you and she gets fucked by other men."

Twenty-Something was on top of him wildly slashing with a knife before any of us could react. I could hear his vocal cords tearing. The circle collapsed into a pile as they pulled him off. His blue gingham had big red spots. Everyone scattered. Twenty-Something was still screaming in pain as he ran down the block. Pock Marks got up and staggered towards Lexington clutching his wounds.

Laughing.

I was still shivering on the steps outside the Kalikow building as the sun came up Sunday morning.

Staring at the blood.

Counting scars.

I never went back to Fight Club.

But I still have the blanket.

Thelma

I once had the privilege to attend the Tribeca Film Festival's fortieth anniversary screening of Taxi Driver at the Beacon Theater in New York City. I arrived to see a heavily waxed, yellow, checker cab out front. It was supposed to look like the one from the movie, but it was a replica of a different model. The real ones are all gone. They also had a GI jacket like the one De Niro wears in the movie. That was a replica too. Paul Schrader donated the real one to the University of Texas at Austin. People took lots of pictures.

The audience was full of the rich and famous.

Michael Moore still looks like a depressed dropout with terrible hygiene.

Danny Glover is a badass.

Jean Reno was there.

Patrick Wilson.

That guy who plays Kick-Ass in the *Kick-Ass* movies.

Jennifer Morrison from *House*.

My seat was in the third row. Four-hundred-dollar ticket. Black suit, black tie. I even brought along my copy of the movie. It has a dark stain on the cover from a night during my third year of college when my blood spurted all over the white wall of my bedroom. It made a wide arc—like a rainbow. I thought it was beautiful, so I left the blood on the wall for the rest of the year. I washed it off when I moved out, but the drops that landed on my special edition of *Taxi Driver* won't ever wash out. I also brought my Bible, but that's just an old habit I learned from my father. I always bring my Bible to church.

I've seen *Taxi Driver* probably fifty times. I'm really not sure. The first time I was fourteen, and I didn't get it. Kind of like the first time I heard Johnny Cash, and my only thought was why is he so sad?

Eventually I got it, though.

I remember the last time I watched it in college. It was about 4:45 a.m., and I'd just finished a final project. All I had left to do was prepare my thesis presentation for later that day. I could have done it in twenty minutes and gone to bed. Instead, I watched *Taxi Driver*, made my PowerPoint, showered, and went to my last college class. What initially created my obsession with Travis, and what is really the final genius of the film, is that for a period of my life I felt like I was Travis Bickle. That character is one of the most perfect articulations of self-destructive loneliness ever created in art, and he came from a momentary synchronization between all the people who made the movie. Most importantly, Paul Schrader, Martin Scorsese, and Robert De Niro.

At the time, these three men understood heartbroken loneliness, depression, and self-destruction better than anyone.

And for a time in my life, so did I. That's why I feel so connected to them and the film. We were Travis Bickle. During that time, watching even a few shots from *Taxi Driver* gave me panic attacks. I had to stop watching it so I wouldn't lose my mind.

But I didn't have a panic attack seeing it at the Beacon.

I'm not Travis anymore.

When the movie was over, they all came out on stage.

Michael Phillips, who produced it.

Paul Schrader, who lived and wrote it.

Harvey Keitel, who plays The Pimp.

Cybill Shepherd, who plays The Madonna.

Jodie Foster, who plays The Whore.

Robert De Niro, who plays Christ.

And Martin Scorsese, who plays God and The Devil.

Seeing the people who made a film that is such an important part of my life ten feet away from my face wasn't any great religious experience—that's what the film is for—but it was something I have always wanted to do. It was like meeting the guy who wrote the Gospel of Mark. He wasn't there with Jesus, and he didn't perform any miracles, but he did something that changed the human relationship with God.

Maybe that's a flawed analogy.

Anyway, they were there telling stories and discussing the movie. I'd heard all of it before, but it was nice to hear it from them. At one point the moderator asked Scorsese what he was trying to say with this movie, and Scorsese gave the same answer he has always given, which is that he cannot articulate it. An interviewer once asked T. S. Eliot what he meant by his poem *The Wasteland*, and Eliot answered, "I meant what I said, if I could have said it any other way I would have."

Even though none of them can put it into words, these people on stage all knew damn well what they were trying to say and how important it was. Paul Schrader was coping with suicidal depression, Robert De Niro had never been socially accepted anywhere, and Scorsese went into a cocaine-fueled, murderous rage when he was told to recut the film. But forty years is a long time. In truth, none of the people on stage were the same ones who made that film. They aren't tormented by the same demons. They don't have the same artistic visions. They've made peace with themselves to some extent and become comfortable. I think the key is that they aren't lonely anymore.

Scorsese was wearing one of his custom-made Armani suits.

Paul Schrader is a revered film critic, screenwriter, and director.

Robert De Niro is far from being a misfit.

And so on.

But that made me happy, too. They had made the movie and miraculously survived, and that is a very good and hopeful thing. It means there's still a chance for all the other Travis Bickles in the world. As they were leaving the stage I yelled, "God bless you, Marty." He turned and waved and said, "Thank you." What I would really like is a chance to talk to Marty and Paul about the film—to ask them questions they have never answered. Not vague, touchy-feely stuff about existentialism. I'm interested in specific directorial decisions and the new meanings they created by synthesizing references to dozens of other films. Maybe I will someday, but probably not. The stage was empty. I left the theater.

I walked out with the rich and famous pressing their way through the lobby. Back to the replicas and the selfies. I made it to the street and looked at the scene. I noticed a little old woman shimming through the crowd toward the doors. No one was paying any attention to her. No one seemed to see her at all. She reached the exit, and still no one recognized her. She came outside and, step-by-step, made her way past the bright lights and winter coats. There were cameras everywhere, but none were pointed at her. She was moving down the block now. I felt a rush of emotion. Someone had to do something. She hadn't even been given a seat on the stage. I sat in the third row, while she was up in the balcony, and now she was just going to walk off into the night like some lost grandmother. It wasn't right. I knew who she was, even if no one else did.

In 1963 she took a six-week film-editing class at New York University. There was a student there named Martin Scorsese who was trying to complete a short film called *What's a Nice Girl Like You Doing in a Place Like This?* But it had been butchered by an incompetent editor, and Scorsese was in a panic thinking that the film would be lost because the negative was ruined. She helped him save the film, which kept him from failing out of school. She edited his first feature too. After graduating, she and Marty worked together editing the documentary of the famous Woodstock Music Festival.

When Scorsese made *Taxi Driver*, his shooting schedule was so tight that he left all the editing until the end. He was over budget and behind schedule. This left him with almost no time to edit the film. He called her to save him once again. With her help, *Taxi Driver* was completed on time. Without her, Scorsese would have been sued, fired, and God knows what would have happened to the movie and his career. Her contribution went uncredited because she wasn't allowed in the guild.

A few years later, when Scorsese finished shooting *Raging Bull*, which is widely considered among the best edited films of all time, he specifically requested that she be added to the Motion Picture Editors Guild so that she could do the editing with him. He was too sick to do it himself and didn't trust anyone but her. She has edited every film Scorsese has

made since and has been Scorsese's most important and closest collaborator. She has eight Oscar nominations, three wins,
and is arguably the best and most influential film editor of
all time. And this tiny, white-haired woman, who had just
walked unnoticed through a celebration of a film she saved,
was Thelma Schoonmaker.

Thelma doesn't wear custom-made Armani suits.

She doesn't sign posters.

And she isn't a replica.

Thelma Schoonmaker is the real thing.

And she was still going uncredited.

Somebody had to say something.

So I approached this artist whose work means more to me
than I can articulate and said, "Excuse me, Ms. Schoonmaker?"

She turned her head, "Yes?"

"Sorry to intrude, but I wanted to thank you for all of your
wonderful work."

She laughed, "Oh well, I work for a brilliant director."

She has been repeating that for years. In every interview
I've ever seen, she always stresses Marty's genius, not her own.
Her security escort stepped up to give me the brush-off, so I
quickly replied, "Yes, well, so you keep saying, but I want you
to know that your tremendous talents have not gone unap-
preciated so, again, thank you very much, Thelma. Have a
great night. God bless you."

She laughed and thanked me in her warm, friendly voice.
Then I stopped and let her walk on down the empty sidewalk
into the night. Her silhouette rocked back and forth in the
dark, and then she was gone.

I turned back to the lights outside The Beacon. "TAKE A PHOTO WITH THIS VINTAGE TAXI DRIVER POSTER SIGNED BY ROBERT DE NIRO!"

iPhones waiting in line.

I went around the block and found the chairs they'd used for the panel sitting on the street behind the theater.

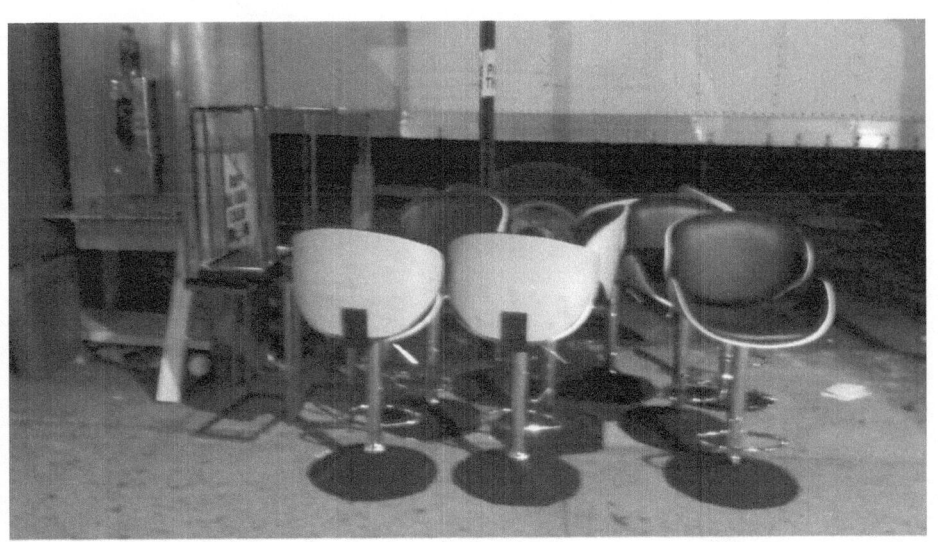

I caught a cab home.

A Long Ride Home

My driver's name was Muir. I got in the passenger's seat instead of the back, and we drove in silence. A song from Bieber's new album came on. Muir didn't flinch. It struck me as funny that he didn't try to change it, so I asked, "Is this what you like to listen to?"

"What?"

"This music—this top forty pop stuff—is this what you like?"

"No. Is for kids, mostly young kids this late," he said with a heavy accent.

"Well what do you like to listen to?"

"You can change if you don't like."

"No, I don't care I just wanted to know what kind of music you like to listen to."

"What station you want hear?" He reached for the dial.

"No, man I don't care about that. I just wanted to—well anyway, what do you think of this Justin Bieber kid?" I asked, trying to change the subject.

"What you mean what I think?"

"Well you know what I mean, just what do you make of him?"

"If you want to change station, is okay."

"No, I—Look, I just—" I shook my head and turned to the window. A thousand lights dancing in the East River. "Well he does a lot of crazy shit, doesn't he? I mean, what do you think about all that?"

"Oh, oh, I see. I see. Well, to me is like this. Okay, he does a lot of crazy shit, right? Well, if you were young kid, millionaire and famous, everybody loves you—you be doing these drugs and so many girls and crazy shit, too. So is no fair hate him. If you hate him—okay. Is because jealousy, not because him. He is just kid. He not know any more than you or me—he just have opportunity and of course he doing crazy drug sex shit and be bad person. Nobody teach him. He just another kid. Is no different."

"Yeah, I guess that's true. God knows, we all do a bunch of crazy, stupid shit when we're young. I bet you've got some good stories, don't you? You ever do any crazy shit when you were young?"

He laughed and pounded the horn.

"Alright let's hear it. Come on Muir what's the craziest shit you ever did?"

"Oh my God. Let me see. Well, okay. One winter in Bulgaria, Soviet Union fall—my friend and I, we get drunk and we take out girls. And between the rebels and the soldiers we lay down in snow and fucking these girls."

"Between the two sides?"

"Yes. But in cold snow how you say, your dick? Prick? You

can't do it because it's your dick is hard keep hard, yes? So, we say okay, okay—we drink more vodka and then is okay."

"You mean you drank so you could get it up?" I couldn't believe he was telling me this.

"Yes. Right. If you drink right amount you easier get hard in snow, but be careful my friend, because drink too much you are soft. All the time, soft. No easy get it right."

"Yeah, right—whiskey dick. Sure. So, did they all see you— the other soldiers and rebels I mean—what did they do?"

"What you think they do? They laughing and yelling. No fighting that night. Everybody happy and singing watch us with these girls in the snow. Everybody drinking."

"Vodka?"

"Vodka, yes. Everybody, all the time, vodka. Both sides, vodka."

"Wow. That's a beautiful story. I've never done anything like that, but I think I got one for you." I shifted in my seat and he smiled in anticipation. "This goes way back, I haven't talked about this in years, but I used to know this girl with a huge crush on Darth Vader. She had it bad, too. She had a Vader backpack, towels, socks, everything. One day she lets me walk her home. I'm alone with this girl in her house and she asks me what my favorite *Star Wars* movie is. Somehow, I end up doing my best Vader impression and I can tell by her eyes that she's into it. She keeps asking for more, and more, and I'm going through every line I can remember until I've got her bent over on the bed, choking her with both hands, and a Darth Vader t-shirt over my face, saying shit like—you are unwise to lower your defenses—and—you don't know the power of the dark side. I was doing the whole breathing thing, too. It was ridiculous, but she was so hot I didn't care. She was sixteen at the time with this long, platinum blonde hair and the ass of a Broadway dancer. God, she was wild. But I guess that kind of thing is only for young people."

"Speak for yourself, my friend," he said with joyous mischief in his plumb-beaded face. He hit the horn again, and we burst out laughing.

"Alright Muir, tell me another one."

"Okay. Okay. Second craziest. Okay—this was few years later in Austria. I had red Volkswagen Beetle and the lake racing. Wintertime lake freeze over, so we racing on the ice. Seven people in my Volkswagen Beetle and racing on the ice with my other friend in his car. Also full of people. But is no really race—we make circles."

"Doughnuts?"

"Yes, yes, big circles. Doughnuts. Drinking and naked in my Volkswagen Beetle and we go one hundred-fifty kilometers per hour across lake."

"Wait—naked?"

"Everybody, yes. Naked, and we take pills. You know this?"

"Taking pills? Yeah, pills. I know pills. What kind of pills?"

"I don't know, but they are working fast, I tell you this, my friend."

"Vodka too?" I was concerned about how this would end.

"No, schnapps. German girl like schnapps, but is no different."

"So, you're telling me you were drunk and speeding across a frozen Austrian lake in two tiny cars full of naked people?"

"Yes, and girls take turns give me blowjob while I driving."

"Jesus Christ, Muir. That's pretty rock n' roll."

"Very dangerous."

"Oh, yeah. I'm sure."

"Yes, because we see big hole in the ice, and car and bodies floating in the water. And so we see this and so—okay, I say—okay, and I drive off ice."

"Oh shit, they died?"

"Yes, not any more fun after this, so we leave."

"Goddamn. Yeah, lots of kids die doing stupid, crazy shit in cars." A huddle of NYU students crossed the avenue through our headlights and I thought about Ben.

"The first friend I ever had died that way. He was trying to show off for a girl. The car was full, and he was speeding down these little weaving streets in our old neighborhood. Drifting, peeling out, and all of that. He lost control and rammed a tree. He sat up and asked, 'Is everybody okay?' Then he just collapsed. Apparently, when they hit the tree the steering wheel bashed in his chest. Crushed his heart on the spot. Everyone else was okay, but he died right there in the car."

I scratched my knee and listened to the turn signal blink.

"I met Ben when I was a month old. First friend I ever had, and my best friend for the first five years of my life. I did well in school. He didn't. We made different friends, did different things—you know how it is. People drift. I remember how much that hurt—watching him turn into a stranger. Losing him a little each day. Seeing the new friends change him. Wanting to run up and hug him and get him back. We were brothers once. His mother is the sweetest woman I've ever known. When I was a baby I loved her more than Santa Claus. She could always make me laugh whenever I started crying. Lost her mind after that accident. Just couldn't take seeing her young son's broken body. We were eighteen when it happened. Ben hadn't spoken to me in years. It's strange, but after all this time I still miss a guy I knew for only a few years before my life had really started. I miss everyone who leaves, but not like Ben. I didn't cry at his funeral, though. Our moms cried, but I didn't. I lost him years before he hit that tree."

City blocks rolled by in silence. White paint. Wet streets. Finally, I had to say something.

"Crazy shit."

"I sorry, my friend. Life is motherfucker," Muir said.

I nodded. Silence again.

"Wait, Muir you said the Volkswagen was the second craziest, what was the craziest?"

His voice went flat. "The craziest was I am from Afghanistan. I spend three years fighting the fucking Taliban and they kidnap my daughter."

"Jesus," I whispered.

"They kidnap my daughter she five years old. Few days later they send her back. And she yelling my name and running toward house, but when she reaches middle of village, she explodes. They put bomb in her backpack. Many people in my village dead. So I spend three years fighting the Taliban. My wife leave. Family gone. House destroyed. Finally, I have nothing left to fight for—this endless war—so, I say okay, I have no life here, why I stay and die? So I say okay, I leave Afghanistan."

"God. I'm so sorry, Muir." Was all I could offer.

"I sorry too. Lot of Yankees die fighting those bastards. Could been you."

"Yeah, they always send young people to do that kind of thing. Crazy shit to have to do when you're so young."

"Is no different. Young man, old man, young girl—no different."

Another long silence brought us to my empty street. Memories kicked my swollen headache. I found a flask somebody must have left in the seat.

"Is vodka?" Muir asked.

"Bourbon."

"No different."

I handed it to him, and he took a deep pull.

The hazard lights clicked.

I turned off the radio.

Ashes

Last night a cathedral burned down in New York.

The Serbian Orthodox Cathedral of Saint Sava.

May 1st. Resurrection Sunday—the most holy day in the Christian faith.

Four alarms. One hundred-seventy firefighters. Barricades and caution tape. Bright lights. Service vehicles. The pavement was littered with debris. Oreos and office supplies. There were cops, firefighters, construction workers, and swarms of gawkers who had just come to see. A bar across Twenty-sixth Street had a great view and was packed with a happy-hour congregation sipping drinks and snapping selfies.

Karaoke night.

Across Twenty-fifth, a restaurant had put out a bucket of menus and extra signs. Taste Good Restaurant—Authentic Chinese Cuisine.

Free advertising.

One guy in the crowd had a beard and shaved head, except for one long braid that went down to the middle of his back. The all-seeing eye on his T-shirt was staring at the wreckage.

He turned to the girl next to him and asked, "What do you see?"

"Ashes," the woman answered.

"I see Freedom."

Then he held up two flowers and took a picture of them and the church.

The flowers were made of fabric and wax.

He kissed her and they walked away.

The whole block smelled like a burned-out campfire.

Steaming black water was being pumped into the gutters.

Slowly going down the drain.

I searched up and down the streets looking for someone who was praying. In a city of ten million people that had just lost a landmark cathedral, there had to be someone who was praying.

I only found one.

Helena was standing alone. Jeans, tired shoes, simple jacket, and a backpack. Tears on worry-lines. No makeup. Her red, shaking hands were clamped together so tight they whited her knuckles. People were pointing and staring—someone laughed. She looked like a crazy homeless lady. I prayed with her for a while, then she just started talking.

"I was born in Serbia and raised by my grandparents. I was only there a few years, but they were such happy memories. I came to America for school and then stayed for university. Then I went back to Serbia to see my grandparents, and it was awful. Bomb holes from the landmines where we went to get water. Running from snipers. They burned my grandfather's church. Awful fighting and wars. So much fear.

"I came back to live here because of this cathedral. Because for me it means hope. I've seen it every day when I wake up since I first came here. I learned English here. So many services, and weddings, and funerals, and christenings. This is my home—you understand? This is my home in this country. And seeing it—this—I just—they said no one was injured, but how can you say that? How could anyone look at this and say no one was injured? It breaks my heart because it will never stop, this madness. The torture, the violent bloodshed. It will never stop until everything is gone."

Helena wept. I hugged her. A man came up and spoke to her in Serbian. We prayed. It got late. I told her I had to leave and let go of her hand. She hugged me and begged me to keep praying.

They don't know what caused the fire that burned down

the 143-year-old Serbian Orthodox Cathedral of Saint Sava in New York City.

Or the one that gutted the Macedonian Orthodox Church of the Resurrection in Sydney.

The cause of the one that destroyed the Valaam Monastary in Russia hasn't been established.

No one knows why the 115-year-old Holy Church of the Annunciation of Our Lady in Melbourne went up in flames either.

The official theory is the fires were started accidentally by ceremonial candles.

Four churches. Three continents. One Easter Sunday.

Coincidence.

If you'd like to make a donation here's a link: http://stsa-vanyc.org/our-church-has-burned-down/

They're going to use the money to restore the building.

I don't know how they plan to rebuild The Church.

* * *

I ate the Oreos—the ones that had been washed out of the church and were sitting in the drain—I ate them.

I bent down and ate the melted, soaked cookies right there in the street.

One of the cops watched me. I guess he'd never seen a guy in a suit eat ruined cookies off the street before.

But I felt like someone should eat them.

And no one else was going to.

So I ate them, Goddamn it.

He stared at me like I was crazy.

Abraham, Abraham

I saw a guy with a three-year-old kid selling drugs on a street corner in the South Bronx once. I was sitting on a bench with my class ring and brand-name jeans—reading a famous book on comparative mythology and searching for meaning—with my stupid mid-twenties, rich-white-guy ennui—and this poor fucker is out on a corner in the Bronx at 2:00 p.m. on a Wednesday trying to sell drugs so he can get high and feed his kid.

I looked at him, and his son, and my book, and I thought, "I am so fulla shit."

Later that day, David called me.

"Give us Barabbas." I always answer his calls with a line from scripture.

"John, you're one of the least full of shit people I know."

I told him about the guy I saw and how I was full of shit and all my problems were stupid.

"Yeah, but you *know* you're fulla shit," David said. "That validates your whole dick. Because that guy is a self-obsessed white guy in his mid-twenties too, but he acts like he's black, roots for the Knicks, and has a kid for no fucking reason. He's only selling drugs because that's all he knows how to do because he drank PBR and smoked shitty weed all his life. He doesn't have *real* problems. Your problems are just as stupid as he is. He's completely fulla shit. And fuck his stupid kid too. That's just a science-fair project eating and shitting until he gets fitted for an orange jumpsuit. They're all fulla shit. Fuck 'em."

That night I remembered a business trip I took while I was a consultant in DC. I'd set an alarm on the clock radio in my corporate hotel room in Baltimore. 6:30 a.m. a voice told me that this morning Mr. So-and-so had decided to run over his infant son's head with his car.

Said, it burst.

Like a watermelon.

After that, they said it was fourteen degrees out.

I never finished the book.

This Is My Beloved Son

"You can't write things like that. You can't say words like F, and S, and G. D.!"

"Why not?"

"*Why not!?*"

"Yeah. Why can't I say words like F, and S, and G. D.?"

"Because I'm your father and I'm tellin' you so! Now the Bible says to honor your mother and father, and I want it stopped. You're supposed to be a Christian. You talk like that—you ought to be ashamed of yourself. I'm ashamed of ya!"

I had just gotten out of bed and I was sitting at my desk in my boxer briefs listening to Dad bark at me over the phone. His call woke me up. Usually, I would have just let it ring, but there's something about family that will make you keep trying even though it's hopeless. I answered the phone and tried to communicate.

"How do you know I'm a Christian, Dad?"

"*What?*"

"Well, I mean—just because I love Jesus, and I read the Bible and pray—doesn't make me a Christian. That's up to Jesus."

"Are you a Christian or ain't ya?"

"Jesus Christ, I hope so."

"JOHN!"

"What?"

"Don't say Jesus Christ like that!"

"Why not? How am I supposed to say it?"

"Stop taking the Lord's name in vain."

"I don't know the Lord's name, Dad."

"You say 'Jesus Christ.' That's bad. You shouldn't say that."

"You just said it twice right now."

"Okay—don't get smart with me, boy. It's different. The way you're doin' it is bad, wrong, and I want it stopped."

"Maybe you're right, but I don't think Jesus would mind me using his name if it makes people think about something besides pornography and Donald Trump."

"That's not—okay—boy, I'm telling you, I'm telling you right now. I don't want to hear any more of your smart mouth. I want it stopped. There's a difference between witnessing to people about the Lord and the filth you're doing."

"I know, Dad."

"Then why do you say that?"

"Because sometimes people say that."

"Well that doesn't make it okay for you to say that."

"I know."

"Then why you say that?"

"It's just more honest."

"What do you mean it's more honest? That's not the way Jesus talked!"

"Well I'm not Jesus, and anyway—"

"YOU'RE GODDAMN RIGHT YOU'RE NOT!"

"—anyway, I think swearing is some kind of prayer, maybe not a good kind, but I know it's some kind of praying."

He took a deep, anguished breath.

"Alright, boy. Now you listen to me. I don't know what your problem is—I don't care about your problems. Whatever you think it is you're trying to do with this—I'm telling you this, I'm telling you this right now. I want this writing stopped and I want it all taken down. You hear me, boy? If you say you're a Christian and you talk about things like that, you're a liar and you're gonna burn in Hell for it. You think people want to read that? You think anyone cares what your problems are? You're embarrassing your mother and father! *You hear me!?*"

"Yeah, Dad, I hear you."

"Okay. Now, are you gonna take this down and stop using bad words?"

"No."

"*No?!*"

"I said no, Dad."

"Ah you, sonofabitch—Look, I'm not—Listen to me. I'm not asking ya, I'm tellin' ya. I want it stopped right now, or I'm gonna come up there and I'm gonna cut ya down, do ya understand?!"

"You're gonna cut me down?"

"YEAH. I'M GONNA CUT YA DOWN!"

"What does that mean? You don't even know where I live."

"It means you better stop all this bad language and go to Church and pray and ask God to forgive ya, or you're gonna burn in Hell for it. You keep going on and on about Jesus, but you don't know him. You're not a real Christian, and you don't know the Lord!"

"Yeah, well maybe you're right. I mean, I've never met Jesus, but I'd like to think he and I would get along. We both have a low threshold for pretentious religious bullshit, and I think we would bond over that."

"*Don't say*—ah—you talk to this boy, will ya!?"

He passed the phone to Mom.

"Hey—hey, John? You there?"

My mother is the best of us. My brother David says she's the cutest fluffy bunny in the whole enchanted kingdom. She's a retired pharmacist and spends all her time gardening, biking, and talking about Jesus.

"Hi, Mom. How are you?"

"Hey, hey, you know what, I'm not doing too good, you know? You know, I agree with everything your Dad said, I don't know why you have to write such awful things like that."

"I know, Mom. I'm sorry."

"Yeah. And by the way, your Facebook picture is ugly—do you know that?"

"I know, Mom, I'm sorry. I love you."

"Yeah, no you don't. You don't love me or else you wouldn't write nasty things like that. What if your employer sees that? Do you think anyone's gonna want to hire someone like you? What about all your friends—and your little cousins? Don't you know they see that? What do you think they're going to think of you if they see that?"

"I don't know, Mom. I guess it doesn't really matter."

"Yeah it does, John. People will see that, and they'll think you're a degenerate. They'll think your father and I are bad people because we raised a reprobate son like you."

"I know, Mom. I'm sorry, but I love you both very much."

"Why don't you shave and get a haircut and smile like a nice boy? Don't you care what people think of you? Don't you care about how you look? You were such a handsome, smart kid, but now you look so ugly and you're wasting your life. You're never gonna make any money trying to make movies, John. Why don't you come home and get a real job?"

"I'm doing the best I can, Mom."

"Well, I think what you're doing is awful, and it's stupid. You're squandering your gifts. And you always try to force God into it somewhere—but that is not appropriate Christian testimony, young man. I'm not debating you. I'm telling you—do not do this anymore. And I don't care what else you've got to say."

"Alright, Mom. I'm sorry you're upset. I love you."

My father took back the phone.

"Hey, boy?"

"Yeah, Dad."

"Now look, boy, I'm telling you this for your own good—okay? This is bad. And it's wrong. And you need to stop doing this and take it down. The Lord showed me that you need to stop doing this."

"Oh, the Lord showed you that, huh?"

"Yeah. He did."

I don't mind ridicule, I don't mind verbal abuse, but I cannot abide a false prophet. The mercury shot up my needle like a hydrogen bomb had gone off.

"Well, I guess that's different isn't it? I mean that changes things some doesn't it?".

"Yeah. It does." I could tell he noticed the tonal shift.

"I mean when you put it that way, I think it makes a lot of sense."

"Alright then. Now are you gonna stop all this and take that filthy trash down?"

"Dad, can I ask you a question?"

"What?"

"Which one of my pieces did the Lord speak to you about? Which one did you read?"

"I don't know—I'm just telling you it's bad."

"Yeah, but which one, though. Do you remember what the title was, or what it was about?"

"No, I don't know. Your mother said the rest of the family has been calling about you, and she read something. I don't know. It doesn't matter what you wrote. If you're using bad words, it's bad!"

"Wait, wait, Dad, wait. Stop. Stop. Stop."

"What?"

"Are you telling me that you called me to tell me all this and you haven't even read anything I've written?"

"Hey, boy, I know everything I need to know about you already. Alright? I can take one look at you and see what kind of kid you are. Okay? You need a haircut and a bath. You look dirty. Now are you going to take this junk down?"

"No."

"*What?!*"

"I said no, Dad. Fuck, no. There's no fucking way, sir."

"Why not!?"

"BECAUSE I THINK IT'S WORTH SAYING! I know you're probably right, and I'm probably wrong, but I don't give a shit. I know Proverbs says that in the multitude of words there wanteth not sin, and I know that I'm probably an irretrievably blasphemous sinner who is going to be damned to Hell. But in Corinthians Paul says it pleased God by the foolishness of preaching to save them that believe, and that God made foolish the wisdom of this world, and that the preaching of the cross is to them that perish foolishness but unto us which are saved it is the power of God. So maybe I do look like a dirty bum, but what do you think Jesus looked like when he was up on that cross? Do you think he remembered to shave that morning? Do you think he woke up and said, 'Jesus fucking Christ— I better shave, otherwise my Father will be very upset with me?'"

"Don't say that!" my father said.

"Man looks on the outward appearance, but God looks on the heart, Dad. And I'm trying to work out my own salvation with fear and trembling. And I may not be doing a very good job, but I'm trying my best. I'm trying to find a way to say something about something. I don't know what—I don't know why—but I know I have to fucking do it. But good or bad, I'm going to do it my own fucking, Goddamn way. Then I'll send you my address and you can either mail me a check or come cut me down."

"Ah, you filth," he snarled.

"And the same goes for God, too. He can stop me anytime he wants, but he can come tell me that himself, because I'm not going to take anyone else's word for it. It shouldn't be too hard for him to get in touch with me. He's got my address."

"You know, you don't listen, you stubborn kid. You're a fool. You know that, John? You're a stubborn, sinful fool."

"Yeah, Dad, I know."

He stopped talking, but he didn't hang up. I could still hear him breathing into the phone. That's my Dad. He'll scream and yell and threaten, but he would never leave the room or hang up the phone—because deep down, he really does love his family very much. He's performatively emotional with very delicate sensitivities. I've seen him cry countless times. These days I find it hard to connect with him. We're very different men. I could have just hung up the phone and forgotten about it, but it was Sunday, and I loved him. I stayed on the line and heard his breathing slow down. When the wind and seas were finally calm, I looked out the window at the sun shining on New York and extended his favorite olive branch—The Great American Game.

"So, how're the Orioles doin'?"

Here Lies John

I found an old man crying on the street last night
on the corner of eighteenth and sixth
I bent down and asked if he needed help
he was on his knees
face to the ground
with drops on his glasses
and dark spots on the concrete
his cane had caught the gray marble corner of a building
I helped him stand
and held his arm
bones wrapped in blue wool
how long have you been here?
forty years
no, I mean on the street
three hours

I hailed a cab
take him home?
no
$100?
no again

two more cabs
two more no's
one said yes if I came too
and the $100

I cautioned him to watch his head and closed the door
my name's john
mine too
he was from England
lived in New York forty years
but tonight, he fell down
and got left out on the street for three hours
in the city that he loved
they both smelled of urine

landlady went up and woke the live-in nurse
I held his arm on the street
Saint Mark's Place
thank you young man
you're welcome young man
he tried to laugh
my hip hurts
the nurse took him inside
I called his son
what's the old fucker done now?
the hospital was more polite
what's your emergency?
broken hip
Saint Mark's Place
Aetna
right away sir
the customer is always right

Here Lies John

I watched them bring him out on a bed
and caution him to watch his head
I looked at the landlady
and the nurse
who the fuck are you?
I left

no sleep again
went to work
came back to ask about him
the landlady told me that john was dead
his son had called to fire the nurse
who are you?

I walked home
tired
alone
I put my knee on the curb and left some dark spots of my own

I made it back to bed
without falling down
this time
and laying here
with muddled thoughts
wrote this

good night

Jury Duty

"Now you all understand the circumstances of the case as the judge has described them to you only a moment ago, correct? Okay great, then I just have a few additional questions for you all. How many of you would say that you regularly ride the subway? Okay great. Silly question I know, but what about this—how many of you would say you regularly ride the subway at four o'clock in the morning? Great. See, the point I want to make here is that—"

"Wait a minute, counselor. I see we've got a hand here."

"Oh, I'm sorry. We have one?"

"Yeah, I see one in the back there."

"Okay great. Thank you, Your Honor. And I see here it's, uh, Mr.—Gillian, is it?"

"It's Gillen."

"Mr. Gillen, thank you. Okay Mr. Gillen, you say you regularly take the subway at four o'clock in the morning?"

"Sometimes."

"I see Mr. Gillen, and how often would you say 'sometimes' is?"

"Well I usually walk, but if I'm too tired or cold or whatever, I'll just take the subway. Maybe a few times a week."

"I see, and Mr. Gillen, would you say that in your opinion a person who's in the subway at four o'clock in the morning is up to something?"

"I would certainly hope so."

No one laughed.

"Very good Mr. Gillen, what I mean is—do you feel that a person is more suspicious or more likely to be involved in some type of criminal activity just because they're in the subway at four o'clock in the morning?"

"Well—no—not necessarily."

"I see. Now, Mr. Gillen, I can't help but notice you hesitated. Something on your mind you want to share with us?"

"No, I was just thinking."

"About what exactly?"

"Nothing, it's not important."

The judge spoke up.

"Counselor, if I may—Mr. Gillen, as I said before, the purpose of these proceedings is to allow the prosecution and defense to agree on a jury. To do that they both must be assured that there is nothing in any jury member's personal experience that might make them biased one way or the other. So, with that in mind, I would ask you to please share with counsel whatever experiences you may have had that might be relevant to this case."

"Thank you, Your Honor. Mr. Gillen, I'll ask you again, is there any reason your experience might make you believe that a person is likely to be guilty of a crime because they are in a subway station at four o'clock in the morning?"

I'd never been called to serve on a jury before, and I didn't expect the first question I'd be asked to answer before a New York State Supreme Court Justice would be about my strange patronage of the Metropolitan Transit Authority. The court-room had a stark linoleum floor and the walls were covered in fake wood paneling, the kind they only made in eighties. There were harsh fluorescent lights and cheap plastic chairs. The whole place had the general feeling of a John Hughes movie set at a state college.

They were all staring at me, so I had to answer.

"Let's just say I'm intimately familiar with what it's like on the subway at 4:00 a.m. and leave it at that."

"Mr. Gillian, may I ask what it is you do that you find yourself riding the subway at four o'clock in the morning on a regular basis? Is this work-related, or some other business you have to conduct?"

"No, nothing like that."

"Something recreational perhaps, or a personal matter of some kind?"

"Not really, no."

"Pardon me Mr. Gillian, but are you saying that you have no reason at all to be out on the street at that time?"

"Counselor, I'm trying very hard not to say anything."

"Well I'd just like to understand what reason you could have to be—"

"My name is John Matthew Gillen. I live in Manhattan, I have a Bachelor of Science in Systems Engineering from the

University of Virginia, and I spend a lot of time wandering around the city late at night by myself for no particular reason that would make any kind of logical sense. As a result, I have been on the subway at four o'clock in the morning a lot of times, and I've seen just about every kind of filth and vice you can imagine. I've seen people puking, pissing, shitting, jerking off, having sex, buying drugs, crying, fighting, gambling, smoking, stealing, and just plain screaming incoherent profanity. I once saw a man stab a fork into a green fungus that had taken over his foot. I've seen people shaving and clipping toenails. I saw one guy doing a back flip off one of the poles break his wrist so bad the bones were sticking out. I've seen people jump down off the platform and run into the tunnels. Once I saw a guy moving an entire Steinway grand piano by himself with just a hand-truck."

The judge had heard enough.

"Thank you, Mr. Gillen. I think that'll do. I believe you're saying that, because of what you've seen, you can't be an impartial judge of the facts of this case. Is that correct?"

"No, Your Honor, not at all. I'm saying the opposite. I'm saying that because I know what it's like down there in the weird hours, I'm probably more qualified than anyone to sit on this jury. Because I understand that environment. I know that, just because I saw a homeless man eating a pigeon on the D train, it doesn't necessarily mean he killed it. It could have been dead when he found it."

The gavel banged.

"Alright, that's enough. Mr. Gillen. I appreciate your candor in answering these questions, but I must ask you to please

return to the jury room and I will remind you not to dis-
cuss the details of this case with anyone after you leave this
courtroom."

"Well, what about this?"

"What do you mean, the trial?"

"No, I mean this—this conversation—can I talk about this?"

His answer dripped with officious annoyance.

"No."

An Objection from Donny

"No, look I support you, I'm just saying, take me out of the story or I'll cut your fuckin' nuts off—that's all." Donny and I were both back home for the weekend. He had read some of my stories and had come to the kitchen table to object.

"It's not about you," I lied.

"He's your brother."

"Yeah, but I changed his name to Donny."

"It's clearly based on me, you fuck," Donny said.

"It's a fictional character—it's all fiction."

"No, it's not, that shit really happened."

"Well it's fiction if I say it is."

"Great, so just take me out of it."

"No."

Donny pointed all his fingers at me. "Look, John, I never said any of that, okay?"

"Yeah, you did, Donny."

His face widened as he yelled, "Well just because I know you need to do drugs and fuck your brains out doesn't mean I want people to know I said that. It's outta context. And you left out the part where I said that if you're asking for other people's opinion about your work, then you're an asshole."

I looked at him without answering. The irony dawned. He stifled a laugh, then in feigned anger said, "Alright—well, how about this—I'm gonna write a story with a character named John Geegan. And he's a blind Vietnam vet who spent, like, twenty years in prison for being a pedophile. But he's a good guy, you know? You root for him because he's got this idea for a business where he can, like—buy and sell—like—drugs— and he's completely addicted to crystal meth."

Our mother came in. "Donny, where were you last night?"

"Mom, I told you—okay? I was up in the titty bar."

"Oh, shut up." She scowled.

"I was in the titty bar rubbing my face on some body-glitter bitches, Mom."

Donny never asked me to change a story again.

Midnight in Graceland

God saw that he needed some rest
and called him home to be with him.
—Vernon Presley

The lifeless body of Elvis Aaron Presley lies under the ground beneath my feet. There is a giant cold slab of bronze and granite above him covered with little white marble angels, flowers, and an epitaph written by his father. It's midnight in Graceland. I'm trespassing, and the Earth is wet with Memphis rain. I've come a long way to stand in this sacred place.

I took the wheel from Donny about eleven last night and drove four hundred miles from Texas to Little Rock, Arkansas. We had taken an impulse trip to SXSW in Austin. Spent a week living in a place called Indra's Awarehouse with something like forty artists and two bathrooms. It was the closest thing to a hippie carnival I've ever seen. The floors were painted with tie-dye patterns and the entire space was littered with incoherent pieces of psychedelic artwork. The owner was a sexy mid-life crisis named Crystal who lives there with her son, her boyfriend, and a wild-looking man named Otto, who introduced himself to me as The House Dragon and would say things like, "If the cops ask, you don't know me, you haven't seen me, and I don't live here." At night he would go around giving people hits of acid out of a bottle and dropper he always wore around his neck. Claimed to have done a hit of acid for every day of his life. My favorite resident was a small, stray dog named Lobo. Lobo came and went as he pleased and was the most well-mannered housemate in the whole place.

I'd spent the week helping with some shows at the South by Southwest Festival in downtown Austin. Setting up stages. Loading and unloading trucks. Mostly though I was assigned the job of keeping an eye on the artists. Giving them pep talks and keeping them sober enough to perform. When the festival was over, we packed up and started the seventeen hundred-mile drive from Indra's back to New York. We were going to stay with one of Donny's buddies in Memphis on the way. I listened to Elvis on satellite radio while I drove. We finally arrived at one of the many inconspicuous homes in a sleepy neighborhood somewhere in the middle of Memphis around six o'clock in the morning. I was bleary with fever from prolonged sleep deprivation. We got into the house and flopped. The last thing I thought of as sleep washed over my fevered mind was the line from the end of *Uncle Tom's Cabin*. The one that says, "Heaven is better than *Kaintuck*." At the time I'd read it, I heartily agreed, but now, as I heard the distant sound of train whistles and the sweet song of birds hailing the gentle arrival of morning light, I wasn't so sure.

I slept until noon in a shivering sweat, then we got up and went to lunch. I intended to go to Graceland afterwards, but I didn't have the strength, so I went back to sleep. When I woke up this time, it was after six in the evening, and my fever had finally broken. I needed a shower and a meal. We went to a place called Central Barbecue. After dinner, we crossed the street to the Lorraine Motel. It's been perfectly preserved—just as it looked the day Martin Luther King Jr. was shot on the balcony fifty years ago. Except now there's a wreath, a civil rights museum, and a plaque with a quote from Genesis about Joseph. The part where his brothers see him and say, "Behold this dreamer cometh. ... let us slay him ... and we shall see what will become of his dreams."

We were awestruck. Everyone stopped laughing and stared in weighty silence.

By the time we got back to the house, it was late and visiting hours at Graceland were over, but I didn't care. I wasn't tired and I'd never been this close before—so, as everyone else went to sleep, I took the keys and drove to Graceland. I went past it just before midnight and parked the car at a gas station down the block. I got out and walked over.

The house sits on a stately hill overlooking Elvis Presley Boulevard. I made my way down to the famous front gates with their music notes. The perimeter wall is covered with graffiti from adoring fans. I noticed that no one was manning the guardhouse. I looked around again just to be sure. No one. Without hesitation, I walked to a dark section of the wall between the streetlights, looked both ways, and climbed over. My feet hit the ground with a dull thud, and I took a slow breath. I half expected floodlights and swarms of armed guards to explode out of the night and take me to jail.

But they didn't. Nothing happened. The crickets kept chirping. The house was still. The smell of damp trees and grass still comforted the air. The peaceful sounds of Graceland were undisturbed by my presence. I felt as though I had permission to be there—as if I had always been welcome. I crouched down and made my way over the green Tennessee lawn toward the house. I had never walked this ground or passed under these trees before, but they seemed like they could have come from my childhood home in Virginia. The familiar feeling calmed and encouraged me. I could have gone right up to the front door if I wanted to, but I hadn't come to see Xanadu. I turned aside and went around back toward the tomb.

Most people don't know this, but Elvis kept a lot of pets. Graceland was home to dogs, horses, peacocks, chickens, pigs, and even a chimpanzee named Scatter. Elvis loved Scatter and Scatter loved to lift skirts, drink whiskey, and generally cause mayhem. The rest of Graceland's occupants were not so fond of the chimp. Scatter caused so much trouble that they persuaded Elvis to build a climate-controlled room for him to live in away from the main house. After being banished from Graceland, Scatter died in his room. There are conflicting accounts as to the cause of death. Some say he was poisoned by the maid. Others claim it was liver damage from drinking too much whiskey, but one theory is that he died of a broken heart. Chimpanzees are social creatures and cannot survive confinement and loneliness, no matter how comfortable their cage is.

Elvis never got another chimpanzee, but he also never tore down Scatter's cage.

He just left it there in his backyard.

Empty,

and dark.

As I approached the Meditation Garden, I could hear water splashing in the fountain and see all the columns and sculptures illuminated in the night. My pace slowed. Alone in the garden—with the solemn stones, the incense of night after a rain, and the statue of Jesus with his arms outstretched—I felt a powerful invocation of reverence. An unmistakable sensation of hallowed ground. Like I was walking through Eden in the cool of the day. I had not come to desecrate or invade, but to pay my respects.

In 1973 there was a satellite broadcast of a concert called *Elvis: Aloha from Hawaii.* It was one of the first things ever broadcast via satellite to the entire world. Back then, the Earth's population was estimated at about four billion. The estimated viewership for the concert was between one and one-and-a-half billion. This means that in 1973 about half of our species stopped what they were doing and watched Elvis Presley sing rock n' roll for an hour. Elvis got more viewers than the moon landing. He will always be one of the most important Americans, like John Wayne or George Washington. It wasn't just music that made everyone tune in, it was him. This dirt-poor, white trash from Tupelo, Mississippi with a funny name and weird haircut carried in his voice and his presence the American Experience. Elvis could sing a song and wave his arm and express everything from the Civil War to the electric light.

But Elvis Presley is not giving anymore concerts. And there aren't one-and-a-half billion people watching him tonight. Tonight, there is just a cold slab of bronze and granite shielding his buried body from the rain and a lonely trespasser who has come across the continent to hold a midnight memorial service in the Meditation Garden of the King of Graceland.

People like to say that God took Elvis home so he could get some rest, but that ain't the truth. God didn't kill Elvis. The truth is Elvis Presley was a sex and drug addict who conquered the world and, like Solomon, realized that it couldn't satisfy him. That's why he built this garden. To make a space in his world for peace. It was one of his favorite places at Graceland. Elvis loved gospel songs and would sing them when he was alone on late nights like this one. I sang him my favorite, a spiritual called "Where No One Stands Alone," and I wished he was there to sing it with me.

When I finished praying, I climbed over the wall and started back to my car. Eleven hundred sleepless miles of American highway will take me back to my Manhattan apartment.

But there will still be a black wreath at The Lorraine Motel. Scatter's cage will still be empty.

And Elvis Aaron Presley will still be in his grave.

It's soon after midnight in Memphis, Tennessee, and there's a man walking alone down Elvis Presley Boulevard singing gospel music with tears in his eyes—and hoping like all Hell—that Heaven is better than Kaintuck.

I feel so alone sometimes
The night is quiet for me
I would love to be able to sleep
I'm glad everyone is gone now
I will probably not rest tonight
I have no need for all of this
Help me, Lord.

—Handwritten note allegedly found in the trash can of Elvis's Las Vegas Hilton Suite on December 7, 1976—less than a year before his death.

Christiane at Pentecost

"Ugh, I look pregnant."

She was looking at her naked profile in a full-length mirror by the foot of the bed and running her hand over toned
abs, trying to smooth out a lump of fat that only existed in
her mind.

"Oh, shut up," I told her.

"I do! I'm so fat and bloated. I hate my body."

For the record, Christiane was flawless. A milk chocolate
bombshell with pierced nipples and a creative mind. I still
don't know how I was lucky enough to end up in her midtown apartment.

"You're crazy. You look great."

"No, I don't. I look pregnant."

"You're not pregnant."

"I could be," she said as she climbed into bed with me.

"How?" I said with concern. I hadn't fucked her. I was sure
of it.

"I don't know. It could happen. What if I had an immaculate conception?"

"What?"

"An immaculate conception. It could happen. My aunt just had one." She nuzzled close and I put my arm around her.

"Your aunt had an immaculate conception?"

"Well she's on the pill, and they used a condom, and Plan B—but somehow she's still pregnant."

"Jesus," I marveled.

"Yeah."

"That's one determined kid."

"Yep."

"Does she already have kids?"

"Yeah just one, my cousin. I'm actually going to stay with her this summer, and I'm dreading it." She rolled her eyes.

"Why?"

"I don't know, my family's just a lot, but particularly my cousin. She has diagnosed OCD and she's transitioning, so she's just like the most complicated person in the world to live with."

"She has OCD *and* she's transitioning?"

"Yeah. I love her, it's just living with her is going to be so extra."

"God, yeah. Good luck."

"Do you believe in stuff like that?"

"Like what, honey?"

"Immaculate conceptions."

I was starting to get suspicious. "What—like virgin birth?"

"Yeah, whatever."   .

"You mean with your aunt, or just in general?"

She shrugged. "I don't know, in general, I guess."

"Why do you want to know?"

"Nothing, just lately I've been thinking about a lot of stories about stuff like that."

"What stories?"

"My grandfather, mostly."

"What about him?"

"Like he literally physically-healed people."

I turned my head and looked at her. "Really?"

Christiane lifted her cheek off my chest and looked back. Her eyes went down to my mouth as she talked. "Yeah. Like, this one time he was at church, and there were all these blind and crippled people there praying. As soon as he lifted his hand up over the congregation, a whole bunch of people fell down. Then the blind ones could see, and the lame ones could walk, and all the sick people were healed or whatever."

"Your grandfather did this?"

"Yeah."

"What was his spiritual background? Who taught him?"

"I dunno. He was a priest."

She laid her head back on the big white pillows.

"What do you mean—priest? What kind of priest?"

"Like, a priest-priest? What do you mean—what kind?"

"Like Catholic? Orthodox? What?"

"Oh, I think Pentecostal."

I sat up in bed. "Your grandfather was a Pentecostal pastor?"

"Yeah, a pastor. That's what he was, a pastor."

I was raised Pentecostal. My father was Pentecostal. "What other stories have you heard?" I asked.

She shrugged again and pulled the comforter up to her chin. "Well, he used to fast and pray a lot. My mom told me this one time he'd been fasting for, like, forty days and she went upstairs and saw him talking to an angel in his bedroom."

"She saw this?"

"Yeah."

"Well, what happened?"

"He put his finger to his lips and shushed her, then she ran downstairs and got my aunt and they both went back up and saw my grandfather talking to this tall white guy with long blonde hair and a white robe."

"She saw this."

"Yeah."

"Your mom saw this."

"Yeah."

"Your mom and your aunt saw your Pentecostal pastor grandfather talking to an angel, and now your aunt just had an immaculate conception." I repeated everything just to make sure I understood.

"I guess, yeah. Why?"

I laid back down.

And told her a story.

"When my Aunt Dottie was five years old, my grandmother took her for a walk and my aunt ran ahead. My grandmother saw a huge black rottweiler barking and charging toward her daughter. Dottie froze. My grandmother was too far away to save her, so she prayed. She saw an eight-foot-tall man with long blonde hair and a white robe appear between the dog and my aunt. The dog leaped into the air, and the man put out his hand. The dog struck his hand, stopped dead in the air, then dropped to the ground and ran away whimpering."

"Oh my God." Christiane cuddled up to me again.

"My grandmother was terrified, but my aunt wasn't scared at all. Dottie said, 'It's alright, Mommy, the angel saved me.' She said it like it was the most natural thing in the world."

Christiane squeezed me and hid her face in my chest. "John, I'm scared. I don't like these stories."

I hugged her and rubbed her back. "Why not?"

"Because if there are angels, that means there are demons."

I kissed her forehead. "You don't have to be afraid, sweetheart."

"Why not?"

"Demons know to stay away from me."

She lifted her head and looked me in the eye. Then she nodded and kissed me. "Thank you, John." She said and laid her head back down. Christiane and I haven't spoken in years, but she's still one of the sweetest and most beautiful women I've ever known. There was something in her voice and eyes that made me feel like a strong, kind man. She was graceful in the truest sense of the word. I miss her.

"What's she going to name it?" I asked after a silence.

"What?"

"Your aunt—the baby—what's she going to name it?"

"Oh, I dunno. I think she's going to get an abortion."

The next morning was Pentecost. I walked to Saint Patrick's Old Cathedral. The pews were thronged, so I stood in the back. I didn't see any angels. And no one was healed. I walked out onto the streets.

Listening to Dylan. Speaking in tongues. Blind and lame.

Resume Padding

I come from the ivy set
the educated adolescents
Tribeca yuppies
elitist brunch spot spring collection sharks

but I don't do their drugs
and I don't go to their parties
last Saturday I went out for a walk
dark summer heat
around four in the morning
I went into the park
at first light I was strolling across the great lawn
green and wet under morning fog

I crossed over to Cleopatra's Needle
a thirty-five-hundred-year-old rock
covered in ancient inscriptions
the bragging words of dead kings

then I found a little green pond
with a tranquil bank

there was a sleepy duck
a white crane in the distance
and two turtles fucking by the water
I sat on a mossy rock
and sang Johnny Cash songs
as I watched the sky changing colors
and the turtles fucking

a few hours later
after sunrise
I finished praying
and walked out past The Plaza

where I saw
in thin morning light
dozens of
pigeons
eating
horseshit
off Fifth Avenue
fighting with each other
for a bigger piece of the pile

The Last Bookstore in Los Angeles

The bald black man with a wedding ring in the wingback chair across from me dropped his hardcover crime novel, and the slam echoed off the stone floor of the last bookstore in Los Angeles. That's how I knew he was asleep.

Through an error of no importance I had ended up with twenty-four hours of shapeless time in the *city of angels*. I'd wandered into this bookstore to read for a while and wait for my flight. The night before, I'd walked around downtown for over five hours. Zigzagging through skid row past two million street people. The weather was perfect. I was listening to a series of lectures about the Gnostic Gospels.

It was a great night for heresy.

I sat down next to a hooker smoking weed in front of LAPD headquarters and asked her where I should have dinner. She said she had the best taco in town.

I went to Chipotle.

A meth addict with fetal alcohol syndrome and a cracked iPhone asked me to buy her some food. Suddenly I wasn't hungry. I gave her my burrito bowl and walked out. A few blocks down, a couple of Lamborghinis were being impounded for street racing. I saw a barefoot man stealing boots from a sleeping bum. The dull sound of him repeatedly slamming the bum's skull against the pavement echoed down the quiet street. The man ran off with his new boots. I kept walking.

The ATM outside the Bank of America Tower is out of order and the top of Los Angeles City Hall is a Masonic altar. Two plastic blondes who were at least a foot taller than me in their heels told me to fuck off when I saw them taking thong shots of each other in front of some 1980s neon street art. A guy under an overpass was fucking a decorative skeleton he'd stolen from the El Día de Los Muertos decorations in Grand Park.

The bald black man with the wedding ring sat up and coughed hard several times. His shoes squeaked as he stamped on the stone floor of the last bookstore in Los Angeles. His arm dropped and he began to snore.

Last night a security guard left the gate open at the Walt Disney Concert Hall and I snuck into the VIP greenroom. Then I went on stage. The hall was dark. I prayed. The acoustics were perfect. The overtone echoes of a concert hall are beautiful, but they carry no answers. I stopped yelling and sat down. Counting footlights. Thinking about the woman I loved and wondering where she was. I missed her so much. She was mercy incarnate. I said the word mercy out loud. Then I shouted it. When I couldn't yell anymore, I stopped. I began asking the echo more questions, but a door clanked open, and I rushed back to the street.

The bald black man with the wedding ring rubbed his face between sputtering grunts then sank back into the chair without waking up.

The bathroom at my Japanese hotel has one of those toilets that washes your ass. There were five temperature settings for the water and five for the seat.

I used toilet paper.

In the morning my body was sore from the miles of meditation and my voice was gone from screaming in the dark, so I checked out and went to the public library to rest. I talked to *her* and worked a little. Later that evening I went to the last bookstore in Los Angeles. I sat in a wingback chair across from the bald black man with a wedding ring. I read dozens of poems and a couple of short stories. Then I put down the books and tried to write something.

But nothing connected.

The bald black man sat up and coughed. He lurched forward and vomited all over the stone floor of the last bookstore in Los Angeles, muttered some angry gibberish, then slumped deeper into his wingback.

I took out my notebook.

And wrote this story.

Watching the bile soak his chinos.

And the acid drip onto his white Nikes.

Two empty stomachs.

One crime novel engulfed in his puke.

One notebook filled with mine.

But only one wedding ring.

It's time to catch my flight. I'll land in New York at sunrise.

It'll be cold, and windy, and dark, and raining, and my apartment will be too small, but at least there I can get fed. I left the bald black man still fast asleep in the wingback chair with his wedding ring on his finger, his puke drying on his legs, and his snores echoing off the cold stone floor of the last bookstore in Los Angeles.

The Opera Singer
and the Sex Slave

Once I went to the opera with a woman I loved.

She didn't like it very much.

And I haven't been back to the opera since.

* * *

I'd heard about Symphony Space before but had never been. My friend was doing a reading there one night and invited me to attend. I arrived a few minutes late and the usher walked me into the darkened theater between readings.

I followed the swinging flashlight and sat down in J10.

Celine was sitting in J11.

Celine was a full-figured blonde woman in her early forties who was there alone. She had big damn blue eyes. I glanced at her in the darkness and caught something in those eyes that I recognized immediately. I waited for intermission and then said, "Wasn't that great?"

"Oh yes, fantastic." She seemed genuinely eager to talk about it.

"I loved the one about the woman who knew she was going to die," I said.

"Me too, that was fascinating. Do you think she died at the end?"

"Well of course she died, the point is, when?"

She laughed. "I guess that's true."

"I think that story was great because it seems like it's about death but really it's about life, and love, and what's important about them. It's really a beautiful piece."

She touched my arm and said, "Yes, exactly. The author didn't focus on the woman knowing when she was going to die, but rather on how much the woman loved her husband and family."

I nodded and turned toward her in my chair. "Right. Yeah. And then she didn't tell you what happened at the end because that doesn't matter either. In the end, all that mattered was that they loved each other."

The eye contact tingled.

"Yeah," she said.

"Yeah—great reading too."

"Oh, I know, it was excellent." She looked like she wanted to keep the conversation going but didn't know what to say, so I just kept talking.

"Yeah ... I'm John."

I am not a clever man.

"Celine."

"Nice to meet you Celine."

Think of something, you idiot. She wants to talk to you. Say something.

"Have you been here before?" I asked.

"Oh yes, many times. I love coming here. I used to come here all the time the last time I lived in New York."

"I've never seen anything like it. It's like an open mic night for A-list actors."

She liked that, "You're right, that's exactly what it is." She laughed harder than she had to. Her laugh was young and full of light.

"I need to get out and see more things like this. I'm always up in some library or watching movies somewhere. I need to see more of the city."

She touched her necklace. "You should come back then, it's such a cultural gem. There's always something good here. Have you been to Carnegie Hall?" She was overflowing with excitement and leaning toward me.

"Yes, but only once. It's an incredible venue though, and the concert I heard was wonderful."

"Well, you should come see me at Carnegie some time." She said with a coy smirk reaching over the armrest to poke me.

"Do you see a lot of shows there?"

"I perform a lot of shows there."

"You perform at Carnegie Hall?" I didn't have to fake my enthusiasm.

"Yeah, all the time."

"Wow, that's a hell of gig. What kind of performances do you do?"

"I'm an opera singer and creative consultant, so I'm always on stage somewhere. I travel and work with production companies across the country. I do a lot of regional theaters too, of course, but New York is home and Carnegie is the best place to do opera in the city."

"I'm sure it is. You must be a world class artist. I'd love to come see you sometime. I haven't been to the opera in years."

She smiled.

The lights dimmed.

I got her number.

Two days later I was sitting on the couch in her apartment in Queens holding a silver chalice filled with ice and ginger ale and popping seedless green grapes. Which was a little ridiculous. But fuck it.

There was a half-packed suitcase laid out on the floor and the TV was playing her favorite Pandora channel. Depeche Mode. "Enjoy the Silence."

She was changing in the bedroom behind a curtain and I called out so she could hear me. "So how long will you be down there?"

"Just the weekend. Four shows and a fundraiser, then a day to myself and a train back to New York."

"Gotcha. You like New Orleans? I've never been, but I feel like it has to be a charming place."

"Oh yes, I love it. Well I don't know. I love most things about it. I could never live there, though."

"What don't you like about it?"

"I don't know exactly. I mean, all the culture and music are wonderful. That's why I keep going back. It's always been a vibrant city, but there's something about it that bothers me." This sounded more like a serious concern than passing thought.

"Bothers you how? What is it, too hot? Too southern? What?"

"No, no, nothing like that—all of that's part of its charm. But there's something else about it. Like a kind of ghost hanging over the city."

"A ghost?"

"Well not a ghost, no, not when you say it like that. But there's something you can feel in the air down there. Something about all the slavery, and the killings, and the hurricanes, and all that death. What really bothers me is how much gluttony and excess there is down there. They've had hundreds of years of whorehouses, and jazz, and riverboat gambling, and Fat Tuesdays. There's just—I don't know—sin. I guess maybe that's what it is. There's just so much sin. I know that sounds crazy, but you can feel it down there. It's—morbid."

"Sinister?" I suggested.

"Yes, sinister. Exactly."

"Like *True Detective?*"

"I don't know, I never saw that show."

I took a sip and popped another grape as she pulled back the partition and emerged in a gold sequin gown with full makeup and jewelry.

I swallowed the grape.

Her hips rolled and her eyes sparked with that shimmer of pride women get when they know that the man they want is admiring them. She strode to the center of the room like a spotlight was on her and took a power stance with her head up, shoulders back, and French manicures on her hips.

"Goddamn," I said reflexively.

Celine giggled her young-woman's laugh.

"Isn't it gorgeous? I've never worn it before but I'm taking it to New Orleans for my performance this weekend. This is what I'm going to wear for the finale and the after-party with all the donors."

"Well I think you're going to raise a lot more than just funds with that. What's it made of?"

She laughed. "It's just sequins and silk. It was hand stitched in Hong Kong in the sixties."

"Jesus, how much did this cost?"

"I don't know. I had it appraised, and they said twelve to fifteen thousand."

"Holy fuck, are you serious? For one dress?"

"Mhm."

"How much did you pay for it?"

"About three hundred."

I put down the chalice and got up off the couch. She lowered her chin and raised her eyes as I ran my hands over the hourglass of gold sequins. My hands rested on her hips and our eyes met. "Somebody got robbed."

She laughed again and turned toward a full-length mirror. "I know. Probably took some poor Asian woman years to make it. Doesn't it look great, though?"

I moved behind her and put my hands back on her hips.

"After all, I'm the star of the entire production. I have to have a dress that's worthy of the occasion. You don't think it's too much, do you?"

I drew her closer and found her eyes in the mirror. My lips gently touched her neck. I could feel the goosebumps.

And this time,

she didn't laugh.

* * *

"Have you ever been in love?"

Her question cut the silence like jagged glass. We were lying in her king-sized bed under white sheets with a thread count higher than Everest. As soon as she asked that question, I knew I was in trouble.

"What?"

"Have you ever been in love before?" she repeated.

"Why do you want to know?"

"I'm just curious."

"You're curious?"

"Yeah."

"Now, you're curious?"

"Yeah, I'm curious now."

"Why?"

"I don't know—it seems relevant."

"What do you mean, relevant?"

"I just want to get to know you better."

"And you want to start with that?"

"Why not? What's wrong with that?"

"It's a little on the nose, don't you think?"

"Oh, calm down, Cellini." She rolled her big damn blues at me.

"What?"

"Nothing, it's from an opera. Cellini was this Italian artist who made this sculpture of Pericles."

"What are you talking about? What does that have to do with me?"

"Well he was madly in love with a woman named Teresa, and his sculpture of Pericles killing Medusa represented Cellini overcoming opposition from the Church and all the other guys trying to win Teresa's love."

"Perseus," I said.

"What?"

"It's Perseus, not Pericles. Perseus killed Medusa. Pericles was a real guy. He was Tyrant of Athens during the First Peloponnesian War."

She looked at me like I had three heads. "How do you know that?"

"Have you?"

"Have I what?"

"Been in love."

"Oh, so now you're asking me?"

"I'm curious." I hadn't been before, but I was now.

"Fuck you. How do you know the difference between Perseus and Pericles?"

"Have you?"

"Ugh! Alright, fine. Yes. Once."

"With your husband?"

Her face and voice fell, and she looked away. A moment of thought passed before she said, "Actually, no."

"Really?"

She nodded.

"I'm sorry," I said.

She looked back at me. "I know. Me too. I always liked him a lot, but I wasn't ever in love with him. He was kind and reliable, but we never had much excitement. We used to go up to Connecticut to the same beach house every summer. Always had separate beds. I never did find him particularly attractive, so sex wasn't interesting to me either. I thought I just wasn't a sexual person, but later I realized it was him. I wasn't in love. There was no spark. No passion. That's what was missing really, passion."

"How long were you married to this guy?"

Her eyes narrowed like a child getting a shot. "Eighteen years." Her voice was a soft apology. I tried to be gentle.

"How did you finally realize you weren't in love with him?"

Girlish playfulness spread over her face and lifted her eyes from the pit of despair. "I fell in love."

Her blushing smile made me laugh. "Oh, you naughty woman, good for you. With who?"

"Jim."

"Who's Jim?"

"My Jim."

"Very funny. Which Jim?"

"The one in the tiniest, shittiest, regional-theater-company production of *Don Giovanni* I've ever seen."

"And what about Jim did you find so enamoring?"

"I have no idea."

"What do you mean—you have no idea?"

"I mean I have no idea."

"How can you have no idea?"

"I don't know, I just don't. I honestly don't know what it could have been."

"Well it must have been *something*. People don't just fall in love with someone else after eighteen years of marriage for no reason."

She rolled over onto her elbows and made her case. "I know, I know. I just don't know what the hell it could have been. He was this ridiculous over-actor and a total misogynist, but I couldn't resist talking to him. He used to eat the greasiest, most disgusting—and he was always making up stories about famous people he'd worked with and beautiful women he'd slept with—but it was all brazenly false. I mean, this guy was a pathological, habitual liar and a gross freak, but I couldn't resist him."

"What kind of stories?"

"Oh, all kinds of nonsense. He had one about getting into a fist fight with Marlon Brando and one where he ran into Johnny Depp at some secret barbecue joint in Vegas at three o'clock in the morning and the two of them robbed a gas station together then gave the money to a children's hospital. Stuff like that. The one about sleeping with Pamela Anderson on a yacht in Acapulco was different every time he told it."

"And it was all lies?"

"Yes, of course it was. But he was such a passionate storyteller. I'd always listen to his stories and then we'd end up talking. The more we talked the more I got to know him. The real him, the one behind all the stories. Before I knew it, I'd discovered this incredible person that I had been needing my entire life."

"Well, what did you find sexy about him?"

"I have no Goddamned idea. I swear to God I don't. He had terrible taste. No sense of fashion or manners. He drove this ugly, broken-down Hyundai with a rusted brown paint job and lived in a filthy little apartment. And the worst part was his hair. He was balding, but he had this awful dyed red ponytail that went down to the middle of his back."

"Ugh," I grunted.

"I know."

"And you fucked his guy?"

She scoffed and smacked my bare shoulder for the blunt remark. "It wasn't like that. I didn't just jump his bones on the spot."

"Well, what was it like?"

"It was like five years of both of us wanting each other more than anything and not sleeping with each other. Like those volcanoes under the ice in Antarctica. We kept getting closer and closer, but I never would do anything with him because I was married. I took a vow before God, and that mattered to me. I told him it would never happen."

"Was he single?"

"No, he was married too. It was inevitable though. I couldn't resist him anymore and we started having so much sex it was like—I don't know—I just lost my mind. I was drunk with passion. I can't even remember how it started. It just did. I've never been so consumed by anything in my life. I had this infinite lust for that man. I craved everything about his mind and body to the point where he physically couldn't fuck me enough. And believe me, he tried. We spent dozens of days and nights in bed desperately making love to each other until we collapsed."

"Alright, alright, I get the picture. Calm down. So, what happened?"

"He promised me he'd leave his wife, and we'd be together."

"Did he?"

She watched her fingertips wander over the pillows.

"No."

The French manicures traced their way across the lines in the linen. I put my arm around her. She laid her head on my chest.

"He swore he would do it, but he was too afraid to leave her. One day he sent me a letter telling me it was over. I mean it was thirty-five pages long, but basically that's what it said. It's over."

"Jesus."

Celine turned onto her back again but stayed cuddled up close to me.

"I have never been so devastated in my life. Of course, my husband knew. It was obvious what had happened. I quit working for two years and just went to therapy—depression medication—the whole thing. I think it was something like five years before it started getting better. I still haven't gotten it out of my system. But I learned a lot from that experience. I learned you should never confuse a life-lesson for a soulmate."

We sat together in the silence. Breathing and heartbeats. I remember the sadness in her eyes as she stared at the ceiling. Tears came.

"My husband lives in Florida now, and I live up here."

"You're still married?"

"Oh, sure. We had to be adults about it. He wasn't in love with me either, but we liked each other, and we're good partners—so we just did the mature thing."

"That's a little cold isn't it?"

"Maybe, but it's realistic, and we're both very happy. I still go down to see him sometimes when I need a break from the city."

"How long have you lived here?"

"I come and go, but I've had an apartment here for most of the last twenty-five years. I remember I had just moved back into my old place right before 9/11 happened."

"You were here for 9/11?"

She nodded.

"What was that like?"

"It wasn't like anything. It was eerie. I was working in Midtown at the time, and I remember somebody screaming and then I saw it on TV. We all went and looked downtown, and you could see it. Long columns of black smoke. Then the second one hit and people screamed and started crying. God, I'll never forget when they started falling. It was so surreal—I don't know what. No one screamed that time, we just watched them fall. I remember feeling the building shake and seeing this huge, dark cloud spread over the entire city. I couldn't get home to Brooklyn, so I spent the night with some friends on the Upper West Side.

"I remember walking through the streets and it just being so—I don't know—it was quiet but not just quiet. Strange quiet. I don't think New York has ever been that quiet. It scared me. That silence scared me more than anything. It said so much that I've never heard anyone be able to articulate. People try, but they never get it right. Years from now, when historians are writing about it and the war and everything that followed—they're all going to give these reasons and try to explain it, but it doesn't have anything to do with politics. Everything you need to know about 9/11 can only be explained by the terrifying sound of unnatural silence that filled the streets of New York City after the towers came down. I'll never forget that. Goddamn—I'll never forget that."

Silence.

I looked at her again. Faraway eyes so full of the past. A beautiful face pallid from experience. At last, she came back to herself and looked into my eyes.

"Why did you ask me if I'd ever been in love?" I don't know why I asked her that, but I did.

"I was curious," she said.

"Why?"

She pulled the covers up with a bashful pout. "I don't want to say. It's embarrassing."

I propped myself up on an elbow and peeked over her fortress.

"Tell me why you asked me that. I want to know."

Celine lowered her guard. "I don't know—it's just—I mean you made me cum like eleven times and you haven't even fucked me yet. No one has ever made me cum eleven times, not even Jim. I mean, Jesus Christ, I almost passed out."

Everything drained out of me.

I collapsed onto the mattress and looked into the ceiling.

Infinite, blank whiteness.

"What's that got to do with being in love?" I said in a low rumble.

"Well I just wondered—I guess I just thought if you can do that to me—I wonder what you would be like with a woman if you were in love with her."

Upon hearing this, I was gone.

My mind fell into the past.

Hurtling through the infinite ceiling.

Searching for something I'd lost a long time ago.

I remembered the night we'd spent at the opera.

Sneaking onto the roof.

The way *she* looked in the moonlight.

Laughing.

Just before I kissed her.

Then Celine touched me.

"John?"

"I gotta go."

Kyo's Monologue: Seventeenth Floor
of the W Hotel, Union Square—
Manhattan—May, 3:00 a.m.

"I'm not like these prissy American women. I'm from Russia. I have a lot of Mongolian blood too, which is worse. Russian women are naturally aggressive, but with Mongolian mixed in it's worse.

"I came to this country for school and graduated Florida State when I was twenty. I moved to the city. Got a job in data analytics. I met a Google exec at a networking event. He bought me a dog collar and paraded me around the city. He took me into a McDonald's and made me masturbate while he ate an ice cream cone. I liked it. Sitting there, wearing a collar and leash, touching myself next to some bums while he slobbered on soft-serve vanilla. I came twice. He kept an apartment as a sex dungeon on the Upper West Side. That's how it started for me.

"Don't get tainted. Don't let anyone break you. A lot of people will try to manipulate you and break you just for the pleasure of doing it. Don't let that happen. You have a gift. It wasn't taught. It's not conditioning. It's a gift. You mustn't waste it or let yourself be ruined by philistine swine. It's too precious for that.

"You'll never be normal, and you shouldn't try. You're too smart, or too loving, or something delicate like that. I don't mean delicate like weak, but there's something inside of you that is special and fragile. And because it's precious, people will try to steal it, or kill it, or break it, or taint it—and you cannot let them. You simply cannot let them. You have to preserve it, but if you preserve it, you'll never be like them. You'll never have a beer and watch the game, never have a wife and kids and an office job, never get excited when Starbucks offers a new kind of latte.

"But if you don't preserve it, your spirit will die and your life will be suffering without meaning until your body dies too. It's your gift, so it's your choice, but I think you should preserve it. Just for spite if for no other reason. They're all miserable, lying, perverted, addicts anyway. You don't owe them anything.

"The man that took my virginity raped me when I was fifteen years old. He beat me, and raped me, and left scars on my body where the ropes cut me. Back then, he was a drug dealer. Now he's the head of cyber security for a Fortune 100 company. He has a wife and two children. He lives in New York. I met him recently, and he tried to fuck me again. He asked me to sleep with him, but I said no. I considered killing him, but it's not worth it. He's already dead. I want nothing more to do with him.

"I had one client who was an executive at JPMorgan. He had an apartment in Nolita. Used to invite me over, and I'd come in to find him on all fours naked and blindfolded with bottles of Dom Perignon and Patron waiting for me on the bar. I gave him chlorophyll enemas. Chlorophyll is good for you. You can get it at Whole Foods. I'd fill his stomach up with that and clean him out, then fuck him with a big strap on and lots of lube. After that he'd fuck me. It was great. This went on for years. He kept trying to find another girl who could handle him like I did, but he never could, so he kept coming back to me. He was married, of course. His wife was an opera singer. He invited me to come see her perform at Carnegie Hall. Not with him obviously, but just to come and see it. It was a huge production of this thing Mozart wrote for the Church, but I can never remember what it's called. It's that thing from the end of *Amadeus*."

"The Requiem," I said.

"What is it?"

"Requiem."

"Yeah, that's it. So anyway, I go to Carnegie Hall and I'm sitting there right behind the orchestra pit, and she comes out in this incredible dress and does this big, emotional opening piece. She was right in the middle of it all. This solitary figure, singing her heart out with all this activity going on around her. As I looked at her, I knew I was filling this big empty void in her husband. A basic need that they both knew he had but that she could never fill. But he was still her husband. I mean she had never been to that apartment in Nolita. She had never used a strap-on on him. But I know she knew. A woman knows, believe me. I was sitting there looking at her singing this powerful, emotional opera—filling the entire room with the beautiful sound of painful death—and I felt—I just—I felt so fucking much. And then, just at the climax of the song, she looked at me.

"Maybe I imagined it, but for a moment I saw her look right at me, and in that instant I admitted everything to her, and she knew. I confessed all my sins, and she forgave me. I stopped seeing her husband after that. He begged and pleaded for years—he even invited me to the opera again—but I refused. He lives in Florida now. I haven't seen him or fucked any married men since. I'm not a sex addict anymore. I've committed a lot of other sins, and done many terrible things, but I'm not a sex addict anymore. I'm tainted, though. There isn't anything that can change that. They ruined me. But that doesn't bother me anymore, because now I can go to the opera to repent from my sins. There's something holy in that pretentious, ancient music. I don't know what it is, but it's something holy. And when I hear it, I know that I'm forgiven."

We sat together until morning. Listening. Without a sound.

I never saw her again.

* * *

Once, I went to the opera with a woman that I loved.
She doesn't love me anymore.
And I haven't been back to the opera since.

Jack

Florida is full of fuckups and washouts
Weird beasts that don't belong
Armadillos and peacocks
Driven mad by the billion-year stare of an unblinking sun

Jack was on the backside of thirty years of suicidal drinking
Lost his mind when his wife Debbie died of cancer
He had broken watery eyes and stringy blonde hair
Turning white
His hands were lumpy and mangled like a boxer's
He worked on cars
Jack needed surgery
Doctor said he had to quit smoking and drinking for thirty days
Thirty days sober, or they couldn't operate, and he'd die
That was on Jack's birthday
He thinks he's somewhere in his late seventies
Says he's quitting after one last party so he can have the surgery

Two days later I walked down to the ocean in the dead of night
Jupiter Island
The winter retreat of the rich and famous
I swam until I lost the shore

Jack

Half an hour after that I turned back
Patrol found me panting on the cold sand
Asked me what I was doing
I told him I was trying to get away
He told me to leave or I'd be arrested

When I got home around sunrise Jack was sitting out back in the dark
He heard me come inside and whipped open the sliding porch door
His yellow eyes were full of brown liquor and hate
Clenched tattoo grease
We stood there in the blue kitchen
Staring at each other
With the colossal weight of angry Death around us
And the frantic orgy of Floridian ambience spilling through the open door

"My Debbie's been sick"
He snarled
"I'm sorry, Jack"
I whispered back

Bella came up and licked his hand and something slumped out of his eyes
He brushed her coat with a mutilated paw
Then turned away
"Motherfuckers"
Jack said
Then shut the sliding door
And went back to drinking
With his cigarette glowing in night
Swallowed by wet, quiet, black

The next morning, I went back to New York
Jack will be very dead by the time you read this
Then we'll both be out of Florida
And Jupiter Island will be a more respectable neighborhood

Donny Saves a Dog

Whenever I get to feeling like a real son of a bitch, I go right out and do some charity work. Something to help the poor, sad bastards who are too sick or too lazy to go out and trade their souls for a dollar like decent people. Now, lest you think me a saint, I want to make clear the reason why I do this. It's not because I want to help any of these poor, sad bastards—because, God knows, no one wants to help them—but doing something nice for a person who is less fortunate brings with it a certain degree of moral vindication. You feel like the Holy Buddha. Like Zarathustra in confident repose. You feel like the eternal prophet of Love and Sacrifice clothed in righteous purity. There's an exquisite sense of gratification. It's intoxicating. Addictive.

People never admit this, but everyone uses charity work the same way they use recreational drugs. And they do it for the same reasons too. Whether it be social pressures, medicinal purposes, or any other pretense for the consumption of spirits, they may, one and all, be meted out with equal validity to charity work. But of course, whether you're getting drunk or helping the homeless, it's really all about you.

The last time I succumbed to this compulsion was in New York City. My older brother John had moved up there and I decided to give it a try too. I got deep into decadence and started feeling like a piece of shit, so I decided to volunteer for a foundation that does nice things for terminally-ill children, which is like the most Disneyland version of charity work that a person can do, so I knew I was going to get a good fix from this. Maybe a free T-shirt letting people know I was a better person than them. Might even end up in a commercial, or on the news, or something. It was going to be a solid Goddamned hit of the pure, uncut shit, and I could practically feel my mesolimbic system coursing with dopamine already.

But right away, it started to fuck up.

My volunteer partner was this officious twat named Rick. Rick was a senior partner at Goldman, and this was part of his annual, corporate-sponsored, mandatory community service—a public relations charade—which cheapened the whole thing. I mean, how am I supposed to pretend I'm a good person when this guy is there reminding me that the entire operation is a cheap theater act?

It's like this one time I was watching porn, and I noticed the video had over one hundred-fifty comments—and I thought that seemed like a lot, so I clicked and starting reading. It wasn't the usual porn comments. You know stuff like, "I'd kill my firstborn child just to eat your ass for five minutes." This thread contained a passionate discussion of the ethics of pornography, as well as an extensively researched investigation into the economic problems of the Eastern Bloc. There was also a lot of fucked up shit about the Russians, and human trafficking, and shit like that.

Meanwhile, I'm sitting there trying to focus on cumming, and I start thinking, "Jesus, maybe Natasha's not really into this." Then I started thinking about how US foreign and economic policy has contributed to inequality in the rest of the world, and how much pain and suffering that's caused for women like Natasha, and how I'm a piece of shit for supporting that system and enjoying the benefits of it. You get the idea. Anyway, that really fucked everything up for me. I mean don't get me wrong—I still came—it just wasn't as good.

Having this "Wall Street Rick" motherfucker volunteering with me was the equivalent of that. He was an old, fat, rich, white man trying to ease a guilty conscience after a lifetime devoted to sodomizing the poor. Like a vampire working in a soup kitchen. I decided to not let it bother me too much and try to focus on doing the job. But then I found out that Rick and I had been assigned to a family of even-richer rich people. Which was the worst thing that could have happened. I'd signed up for this thing thinking I'd get to help some terminally ill son of an immigrant single mother living on food stamps in the Bronx, but these people had a penthouse apartment on Central Park West. It almost wasn't worth going, but I figured I could just make up a more heartrending version to tell at parties and save myself the hassle of having to visit a shitty neighborhood.

As Rick and I walked through the gilded, marble lobby,

I knew this wasn't going to end well. The elevator smelled like a mahogany forest, and entering their apartment felt like taking out a loan. I was worried that if I took a deep breath, they'd send me a bill for more than my rent. The whole family answered the door in business-casual dress. They were too clean and too quiet. What kind of family of four lives in an apartment with white carpet and white couches that aren't covered in Cheeto dust? The parents were especially strange. They behaved more like awkward caricatures from a comedy sketch than real people.

The kid, the one we'd been sent there to help, really sucked too. He wasn't right at all, which wasn't fair to me. I was supposed to get to play "White Savior" to a brown-skinned Tiny Tim—a cherubic racial minority who was sweet, and adorable, and full of human goodness, and wonder, and gratitude. Instead, I was stuck with this seventeen-year-old rich kid who looked totally healthy. He was just some fucking B-student who probably spent all day masturbating to unethical porn and playing video games. It was fuckin' bullshit. He wasn't tragic at all. He and his sister shook our hands and left the room without speaking or making eye contact.

Rick and I sat down on an oversized antique couch and explained to the parents that we had all these gifts for their son. We told them we were looking forward to talking to him and finding out more about his condition. They'd sent us some basic info, but we wanted to hear it from him. They both grunted a lot and said, "Fine."

Then the father got up and left. We thought that he was going to have the kid come in and talk to us, but instead he just stood in the kitchen like he had no idea what he was doing there.

We waited. The mom sat with folded hands on crossed knees and a painfully rigid smile. Then she said, "Excuse me," and got up and left too.

I looked at Rick. He shrugged his fat, dumb, shoulders like a pointless blob. Then we saw a squeaky clump of fluff scamper across the white marble kitchen, and the mom squealed and did baby talk to it and said, "Let's get you a treat."

We heard the treat box shaking and the dog panting.

Then silence.

The mom said something that sounded concerned.

The dog made hacking noises.

More silence.

Then she let out this horrific scream that made me jump up off the ancient red couch.

"He's choking! He's choking! Somebody, do something— he's choking!"

I ran into the kitchen to find her waving this little eight-inch dog around the room and screaming for help while her husband leaned on the counter by the sink and the kids sat in the living room watching reality TV. No one seemed to care that she was hysterical. Rick waddled in next to me and she turned to us with this tiny carcass and said, "Please do something!" Rick starts googling dog CPR, while this woman dumps her dead ball of pampered fur into my hands, and suddenly I'm the one responsible for saving the little bitch's life.

My first instinct was to just throw it in the trash and walk out, but then I realized this was my divine opportunity. If I saved her dog's life, I'd be a hero—and not just to this silver-spoon, freak family, but to the entire bullshit organization. They'd trot me around like the second coming of Christ. There be a photo-op for the press with me and the dog. Media coverage, parties—hell, they might even build an entire ad campaign around me. From there, who knows? Live appearances. Speaking engagements. Book deals. Oprah. God knows what else. I'd be a lifelong symbol of hope and salvation. I could make millions and never have to do any real work ever again. Like Tony Robbins.

So, I started trying to pull a Lazarus out of my ass on this domesticated rat. I tried the Heimlich, but the dog was so small I felt like if I squeezed him, I'd crush him, so I put my finger in his mouth and tried to find the obstruction. I felt something, but it might have just been part of the dog's throat. Then I turned him upside down and smacked his ass like a ketchup bottle hoping whatever it was would just fall out. Nothing. I shook him harder. Still nothing.

I got more and more frantic. Slapping and squeezing and shaking and anything else I could think of to try and jolt some life into this creature whose revival would change the course of my life, but nothing worked. He'd been deadweight for a while and was totally unresponsive, so after a few minutes of me fumbling around with the body like a meat slinky, I decided it was dead.

I looked at the woman closely for the first time.

The anguished look on her lifted face.

Her straining turkey-neck.

The garish jewelry she wore for no reason.

The Chanel dress and excessive makeup.

Dyed hair.

Fake eyelashes.

Weird veins.

I almost pitied her.

She'd lived so long in luxury that she was completely dependent on other people. And now, when the being she loved needed her, she was totally helpless. I dropped her beloved corpse on the counter and said, "He's dead."

She started wailing like it was the worst thing that had ever happened. "Oh, God! My baby, my poor baby!" She turned to her husband. "Fuck you, Chad! I know you're happy he's dead. You never loved him. You never loved anything in your whole life!"

Her husband still leaned on the counter with crossed arms and a blank stare. The kids stayed on the couch and didn't make a sound. Then a short, smiling, Latino lady brought in a pizza and presented it to me and Rick. "We order for you," she said. She acted as if she didn't even see the dog or the screaming woman.

I knew we had to get out of there, so I said, "No thanks. I think we should be leaving now." I'm not a particularly polite individual, but even I know it's rude to intrude on someone's death.

Rick, the dollar-sucking tool bag, went around the room saying goodbyes. The husband, whose name was apparently Chadwick of all Goddamned things, said something to him, and Rick laughed and said something back, and then they both laughed and shook hands. I didn't say anything. I looked at the kids on the couch. The girl had started fake crying, but the boy—the one who was supposed to be terminal—was staring at his mother with a disturbing intensity. He didn't move, or blink, he just looked at her.

I wondered what he was thinking.

And what it would be like when he died.

I walked out leaving Rick and the father networking by the sink, and the children on the couch staring at their mother, and a dead dog voiding its bowels on the white marble floors of a misplaced corner of Hell on Central Park West.

I asked to be reassigned to a different case after that. They said no, so I backed out of the whole thing. Never heard anything more about the family or that kid, but somehow, I think he got exactly what he wanted. I certainly didn't. The whole point of this was to make me feel better about myself, and now I felt even more guilty than when I started. But I know exactly who's responsible for all of this, and I want to go on record, so he'll be held accountable.

It's all God's fault.

He killed that wretched little vermin on purpose to deprive me of my chance to atone. He did it because—ever since He sent His precious little boy down to Earth to live a perfect life and die a horrible death to sacrifice Himself for the whole sinful, unworthy world—He's been very touchy about anyone else doing something similar. He wants to keep all the fun for Himself. The greedy miser won't share his jollies with anyone else. Instead, He demands that we take part in his little game of salvation.

Well, I don't think that's fair at all. God killed that dog

when he should have let me save it. It was my moment of glory, and he stole it from me. So, as far as I'm concerned, he owes me big time. I left New York and went back to Virginia. John's still up there, but I'm in no hurry to go back. A few months later, John asked me a lot of questions about this and I barely remembered it. He'd taken a lot of notes on it when I first told him the story, though, so I guess he knows what happened. For some reason, John seemed to think it was important.

Anyway, about a week later my friend took a fuckload of Klonopin and vegetabled himself into the hospital, and my ex-girlfriend Cassie called in a fake suicide report on me that sent a SWAT team busting into my apartment in the middle of the night, so I had bigger things to worry about than God.

The Answer

The first week of July 2016 was one Hell of a week. For me it began back in Austin, this time just visiting a friend. I took a tour of the Lyndon Baines Johnson Presidential Library on the fourth of July. Independence Day. I listened to audio recordings of phone calls between Johnson and the Reverend Doctor Martin Luther King Jr. A holy ghost African American tremble and a thick Texas drawl talking about how they were going to pass civil rights legislation together. Talking about peace, tolerance, love, brotherhood, and their own friendship. They worked on a lot of things together, including the Civil Rights Act of 1964. In 1966 Charles Whitman shot forty-nine people from the top of the University of Texas at Austin clock tower, which is just a few blocks away from the LBJ library. Charles was twenty-five years old and he killed seventeen people before the cops shot him.

That night I flew to Dallas, where they shot John Kennedy, to make a connecting flight to Dulles in Washington, D.C., before taking a bus back to New York at the end of the week. As my plane rose into the night sky over Dallas, I saw the natural beauty of America. The sun was well into setting and cast a huge swath of crimson across the wide horizon. There were storm clouds lumbering in the distance with their electric light surging against the growing darkness. Below that were ten million lights of a city I had never visited, and across the land, fireworks were jumping into the sky, dotting the Earth with sparkling color. I sat in my empty row and stared out the window. Such dramatic light. I remember thinking that Dallas almost looked like a war zone. Three days later, an American named Micah Xavier Johnson ambushed a group of police officers in that city. He killed five cops and injured nine others plus two civilians. Micah was an Army Reserve Afghan War veteran. He was angry about police officers killing black men. He stated that he wanted to kill white people, especially white police officers.

There's a madness in this country. Angry young men with guns trying to start wars in South Carolina churches—trying to start wars in Orlando nightclubs—trying to start wars in schools, movie theaters, homes, in the streets. Everywhere you turn there is someone killing, and hating, and blaming, and protesting—and there doesn't seem to be anyone anywhere who knows what to do about it. There are endless social media conventions, Instagram committee meetings, 140-character political campaigns. Do this, vote that, he's Hitler, she's Hitler, everyone is Hitler. The cops are racist. You're racist. Everyone is racist. Endless statistics. Talking heads. Arguments about which lives matter—and when, and which hashtags to use, and why, and why not, and where, and for how long.

The main thing missing from all of this is an answer. Everyone keeps looking for clear, neat, simple answers. Some people think that they've got the answer, but thinking that you've got the answer is the only guarantee that you haven't got it. While all this was going on, I attended back-to-back performances of the same concert, in different cities, in the same week. I saw Mavis Staples open for Bob Dylan and his band, live and in-concert. Twice.

Mavis sang a song her father had written back in 1965 called "Freedom Highway." He wrote it for the famous march from Selma to Montgomery. Mavis was there for that Alabama march along with her friend Dr. King. She's still marching, God bless her. In 1963 The Reverend Doctor Martin Luther King Jr. led a march on Washington. LBJ was there too. Bob Dylan and Joan Baez opened for King. They sang "When the Ship Comes In," and "Only A Pawn in Their Game," a song Dylan wrote about the murder of Medgar Evers, the civil rights leader, and about how racial hatred is used to manipulate Americans into destroying their own country. Peter, Paul and Mary, sang "Blowin' in The Wind." Then Martin Luther King Jr. came out on stage and said that he had a dream.

Fifty years later, as I was listening to Bob sing "Blowin' in the Wind" I heard angry voices behind me getting louder. Someone was drunk and someone asked them to quiet down, or something. What caused the fight didn't matter, what mattered was Bob Dylan was singing, and they were yelling over him. Bob doesn't sing many of his "old" songs anymore. His body and voice are too worn down. He's been on the road longer than anyone. It's a miracle he's come this far. But recently, Dylan has started doing an encore performance at the end of his shows where he sits down at the piano and plays a lower, slower version of "Blowin' in the Wind." He wrote it in about ten minutes one day back in the early sixties. Back when the songs were coming out of him so fast, he said he was afraid to go to sleep because he might miss some. After a minute or so of listening to these drunk strangers shouting back and forth, I stood up and offered my seat to one of them. They were separated, and the fighting stopped. I crouched on the floor to listen. Almost immediately I heard different raised voices arguing over an armrest. Two tombstones fighting over where they would put their elbows for three minutes.

Madness.

The question is, what should we do about all of this?

What is the answer?

Well.

The answer, my friend, is *blowin' in the wind*.

But the air is full of smoke, from guns, with triggers, pulled by fingers, on hands, belonging to Americans with blood full of hate, and anger, and fear, and God only knows what else.

So, what is the answer?

More laws? Fewer laws?

More guns? Fewer guns?

No people? No America?

Maybe everyone just needs their own armrest.

Bob Dylan and Mavis Staples dated off and on for about seven years in the sixties. Near the end of the decade, Bob asked her to marry him. She declined. Her given reason was, "I was young and stupid, and I was thinking Dr. King wouldn't want me to marry a white guy." They never got back together until this tour fifty years later. They're not going to get married this time, though. They're just running out of people to march with. A lot of years have passed since Dylan opened for King. Bob doesn't sing about the hour when the ship comes in anymore. Now he sings a different tune. Now when Bob Dylan walks out on stage the first thing he says is, "I used to care, but things have changed."

On March 31st, 1968, President Lyndon Baines Johnson announced that he would not seek, nor accept, his party's nomination for another term as president. Five days later, the Reverend Doctor Martin Luther King Jr. was shot dead on the balcony of the Lorraine Motel in Memphis, Tennessee.

I'm back in New York now.

Bob Dylan is still touring.

And America is still looking for the answer.

Jesus Christ.

Scorned

There is no fate that cannot be surmounted by scorn.
—Albert Camus

In the early morning of November 9, 2016, the world learned that Donald John Trump had become the president-elect of the United States of America. Clinton and Trump were both in my neighborhood in midtown Manhattan to watch the results. As I walked the streets between 3:00 and 5:00 a.m., I saw more people than usual. Most of them were crying or yelling.

A honking Humvee with an old, fat, white man waving a sign from the sunroof and telling people they'd won their country back almost clipped me. I saw two women taking off their clothes and screaming profanity at police officers. A missing-tooth man was selling counterfeit "Make America Great Again" hats outside Trump Tower. I saw a roving gang of teenage white girls chanting, "Fuck Trump, that's what he wants." A six-foot-five, 250-pound, red-faced, sloppy-drunk ginger came down Sixth Avenue pumping his arms in the air and screaming, "AHH! FUCK!"

My Pussy Grabs Back signs.

Media circus.

No peace.

By the evening of the same day, approximately one hundred thousand angry New Yorkers had clogged the streets of Manhattan in protest—many of them marching from Union Square up to Trump Tower. There was a lot more yelling and crying. I was going the other way, so I stepped aside and waited for them to pass. Tanya was pissed off long before she saw me and asked, "Why ain't you marchin'?"

I said nothing.

"You—white boy—why ain't you marchin'?"

Don't talk to strangers.

"Hey motherfucker, I'm talking to *you*. Why ain't you marchin'?"

Fuck.

"Ain't you hear me, white boy? Don't you give a shit when I'm talkin' to you?"

I couldn't move, too many people.

"I bet you voted for that racist asshole, didn't you?"

No way out.

"I bet yo' red-tie-wearin', white-collar, cracker ass voted for that stupid, racist, sexist fuck."

I wear neckties, some of them are red, this one was red—clearly that was a mistake.

"Well?"

People were starting to gather. I had to do something.

"Well, what?"

"Cut the shit, asshole. Did you vote for that motherfucker or not?"

People were watching.

"It doesn't matter, she won New York, what difference does it make?"

In hindsight, this was a poor answer.

"So, you voted for him?"

"I didn't say that."

"I knew it, I knew you did it. I knew you voted for him the minute I saw you wasn't marchin'. You're just another rich, racist, sexist white man."

"Lady, please I—"

"You make me sick, you punkass bitch with your dumbass bullshit. You think you're gonna get away with this? Huh? This is revolution out here, Mister One Percent!"

Another woman spoke up.

"Tanya, this guy bothering you?"

"Fuck yeah, he's fuckin' botherin' me."

"I'm just trying to go grocery shopping, and she—"

"Oh, so what're you sayin'? Women and minorities and Muslims are all going to get fucked over and what—you don't have time to go march because you have to go get groceries?"

"No, I just—"

"Mhm, that's fucked up."

"Get 'im, Tanya."

"You know what? No, you're what's wrong with this country. No, excuse me, you miserable piece of shit, because you can't be bothered to stand up for what's right? We righteous out here marchin', and you can't be bothered 'cause why? Because you got better things to do? You ain't got time to be a decent human being?"

There was a group forming around me. I felt the wall against my back.

"What's going on?"

"This guy's a huge Trump fan, and he's been saying all sorts of racist stuff to Tanya."

"That's fucked up, man. We're out here because we love everybody, why do you have to bring your hate out into this beautiful community?"

"I'm just going to Trader Joe's."

"Well you said you voted for Trump and that's the same thing as a rape or a lynching because that's what he wants to do to people."

"What? No, I—no, I don't support any of that. No one does. Please just leave me alone, I'm—"

"Well then tell me why you voted for Trump then?"

"I never said I voted for Trump."

"Oh, sure. Yes, you did. I know you did. You white boys are all the same. Are you tellin' me you're a big Hillary fan then?"

"No, I'm not."

"See!? Right there, I fuckin' knew it—you love Donald Trump, don't you? You racist shitbag!"

"No, I don't!"

At this point, Tanya got in my face and really started yelling.

"Well which is it, bitch?! Because you can't have both, so what are you?! Are you a Republican or a Democrat?! You better answer me right fucking now, white boy—are you a Democrat or a Republican?! Which is it?! What are you!?"

There was a moment that sort of hung in the air. The streets were full of people and noise, but after she screamed in my face and stepped up to me, there was a second of space where a lot of people were waiting to see what would happen. My first instinct was to cold cock the bitch with a right cross and run like hell. Now, I am not a smart man, but I know that a white man in a suit punching an irate black woman in the street while surrounded by thousands of pissed-off Democrats and hundreds of nervous NYPD officers the day after Trump's election is a white man who is about to get his shit wrecked.

So, that was no good.

My next instinct was to yell back at her. Something like, "I think both of them are hopelessly immoral, habitually lying, manipulative sociopaths who are better suited for prison than for elected office—and the fact that either of them can be considered candidates for the presidency is a disgrace to our Republic and an insult to everything in this country past, present, and future!"

But I felt like that would probably end badly too. Fortunately, I'd been in situations like this many times before, and I'd long ago discovered through trial and error the best way to handle them. During my childhood, I was yelled at and beaten many times, for many years. There was rarely a reason, but this kind of thing isn't rational. Being hit in the face because your brother is bored or being screamed at for an hour by your father because you didn't finish your milk teaches you how to handle this kind of anger. You can't reason with it, you can't calm it down, you can't run from it, you can't yell back, and you can't hit back. I've tried all of those and none of them work. The only thing I've found to be effective is a piece of advice I learned from the Bible.

Proverbs 15:1 says "A soft answer turneth away wrath …."

I told Tanya that I was a Christian. I calmly told her that I was a Christian, an American, and her brother. I told her that I loved her and—if she was hurting and it was important to her—I was more than willing to march to Trump Tower and stay with her until she felt like someone in this country gave a shit about her.

Of course, I didn't really mean what I said in that moment. Tanya assaulted me. I was afraid, and I could have reacted with anger—but I recognized that she was dealing with her own fear and anger. As soon as I said what I said, she came back to herself and grabbed her cross necklace. Her tone was much different as she said that it didn't matter to her one way or the other, and that if I needed to go grocery shopping, that I should just go. Then she and the rest of the protesters went on their way. We were all just Americans who loved our country walking in opposite directions on a Manhattan avenue. Because *a soft answer turneth away wrath.* Maybe if more people remembered that, then we'd get rid of all this fear and anger and finally have a chance to make America great again.

Maybe.

But probably not.

We all know that's not what's going to happen. There's going to be a lot of violence. A heinous kind of homemade evil and death. No Messiah is coming. So, I want to remember the chaos I saw that day on the streets of Manhattan and the prophetic words it left pressed on my spirit.

No peace.

No peace.

No peace.

Incoherence by Riverside Drive

I am writing this in a closet-sized room on the seventeenth floor of a dormitory of what I believe is the Manhattan School of Music. There is barely enough moonlight bouncing off the Hudson for me to see my breath. The only sound is the snoring of a young woman who is studying to be an opera singer. Her roommate is out of town, so she invited me over. She ordered Chinese food for dinner but was all over me before we had a chance to eat.

She kept biting my lip. I tasted blood. Finally, I got mad and bit her back.

Hard.

She asked me to eat her out, and I said no.

We awkwardly ate cold Chinese food on the floor of her dorm room and watched *Thelma and Louise*, but she wanted to go to sleep, so I couldn't even finish the movie. I brushed my teeth, and now it's three o'clock in the morning and I'm looking through a huge window at the dark silhouette of Riverside Church looming in the night sky against the Hudson River while she sleeps in the twin bed. Rockefeller built this monstrosity so his cronies would have a place to worship him. Beside it is a gigantic edifice that serves as the tomb of Ulysses S. Grant. The dome of the tomb is illuminated by turquoise lights signifying nothing. I have no idea what the S stands for, I have never read *Ulysses*, and I doubt Homer's poem has anything to do with this situation either.

The reason I took out my notebook and pulled her desk chair over to the window so I could sit here shivering out these scribbles is that I have never considered what a strange curiosity is Grant's Tomb. The inexplicable stone was staring at me and keeping me awake, so I felt compelled to address it.

Primarily, because I can see no reason why Grant was buried here. He was born in Ohio. Fought in the South. Presided in Washington. I guess it's true he died in New York, but not in Manhattan. And he never lived in this city either.

So why the fuck is the largest mausoleum on the whole Goddamn continent sitting on the Upper West Side of the Island of Manhattan and housing the bodies of two people who never lived here? And why the fuck am I sitting in my underwear in a freezing cold dorm room, with blue balls, bit lips, and a headache—writing this bullshit in a notebook next to an opera singer's extra packets of duck sauce?

Before I came here tonight, I was helping a Broadway star make an audition tape for a submarine movie Tom Hanks has written. I agreed to stay late to help him out, so he brought me a gift. Single malt scotch. The note said, "Thanks for all you've done for me. It's been a pleasure to work with such a gifted director."

I don't drink.

Ezra Pound set out to become the greatest poet of all time. His poem, *The Cantos*, is the most ambitious authorial project ever attempted. He wrote a lot of it in a mental hospital in Washington, D.C. Like Satan facing the chaos of Hell in *Paradise Lost,* or Odysseus in the Cyclops's cave—Pound, in his mad hubris, tried for something only God could do. Pound's last completed verse says,

Tho' my errors and wrecks lie about me

And I am not a demigod,

I cannot make it cohere.

When I was in elementary school, I read a lot of Greek mythology. I've forgotten most of it, but somewhere I ran across a poem Sophocles wrote about the dying words of Hercules. The words have been stuck in my mind ever since:

"WHAT SPLENDOUR / IT ALL COHERES."

I think the whole project of literature is to recreate that Herculean epiphany.

That's what Pound wanted.

And so do I.

I guess that's why I'm writing this.

But Pound never finished *The Cantos.*

And neither will I.

Groucho Marx used to ask people who was buried in Grant's tomb.

I think he was right.

Daffodils

When I was back there in elementary school, they made us read a poem about daffodils. This guy was remembering a time he had seen thousands of daffodils on a summer's day, and, at the end, he said something about how when he remembered that experience, "my heart danced with the daffodils."

Something like that.

I mention this because last night I woke up at 4:00 a.m. in a panic, dreaming about the time I found a bunch of bums gang-raping a whore in the street on a summer's night. I tried to save her, and they beat the shit out of me. Turned out she didn't want to be saved. Also turned out she wasn't a whore. Just an Upper East Side-wife who happened to enjoy dressing like a whore and getting gang fucked in the street.

They beat the shit out of me anyway.

For some reason, when I woke from this nightmare I remembered that poem from decades ago in elementary school.

"My heart danced with the daffodils."

As I was sitting up in bed, gasping through cold sweat,

I said something out loud that woke the young Broadway dancer next to me.

"Go fuck yourself with your daffodils."

"What?" She asked.

"What?"

"What daffodils?"

"Nothing. Go back to sleep," I said.

She opened her sleeping eyes. "Jesus, are you okay? You look like Hell."

"Just go back to sleep."

"Go shower. You're soaking my sheets."

"Fine. I'll shower. Go back to sleep," I repeated.

She rolled over, and I went to shower.

Cold water. Pink towel. Floral pattern.

I went to her desk and found a pen.

Ginsberg and Bukowski clasping assholes in America.

I felt around on the floor for my pants.

I got dressed, put the note in my pocket, and went home.

David's Baptism

For a few months, I lived illegally under an old woman's stair-case in Queens. My brother John set me up with the place. I was between jobs and driving for a guy who did real estate and insurance. He mostly sold meth, coke, weed, and what-ever else he could find. He had to make a trip to Indiana, so I had Sunday off. The old woman spent Sundays at church, which left me with the whole place to myself.

I made a day of it. Big steak sandwich. Plenty of fries.

Got a call she was in the hospital. Cardiac. Happened during the service. The pastor was very upset.

I went down to the hospital.

The old woman shared a room with a five-year-old girl with platinum hair and a *Little Mermaid* onesie. The little girl got excited watching Barney and accidentally pulled out her feeding tube. It spilled out all over the floor. Interrupted the old woman's prayer circle. The pastor was very upset.

While they cleaned it up, I grabbed a handful of pills. The real good shit.

I went home and got down.

I smoked up and took a few pills. As the setting sun filled the room, I lit some incense and put on Muddy Waters loud as fuck. It took about thirty minutes to submerge myself in the warm tub. Chicago blues under deep opium oceans. The water was scalding hot, but I was numb. The incense-mingled weed smoke was spirituous. I had lined the lip of the tub with five ripe grapefruits and a ten-inch hunting blade. As the blues played on, I alternated between slurping lacerated grapefruit and masturbation.

Slow cuts. Bitter juice. Easy strokes. Stringy pearls. Ecstasy doldrums.

However, apparently, a big steak sandwich, plenty of fries, five grapefruit, Muddy Waters, weed, incense, excessive masturbation, and a heroic dose of medicinal-strength opium don't mix well. The first time I threw up, I was still in the tub. A long, dark stream gushed out of my belly and splashed into the water.

"Oh, Jesus."

Now I was sitting in a hot stew of puke, cum, and bathwater. Little bits of chewed steak and grapefruit pulp floated all around me. Right away, I started sifting through the water for the half-digested pills. I found one and swallowed it again.

I had to get out.

Lifting myself over the lip of the tub was a Herculean struggle. My water-logged noodle arms had no power and my heart was fighting to keep tempo. My hands slipped and the lip hit my stomach. A second stream of vomit spilled across the floor.

Dull thumping.

"Oh, God—Jesus—fuck."

I groaned and rolled onto the floor. A cold touch stickeled my side and I knew that I had landed on the hunting blade. I pulled it out and felt the wound. Long and wide. My breathing carried involuntary whimpers, like a frightened animal.

"Fuck ... help ... Jesus ... fuck."

I was naked and drenched with my own blood, cum, and vomit, as I crawled through the humid blues searching for my cell phone like a blind pig. The air was foul and thick with putrid steam. My skin was burning but my body was cold. I was breathing harder and getting less air. No strength. No pain. No light. Fading out.

I slipped again and landed face down in the cesspool on the bathroom floor. My unfocused eyes lazed open.

"Fuck ... Jesus, please."

I thought about the old woman—all the Sundays she'd invited me to church. The prayer circle at the hospital.

Jesus was going to heal her.

And she'd come home.

And find me like this.

And the shock would kill her.

"Christ—fuck."

Then I saw the screen light up. With the last of my will, I pushed myself up, grabbed my phone, and flung my body over the toilet. I'd texted Erik before going in, and he hadn't replied. Now his answer was vivid on the bright screen.

"im att bible stdy"

I puked again.

This time in the toilet.

Like a normal person.

I dropped the phone and passed out with my head in the bowl.

American Standard.

The last thing I remember was voiding my bowels.

* * *

I awoke to the sound of my phone rattling on the tile. I answered. It was a job offer. Finance gig. Upstanding citizen. White shirt—neckties.

Hallelujah.

I hung up the phone and immediately called John to tell him the news.

The dealer got arrested and never came back from Indiana. The five-year-old girl with the feeding tube and *The Little Mermaid* onesie died laughing at Barney. The old woman died in a prayer circle next to an unopened bottle of pills. The pastor was very upset. I moved back in with my parents in Virginia and started the new job.

John cleaned up the bathroom.

For Ben

The fastest I've ever made anyone cry was the time I told my
mother that Ben was dead.
She was standing in the kitchen, folding laundry,
and I said,
"Mom?"
"Yes, honey?"
"Mom, I have something to tell you."
"Okay."
"There was a car crash—Ben's dead."
She burst into tears and moaned the word no like a sad wound.
I've never heard my mother make a sound like that before.
I hugged her for a long time while she cried.
She and I went to the funeral together.
I saw Ben's mom carrying his ashes.
This woman who had changed my diapers was inconsolably sob-
bing and carrying the ashes of my first best friend.
The ashes and I were eighteen and had just graduated high school.
My mom cried again.
And I thought about Ben.
Learning to ride a bike so I could ride two blocks down to his house.

Playing PlayStation for the first time and trying to figure out what
Bandicoot was.
Exploring the crawlspaces and attic in his house.
Learning numbers and letters.
Going swimming.
Nerf guns.
Summer.
Grass and sunshine.
I remember the first time I saw him in public school.
I ran to hug him.
And he wouldn't hug me.
He looked so embarrassed.
He was cool.
And I wasn't.
And that was that.
But tonight I didn't think about any of these things.
Tonight I remembered something else.
Something I haven't thought about since it happened.
I was three years old and playing at Ben's house and my mother
came to take me home.
We hid under his bed because I didn't want to leave.
While hugging each other in the dark, I asked him how long we'd
be friends.
And Ben said,
"I don't know.
Forever, I guess."

This Isn't Your Usual Cocaine Rant

My best friend lived on my couch for a month while waiting tables at a fancy hotel restaurant in Nolita. He came home very late one night talking as fast as I could write.

This is what he said.

* * *

Cocaine is fucking amazing.

You feel like you want to talk to everyone right now. Like, hey, listen to me. Here's what I have to offer. Value. Value right now.

Every person you meet has the ability to astound you.

Tonight I met a friend of the guy who owns the hotel. He's been there like ten times. Only orders steak and eggs.

This is the first restaurant I've been to where they charge for water. Water is a non-zero item. Three dollars for hydrogen and oxygen and some covalent bonds.

Multivalent is a word I tried to use in an English essay one time, and I got called out on it, but I feel like it's a good word.

My socks are comfortable. My pants are not. I need a U-shaped crotch. This one is V-shaped.

Cocaine is a fucking hell of a drug.

Also, why are you hanging your mirror on this plastic, amateur shit?

You should have, like, brass—

This isn't your usual cocaine rant. Last time I had cocaine I was silent. I've never felt like I had to say something more than at that moment, but then didn't say it. Which is a little sad. But I did a lot more cocaine tonight.

Also, if you could look up the Deadpool sexuality article online that would be great. There's a Deadpool article, but it's like hetero-something is the new homophobia.

Silverado is the SUV, right? We did cocaine in there. And in every bathroom we went to. And I talked to various gay dudes. Mostly about content marketing.

I feel like that's what I excel at, you know? Short-term memory.

I might have gotten two or three cards tonight because— let's be honest—this stuff makes you do fucking business.

Don't publish this under my name, please.

I met several Puerto Ricans too.

I hope my head movement isn't disturbing you.

I feel like I was really, really, smart at one time. Like, I was incredibly smart in high school. And I was surprisingly smart in college. I would write something and the teacher would write it up on the board and be, like, look at this. Look at what this kid did. This is great. But you get out of school and then it's just like—I don't know, man. Nobody fucking cares about Walt Whitman. Or Epicurus. Or Swinburne. Have you read Swinburne? You should look into Swinburne. He's a pre-Raphaelite. They were the guys after Tennyson and before T. S. Eliot. He wrote a really good poem about Sappho. She was this lesbian poet in Ancient Greece before Christ. It was really violent and—you know—awesome. It just really tickles you.

There's a really good poem called "The Woodspurge." It's this, like, dandelion they have in England. It's basically this three-pronged weed. And it's about this person who's had his heart broken. And it's like all he can remember from all the grief is that he saw a woodspurge and it had three prongs. All that pain and torment, and you don't learn anything in the end. It's just chaos, you know? Or maybe it's like sometimes when something really significant happens to you, you can only focus on the most insignificant things in your life.

I should memorize more poems. The only poem I've ever memorized is "Desiderata." It's, like, the most poem-est of poems. But I just can't right now. My mind is electric you know. It's circuits.

I feel like kissing somebody on the forehead is really like a cheesy move. You know? Like, I really care about you, but only from here upwards. Only from your eyebrows to your fucking hair.

I recited that poem on the last day of college. "Desiderata." That day was just so full of tears. It was also the day we drove to Myrtle Beach. The dotted lines kept turning into solid lines. But when we got there it was so great. Except that one night on the beach that didn't go well. When you came back to the room, you looked so sad it really hurt. I couldn't sleep I was so worried about you. You said you couldn't find the right thing to say to her. That made me sad. The look on your face like your insides were dying. God, there were so many tears that week.

This city is so great. The newness is so great. Every person you meet has never met you. They don't have any reason to hate you yet. You just have to be there to tell them what you're about. What you stand for, who you are.

I met a guy who's written for Comedy Central.

I'd read this headline today, and that head implanted itself in my head.

Let's write a story right now. A story I would write would be about a kid who grew up where I grew up, but who worked his way up to working at a building like the one I'm looking at right now. But that's not an exciting story, that's just following the rules.

You know who sucks? People ignoring their father, who's gonna pay for whatever it is they're buying. This guy with quaffed, brown, wavy hair orders a seven-hundred-dollar dinner and doesn't even look up from his phone.

I don't know.

Is this productive for you at all?

Usually when I get home from work I just kinda scratch my inner thighs. 'Cause it feels so-o-o good.

I'm so glad that guy likes me. I had such a great time bonding with him and doing cocaine in the bathroom of a gay bar. When's the appropriate time to broach the subject that you're not gay?

Who's that philosopher who's all about sets? Wittgenstein? No, Bertrand Russell. Yeah that's the guy. Set-theory guy.

There are guys who you find attractive, but it's like a small, small set. Like you see yourself in the mirror, and you can see how that could be attractive to somebody. And you reinforce your attractions to what you look like.

There's this guy there who everybody hated who styled himself exactly like me. He told the hostess he wanted steak and eggs waiting for him when he got there because he knew the owner. He's achieved a level of success where he can walk into a restaurant and order anything he wants—even if it's not on the menu—but he was by himself. He sat at a table for four, but he was by himself. I don't know what to make of that.

Do you see a story in here yet?

This other guy I met—the gay guy—he had to coach me on how to do cocaine. First time was the Calvin Klein, which is cocaine and ketamine. Ketamine isn't a fun drug after a while. It also makes your poop really thin. Like undergrown carrots.

I'm sorry I went to Trader Joe's without you that one time.

I could speak poetically if you'd like, but I feel like all my kinetic energy is spent on my neck movement right now.

I'm so glad I'm here. I met a guy who writes for a show on Comedy Central and did cocaine with him in the bathroom of a gay bar.

The great thing about cooking is you never come up with the same thing twice. Herodotus said that. You never step in the same river twice.

Alright let's try some fucking poetry.

It's so humbling to walk past a pillar on a bank that's worth more than you are. In terms of marble. My weight in marble is not worth what I am as a human being. That's a crazy thing.

I was watching *Mad Men*, and Pete Campbell's apartment was exactly like this one.

I feel like cocaine is like a ten-minute drug. The inspiration might be waning.

You have to search your top competitors for things people need in the comments. Sniper advertising. That'll show you what people want in the area you're in.

All these developers are just living for their next demo day. After demo day the dust they've accumulated will be a beautiful sandcastle or it will just blow away with the wind.

I've seen the upstart Czechoslovakian with his bus business.

I don't know.

"Fuck" is such a great word. Because you can intersplice it anywhere. It's un-fucking-believable.

If you want to write something, I'd be happy to be productive.

Let's write a New York story. Everybody likes a New York story. That's why everybody likes John Cheever. He's so good. He's also unpredictable—but whatever.

I haven't fucked enough girls to start fucking dudes.

I hope I meet somebody like me. In some kind of way.

Hey, let's read a story from the Calvino book of *Italian Folk Tales*.

How do I look in this all-black shit?

Alright this folk tale is about Jesus and Saint Peter.

It's called "How Saint Peter Happened to Join Up with the Lord."

Hannah studied geography. And it's like why would you study fucking geography? Don't we already have enough maps?

Okay wait, "How Saint Peter Happened to Join Up with the Lord." That's such a great title for a chapter. It's just like—I mean there are like so many prosaic words to use for it. It's like one day Saint Peter was just around the Lord and this is how he found him.

I feel like I should teach my children Christianity if I have them. At the very least it's a true narrative. I don't know that much about Christ—I'll admit that—but I think that—you know, obviously Abraham's sacrifice is huge. I don't even know what he represents in the sense of everything. But we humans are fucking terrible. We're fucking fucked up. We all have flaws. Nobody is really a good person. Or at least every good person has sort of a side that belies that. I have good characteristics, but I have others that disenfranchise me from that category of good. Christianity is like this collection of narratives—plus what Jesus represents. I think what most pastors hope for is something so massive that people can't understand it. That it just takes you and makes you part of it. People are so amazed and dazzled that they believe something that they haven't personalized.

It's all about your relationship to the story. If there were a parent who didn't entirely believe the story of Christ, I can see why they would embrace that narrative to teach their children. We've lost religion, and then you end up with people who don't believe in anything. Everything becomes momentary, and you're not connected to anything. You're just critical of everything. Like some dumb, sentimental, Easter Sunday-post on Facebook by some bimbo who gets sixty-five likes from a bunch of fuckboys who just like her boobs. That's just fuckin' shit. And that Calvino story I read was fuckin' shit. But your essay about why you believe in Christianity would be like one of the seminal works of all Christian literature. Your discipline is like a fucking drug. It's just unbe-fuckin'-lievable. But you also have a deep interest in what the human spirit wants. And you try to understand it. I just think that you—I don't know.

I don't believe in God, but I would go to your church. Even though you're not a pastor. And I know you don't like Christians.

I can understand why people fucking do cocaine.

I like to think that I'm pretty good with words.

I gotta pee.

A Nightmare with Johnny Cash

I dreamed I was wandering in the Death Valley desert
When I came upon a black muscle car blazing in the night
I walked toward the fiery wreck

He was sitting on the ground leaning on the many rolled crash
Wild energy emanating from this creature of unending darkness
Pandemonium in a black suit
The twisted steel frame was wrapped in a fireball
And the stinging smell of kerosene
His guitar was charred carbon black
Scratched and splintered all to hell by his savage frantic picking
The broken neck dripped blood from his lacerated fingertips
Shattered bottles and spilled pills
Blood-soaked sweat

He looked at me with tears and said
"I have learned the secret song of God"
Then with a voice of gentle power, like many troubled thunders,
he sang the song of Revelation
The one that cannot be learned except by the redeemed

And a voice said
"Johnny Cash, you're like a thorn tree in a whirlwind"
He set down the guitar
And replied
"The whirlwind is in the thorn tree"

And when he had made an end, he laid down on the restless sand
and died

I remember it so well
The cutting wind
The pain in his voice
The angry fire and blood
The thick darkness where God was
I remember every detail
except one

I can't remember how the song goes

The Light-Bearer and
the Heart of Darkness

And when the sun was going down, a deep sleep fell
upon Abram; and, lo, an horror of great darkness fell
upon him.
—Genesis 15:12 (King James Version)

On the last weekend I spent in Virginia before I moved
to New York, I left my home and drove west into the
Shenandoah Mountains. My family had fallen asleep, and
the humid dark smelled good. The sky was black clouds. I
parked on the side of the highway and walked into the woods.
There was no moon, no stars, almost no light of any kind. I
was out there about six hours. I don't know how many miles
I walked or where I went. When at last I was exhausted, I sat
on a cracked boulder near the top of some mountain. I stayed
there till sunrise. Thinking.

Heart of Darkness and *Apocalypse Now*

"And this also has been one of the darkest places of the Earth."

This line comes from the beginning pages of Joseph Conrad's 1902 novella, *Heart of Darkness*. In 1979, Francis Ford Coppola released a film based on this story, called *Apocalypse Now*. It's about an American colonel played by Marlon Brando, who must be killed because he has succumbed to violent madness during the war in Vietnam. Near the end of the film Brando delivers a monologue about horror. He describes the face of Horror and speaks of Horror and Moral Terror as though they are dear friends. Then he tells a story about a pile of little arms:

I remember when I was with Special Forces. Seems a thousand centuries ago. We went into a camp to inoculate some children. We'd left the camp after we had inoculated the children for polio. And this old man came running after us, and he was crying. He couldn't say. We went back there, and they had come and hacked off every inoculated arm. There they were, in a pile—a pile of little arms ...

Earlier that week there had been a forty-nine-year-old black Army veteran sitting next to me in a waiting room. He had never seen *Apocalypse Now*, nor had he read *Heart of Darkness*, but he told me stories about the horror and the darkness. He had seen people murdering each other and committing all manner of evil in the name of religion, money, power, even water. He had been in Somalia in the nineties. Once his unit vaccinated the children in a small village there. When they returned a few days later, they found that the warlords had come to the village. They had come and hacked off every inoculated arm. *There they were, in a pile. A pile of little arms …*

He said his unit hunted these men, and when they found them, they tortured them with hatred and malice in their hearts. He said they took their machetes and chopped off every limb and member from the bodies of dozens of these men they judged to be monsters. Then they made their own piles. Not just piles of arms, but piles of legs, ears, noses, penises, tongues, and heads. They burned them all. The stench of that holocaust haunts his dreams. It's been over twenty years since he made those piles in the Somalian highlands, and over fifty years since the piles in the jungles of Vietnam— but men will go on making piles as long as there are people to make into piles.

This veteran showed me the potent drugs he depends on. Without them he can't function. He can't sleep because of the dreams. The drugs are his only defense. They are the only love he has, and only love can hold back the horror and the darkness.

Apocalypse Now ends with Coppola cross cutting between a ritual slaughter of a bull and the killing of Colonel Kurtz. Both Kurtz and the bull are helpless beasts being hacked apart with machetes. The weary dying voice of Marlon Brando groans the film's final words, the famous lines from Conrad's story, "the horror … the horror."

Conrad's novella is set up as a story told by men on a boat going down a river at night and ends with them floating off into darkness. "The offing was barred by a bank of black clouds, and the tranquil waterway leading to the uttermost ends of the earth flowed somber under an overcast sky—seemed to lead into the heart of an immense darkness."

Conrad and Coppola have agreed that despair, horror, and—above all—*darkness* lie at the heart of human existence, and their art plunges us into it to fend for ourselves.

Evil

The problem of evil is a major point of contentious debate among philosophers and theologians. It asks how we can reconcile the existence of evil and injustice with that of an omnipotent, omniscient, and omnibenevolent God. A good Christian at this juncture would begin a discourse on Leibniz, Malthus, Kant, and maybe even Epicurus. They would give a nice scholarly answer with a biblical foundation that venerates Aquinas and points out how the question misunderstands slippery metaphysical subtleties.

But I am not a good Christian. My answer is the book of Job.

However, none of these answers are any good when you're looking at a pile of rotting infant arms. That is *evil*. It's there. It exists. Never mind how, never mind why. Philosophy and theology are reduced to pedantic babbling once someone starts swinging a machete at babies. All that matters is— what do you do about it?

That answer is simple: oppose it.

But how? What is the greatest thing that I can do to oppose evil?

Again, the answer is simple: expose it.

People always oppose evil when it is exposed to them, so if you can expose evil, you can begin to destroy it. That, however, is not so easy. Even the few who are not blind cannot see in the dark, and evil is shrouded in darkness. Thick darkness. Immense darkness. I'm not concerned with ugly, blatant evil that is done in the open. The kind of evil that worries me is infinitely more sinister, namely the kind of evil that men believe is good. Pernicious is the closest word for it—something evil that appears good. Isaiah says, "Woe unto them that call evil good, and good evil; that put darkness for light, and light for darkness."

A familiar example to illustrate the danger of this confusion may be found in *Star Wars*. Emperor Palpatine tells Anakin Skywalker, "good is a point of view," and later Anakin becomes Darth Vader and tells Obi Wan, "from my point of view the Jedi are evil."

This kind of deception causes more pain and damnation than anything else.

The Anointed Cherub

Now that we're talking about true evil, we must introduce its main character. The God of this World. Satan. Lucifer. The Goddamned Devil. The Prince of Fucking Darkness. If I am to oppose evil, I must oppose the Devil—and if by exposing evil I can destroy it, then maybe by exposing Lucifer I can help destroy him. The problem is that most people don't even believe in the Devil, let alone know anything about him or what he has done.

In Bryan Singer's 1991 film *The Usual Suspects*, Kevin

Spacey says, "The greatest trick the Devil ever pulled was convincing the world he didn't exist."

This line by Chris McQuarrie is paraphrased from the French poet Charles Baudelaire's words, "The Devil's finest trick is to persuade you that he does not exist."

But I'm not going to summon Lucifer here to stand before you, and even if I did, I don't believe it would convince anyone. When God brought the Israelites up out of the land of Egypt with a pillar of smoke by day and fire by night, he parted a sea and drowned the most powerful army in the world right before their eyes. He spoke to them with a voice of many thunders and they sent Moses to climb Sinai and listen on their behalf because they were afraid the sound alone would kill them.

"And Moses said unto the people, fear not: for God is come to prove you, and that his fear may be before your faces, that ye sin not. And the people stood afar off, and Moses drew near unto the thick darkness where God was."—Exodus 20:20–21, KJV

Moses was gone for less than forty days, and the children of Israel built a golden idol and had an orgy to worship Lucifer. So, I don't want any one-hour Christians. I have not come to save your souls. I have come to show you what the children of Israel saw in Egypt. "A horror of great darkness, even darkness which may be felt."

I want to submerge you in immense darkness so that you will see the light and be able to tell the difference, which is not as easy as it sounds. Destroying the Devil is the most important work that can be done. The Bible says in the book of Jude, "For this cause came the son of man into the world, to destroy the works of the devil."

Maybe the best way I can serve Christ is to expose the Devil and show how he is affecting the world around you. Then whether you believe he exists or not, you must acknowledge that he is influencing your life and decide how to respond to him.

It's Only Rock n' Roll

The easiest way to do this is to show Lucifer's presence in music rather than politics, religion, or other parts of our culture where he has established his kingdom. Because music is where Lucifer is most obviously prevalent. On this point, the artists speak for themselves.

Peter Criss of KISS said in a *TV Guide* interview, "I find myself evil. I believe in the Devil as much as God, you can use either one to get things done."

The Rolling Stones have an album entitled *Their Satanic Majesties Request*, and Mick Jagger did the music for several films produced by Kenneth Anger, a high priest in the Church of Satan.

Brian Wilson of The Beach Boys said in an interview, "We were doing witchcraft, trying to make witchcraft music."

Carlos Santana claims that a demonic spirit called Metatron gives him the music and lyrics for many of his songs, saying in *Rolling Stone* magazine, "You meditate and you got the candles and the incense and you've been chanting and all of a sudden you hear this voice saying write this down."

Snoop Dogg, in his autobiography, *The Dogfather*, claims

that the Devil came to him and offered to make him rich and famous in exchange for his soul. Snoop accepted the offer and identifies that moment in his life as the birth of Snoop Dogg.

Ozzy Osbourne said in *Hit Parader* magazine in 1975, "I really wish I knew why I've done some of the things I've done over the years. I don't know if I'm a medium for some outside source, I hope it's not what I think it is, Satan."

Kurt Cobain once said that his life's goal was to, "get stoned and worship Satan."

Jim Morrison of the Doors, speaking of what started his musical career, said, "I met the spirit of music. An appearance of the Devil on a Venice Canal. Running, I saw Satan."

Eminem said, "I'm trapped. If I could go back, I never would have rapped. I sold my soul to the Devil. I'll never get it back."

Kanye West said on stage during a live performance, "I sold my soul to the Devil. I know it's a crappy deal, least it came with a few toys—like a happy meal."

When asked how he got the energy to perform, Van Halen's David Lee Roth said, "You must fall into supplication of the demon gods."

Dr. Dre's producer early in his career was a man named Griffy, who claimed to be present when Dr. Dre sold his soul to the Devil, adding, "I swear the devil got a receipt for his ass."

Little Richard said of Rock n' Roll music in his book *The Life and Times of Little Richard*, "I believe this kind of music is demonic. A lot of the beats in popular songs are taken from voodoo, from the drums. I believe this music is driving people from Christ."

Later he says, "I was directed and commanded by the power of darkness. The power that a lot of people don't believe exists. The power of the Devil, Satan."

Bob Dylan once said to Ed Bradley in a *60 Minutes* interview, "I made a bargain a long time ago." Bradley asks, "With who?"

Dylan replies, "With the chief commander." Bradley asks, "In this world?"

Dylan responds, "In this world, and in the one we can't see."

Jimmy Page, lead guitarist for Led Zeppelin, was involved in the Church of Satan and lived in a house formerly owned by Aleister Crowley.

Do What Thou Wilt

Aleister Crowley is known as the father of modern satanism. He wrote books on witchcraft, sex magick, and a book called *The Diary of a Drug Fiend*. In his book *Magick*, Crowley discusses sacrificing children to Satan and was exiled from Italy for holding satanic orgies and ceremonies. The Italian newspaper headlines called him, "the wickedest man in the world."

In 1904, Crowley wrote *The Book of the Law*. In it he states, "Do what thou wilt shall be the whole of the Law. …. Love is the law, love under will. …. There is no law beyond Do what thou wilt."

In 1980, John Lennon told *Playboy Magazine*, "The whole Beatle idea was to do what you want right? Do what thou wilst."

Lennon is clearly familiar with Crowley's maxim and

implies that the goal of the Beatles and the movements they inspired, was to promote the philosophy of the most influential Luciferian of the twentieth century.

So, what?

How does this affect people living in the world today?

During my third year at the University of Virginia, a Christian friend and I were arguing a point of Christian doctrine. Unable to reach an agreement, I turned to another friend of ours who knew nothing of Christianity, satanism, or the Beatles—and asked his opinion. He said he believed that if you really wanted something, you should do it. Regardless of what anyone else says, he believed you should "do what you want," which is a paraphrased quotation of Crowley, the way of Lucifer, the teachings of the Prince of Darkness. The key piece of this story is that my friend was not taught this in the Church of Satan, but by secular American culture. This means that American society is teaching Satanic ideas. Therefore, America is becoming—or will become, or has become—a satanic nation.

Darkness for Light

My friend said, "Do what you want."

Just before he was killed, John Lennon said, "Do what thou wilst."

And the wickedest man in the world, Aleister Crowley, claimed that Satan himself told him that, "Do what thou wilt shall be the whole of the law."

This idea can be traced back through the history of philosophy and religion all the way to the serpent in the Garden of Eden. The one who told Eve, if you rebel against God you will become like God. You can make your own rules. If you reach out and eat, then do what thou wilt shall be the whole of the law.

This lie is the infernal gospel.

Lucifer means *light-bearer*, and there are many myths about Lucifer, or Prometheus, or countless others—but they all tell the same story. The story of a spiritual being that gives men knowledge that God did not intend for them to have. Luciferians claim that this is the better way to live, and it is appealing. Be your own God. Make your own rules. Do what thou wilt. It sounds like freedom. Lucifer appears to be the light-bearer, trying to free us from forced submission to a jealous, tyrannical God with rules that take all the fun out of life—like rape, fornication, drugs, gluttony, and greed. No more boring church services or giving money to the poor. John Lennon's song "Imagine" is the most profound satanic manifesto ever set to music. It speaks of a world of perfect peace without God ruining everything. It's very sweet music and the lyrical imagery is so beautiful that it convinces everyone that it must be light.

This, at last, is Satan's magnum opus. This lie is his greatest achievement. Kevin Spacey and Charles Baudelaire are wrong. The greatest trick the devil ever pulled was not convincing Man that he did not exist, but convincing Man that he could be God. This is the horror, the great darkness at the heart of this world. And the darkness has deepened with Lucifer's rising.

In the eighth chapter of the book of the prophet Daniel,

one of the most important of God's prophets, God shows Daniel a vision of the end-times and sends the Archangel Gabriel to speak to Daniel, saying:

Understand, O son of man: for at the time of the end shall be the vision …. Behold, I will make thee know what shall be in the last end of the indignation: for at the time appointed the end shall be.

And in the latter time of their kingdom, when the transgressors are come to the full, a king of fierce countenance, and understanding dark sentences, shall stand up. And his power shall be mighty, but not by his own power: and he shall destroy wonderfully, and shall prosper, and practise, and shall destroy the mighty and the holy people. And through his policy also he shall cause craft to prosper in his hand; and he shall magnify himself in his heart, and by peace shall destroy many.

The Apostle Paul said, "Satan comes as an angel of light, as a wolf in sheep's clothing seeking whom he may devour." Bob Dylan said, "Sometimes Satan comes as a man of peace."

This is done to deceive people who are seeking light. They think they have found it, but they are in darkness. Solomon writes in Proverbs, "There is a way which seemeth right unto a man, but the end thereof are the ways of death."

The Bible refers to Jesus as "the Morning Star" and to Lucifer as "thou son of the morning." If you understand astrology and astronomy you know that it likens Jesus to Venus and Lucifer to Sirius, but most people confuse them for the same light-source. Lucifer (Prometheus) brings false fire, Frankenstein's monster. It appears to be light, but it is thick darkness in the end. In the Gospel of John, Jesus says, "I am the light of the world: he that followeth me shall not walk in darkness but shall have the light of life."

The Light of The World

About the time I drove out into the Shenandoah and walked up that dark mountain, I had been having a strange recurring dream. My mind would go black in the midst of a dream, and I would hear a deep, ominous voice repeating the words, "I am the gathering darkness," over and over for what seemed like hours. I've seen horrors, horrors that you've seen. I've wandered lost in the darkness too. I'm no different. But in 2 Chronicles it is written, "The Lord hath said that he would dwell in the thick darkness."

Christ has not forsaken me in my darkness. I dwell there and he with me. When you bring the light of the world into thick darkness you can finally see them both for what they are. As Anne Frank wrote in her diary, "Look at how a single candle can both defy and define the darkness."

Lucifer claims to bring light, Crowley claims to worship love, but without Christ there is no light, and without God there is no Love. For God is Love.

Martin Luther King Jr. said, "Darkness cannot drive out darkness: only light can do that. Hate cannot drive out hate: only love can do that."

I want to see light in darkness and know the difference. Above all, I want to walk in the light of life and love which is Christ Jesus, the Messiah of Israel. This is the only way I see to drive out the horror and the darkness.

I Am the Gathering Darkness

But, like everyone else, that forty-nine-year-old Army veteran I met in a waiting room is still in the grip of the horrors of Satan's evil. He told me that he didn't believe that any God could take away the horror and the darkness. A good Christian would have assured him that he was wrong. A good Christian would have told him that God can ease all suffering and heal all wounds. But I am not a good Christian. I am the gathering darkness. I sat on that Shenandoah mountaintop and I thought of all the evil I have done. Jesus said, "if a man knoweth to do good and doeth it not, to him it is sin."

He who is guilty of part of the law, is guilty of all.

The morning star crossed the horizon. The sun rose. I wondered at the light of the world.

As a child, sunrises gave me a feeling of hope and joy—but as a man, I have spent hundreds of sleepless nights sitting alone in darkness, and the dawn doesn't rescue me anymore. These days I see horrors. The light-bearer and the heart of darkness. Closer now. Much closer.

I rose from the boulder and walked back to the highway.

No one knew how I had passed the night.

But the drug-addicted veteran still sits in the boat on Conrad's river.

Still sits on Coppola's pile of little arms.

Still sits on my Shenandoah mountain top.

Still sits in every chair in America.

Still sits in the heart—*of an immense darkness.*

Sweet Rolls

I remember the smell of my grandmother's house in Huntington, West Virginia when I was four years old. My grandfather had been one of the top civil engineering students in Hungary before coming to the United States to escape the war. By the 1950s, he'd married my grandmother and started a family. He designed and built that house himself. His name is on the blueprints. Fifty years later, I woke up before sunrise in one of the upstairs bedrooms.

My mother had one older brother, Joe, and two younger sisters, Aunt Cherie and Aunt Dottie. Donny was sleeping in Aunt Dottie's bed, and David was sleeping in our mother's old bed. I was lying in Aunt Cherie's bed. I was always the first one awake in those days, and this morning was no different. It was still dark. I drew back the sheets and silently got out of bed. I thought about my mother waking up here when she'd been a little girl. I couldn't imagine her as a child, but the room must have been almost the same. There was a big toy chest with circus animals dancing on the sides. A tall bookcase full of children's books stood against the wall. Dr.

Seuss. Winnie the Pooh. Aesop's Fables. Bible stories for kids. Books about gardening and baking. My mother is very fond of gardens and growing things.

The door made a friendly creak as I opened it and toddled down the hall past the blue bathroom where my mother had brushed her teeth before bed every night for twenty-two years. My socks slid like magic over the polished wood floor. I heard my father and grandfather snoring from their respective bedrooms as I looked down the staircase. Dad always complained about that staircase. He said it was dangerous. Slicker than ice and so steep it was almost a ladder. But that's the way they did things in the old country. I went down.

The first sip of light was spilling through the wide window by the front door and pouring gold over the musky rugs and antique sofas that filled the front living room. The rugs had been there since before my mother was born. My grandmother told dozens of stories about the prayers God had answered for her there. She believed in kneeling. I examined the spot where her knees had worn through the rug, running my fingers over the threadbare holy ground. My grandmother is a bonafide, *Gone with The Wind*, Georgia Peach, and you can hear the echo of old Savannah when she lifts her hands and says, "Thank ya, Jesus."

I took a deep breath and tasted dew coming in off the green leaves in the front yard mingled with the smell of cinnamon sugar from the kitchen. I walked into the den and found my grandfather's big rocking recliner empty and the TV off. My grandmother was perched on the couch wearing a nightgown and reading Isaiah. The clock over the great hearth chimed five o'clock, and my grandmother looked up and saw me watching her read.

"Honey, John's up," my grandmother said.

My mother came in from the kitchen wearing green and brown mismatched oven mitts and carrying a tray of fresh-baked sweet rolls. The love in her smile was soft and warm as she said, "Good morning, sweetheart."

"Good morning, Mommy," I said to her. I was very particular in those days about always calling my mother *Mommy*. I had decided that Mommy was my favorite of the various names one could use for a mother. Later, I switched to *Mom* because it made me feel more grown up—but when I was very young, I liked Mommy more than anything else and I stuck to it loyally. Mommy put down the sweet rolls and took off the mitts, then came to pick me up. My mother wasn't very affectionate with us as children. She loved us, of course, but she didn't like being hugged by three boys at the same time. David got a lot of attention because he made trouble, and Donny got a lot of attention because he was the youngest, but I always felt like she didn't notice me very much. However, on this morning in her childhood home with her mom in their kitchen, making her favorite family recipe, my mother was overflowing with adoration. She squeezed me and kissed me and told me she loved me, then she sat me down beside my grandmother and went to finish icing the sweet rolls.

"Honey, do you know who you are named after?" my grandmother asked.

I shook my head, even though I did.

"Why, you are named after the Apostle John. Now, do you know who the Apostle John was?"

I shook my head again with my little mouth hanging open. My grandmother is the greatest storyteller who ever lived. She always holds me in rapture.

"Well, now you wanna hear something? Let me tell you, sweetheart—I mean, do you realize that he was a great man of God? The Apostle John was beloved of God. He was Jesus's best friend. The Bible says that he was the Beloved Apostle and that Jesus loved him dearly. Now, do you know what your middle name is?"

"Matthew," I said.

"That's right. And what does Matthew mean?" She waved her fists like this was the most exciting conversation she'd ever had.

"Gift from God." I'd been taught this by my father.

"That's right. And John means that God has been gracious. So your name is John Matthew, and that means that you are God's gracious gift, doesn't it? Do you know why your mother and father have named you that?"

I shook my head, knowing that feigned ignorance would keep her talking with that spirited passion that I found so engaging.

"Because they love you very, very, much. And just like the Apostle John, you are beloved of God. You're going to grow up in the grace and favor of God and, someday, you are going to be a great man of God. Isn't that wonderful?"

My mother came back from the kitchen with a cold glass of milk and a plate of hot cinnamon sweet rolls covered with melting vanilla cream. She picked me up and sat me on her lap. "Read him the Gospel of John," my mother said, "That's my favorite. Read it to him, Mom."

As my brothers, father, and grandfather lay sleeping upstairs, I sat on my mother's lap and ate sweet rolls and drank milk while my grandmother covered me with prayer and blessings. I've been to a lot of churches, but I've never met another Christian like my grandmother. I suppose this is why I don't get along with most Christians. I have seen and tasted and I know the difference between store-bought and the real thing. As for me, I pray just as much as she did, but I don't do it the same way. I believe that God must teach everyone to pray, just like he did with the apostles. My grandmother had her way and I have mine—and even though I may never wear holes in any rugs, I pray without ceasing. My grandmother held up her Bible so I could see, and we read together from The Gospel of John.

"In the beginning, was the word ..."

My mother kissed the back of my blonde head as I received the elements and my grandmother's Holy Ghost hallelujahs greeted the sunrise with our family's sacred mantra.

"Thank ya, Jesus."

* * *

When my grandfather died, mom and her siblings sold the house he built for them and moved grandmother closer to them. I'll never set foot in that home again, but I remember the way it smelled when I awoke that morning before dawn and came downstairs to find my loving mother making sweet rolls. I also remember when Mom told Grandmother that they'd had to throw out her prayer rugs.

"They fell apart when we rolled them up, so I had John put them in the trash."

My grandmother looked at me. White hair. White turtle-neck. White pants and socks. Strong, blue eyes that had seen angels walking on Ohio farms and sent demons fleeing into the pines of Georgia.

A righteous Southern voice that spoke the word of The Lord.

"Goddamn you, John,"
my grandmother said.

The Gadarenes

And they came over unto the other side of the sea, into the country of the Gadarenes.

And when he was come out of the ship, immediately there met him out of the city a certain man, which had devils long time, and ware no clothes, neither abode in any house, who had his dwelling among the tombs; and no man could bind him, no, not with chains.

And always, night and day, he was in the mountains, and in the tombs, crying, and cutting himself with stones.

But when he saw Jesus afar off, he ran and worshipped him,

And fell down before him and cried out with a loud voice, and said, "What have I to do with thee, Jesus, thou Son of the most-high God?"

"I adjure thee by God, that thou torment me not."
—from the Gospels of Matthew, Mark, and Luke

Paulina was a transsexual hooker up on 101st Street who was addicted to ketamine and cigarettes. She had a fetish for fishnets and drank Tortilla Gold by the bottle. Up until now, the only people who knew this story were Paulina and me. I planned to take it to my grave, but the wild bitch up and died this winter and nobody gave a shit except for me and a handful of dudes she was fucking, so I decided to write this because I feel like I owe it to her. And so, to pay a debt to a dead whore, this story is dedicated to Paulina.

* * *

I first moved to New York City and started a new job in a desperate bid for survival.

Right away I started having nightmares about Gandalf.

You know that scene from the beginning of *The Two Towers* where he's fighting the Balrog and they both fall into this huge underground cave and then when he finally kills the demon he collapses and says, "I threw down my foe upon the mountainside?"

That's what he looked like.

Gandalf, I mean.

In the dreams.

All cut up and out of breath.

Singed and panicked.

He would come bursting into my dreams out of nowhere. Crashing through walls, erupting from the ground, or falling out of the sky. Sometimes I'd dream that I was falling with him and the Balrog, and they were both yelling and trying to grab me. I can't explain why, but I knew he was trying to warn me about something. I had this deep sensation in my spirit that I was in mortal danger. I never found out what the wizard wanted to tell me, though, because he always came at me in this terrifying rush—yelling like hell, swinging his staff with one hand and his sword with the other—and it always scared me so badly that I'd wake up. I've had many recurring nightmares, but this one kept coming back more and more frequently, getting stronger each time, until I was tormented to the edge of madness.

Sleepless terror.

The job itself was high pressure and low intensity. Silent cubicle. Twelve-hour days. Outlook, Excel, PowerPoint, shared drives, you know the deal. Standard-issue, overpaid dehumanizing office job. I'd been working and living in midtown for about two months when all of this happened. It was December. My first Christmas in New York City. For most people, Christmas in New York is a magical wonderland, but I felt something distinctly evil about the whole thing.

Like I'd been marked for death.

Like wearing a bull's eye in a warzone.

Like Hell was following me home at night.

My office was high inside a million-ton monolith of black steel located at 666 Fifth Avenue on Fifty-second Street. The interior looked like something out of *American Psycho*. Polished white-marble floors. Sleek silver elevators. Dry-cleaned toilet paper. Ivy League frat boys. Cold-cash women. Free catered lunches. The desk chairs cost more than my rent. I used to walk around the office like a child at the circus and just look at everything. Trump stickers. Baseball bats. Pin-up girls. Golf clubs. Hermes neckties. Leather. Granite. Silk. Gold and glass. I've never seen people who worshipped Money like that. They all looked like they went home and fucked their bankrolls every night.

One of the most damnably confounding places in the whole Godless world is the stretch of Fifth Avenue that runs between Forty-ninth and Fifty-first streets in Manhattan. The biggest store on the block is Saks Fifth Avenue. Before Christmas, even before Thanksgiving, the storefront of Saks Fifth Avenue turns into this mesmerizing music-and-light show of holiday debauchery. Ten stories of multicolored lights set to music like "The Ukrainian Bell Carol" and "Somewhere in My Memory" from *Home Alone 2.* The streets are lousy with people who stop and stare at the pretty lights, and the music echoes for several blocks in all directions. When you're up close, it seems festive, but from a distance, it takes on an eerie, foreboding quality. They've also elevated window shopping to a gaudy art form. Each window, all around the block, is stuffed with animatronic holiday scenes that advertise their merchandise and make you feel like you're in an amusement park instead of being subconsciously manipulated into credit-card debt. It's so crowded that you have to stand in line behind red-velvet ropes just to get inside, and the inside is even worse. The whole building is crammed with people tripping over each other trying to buy something that will bring meaning to their lives, and they sell just about any Goddamn thing you could want. Brand-name and tailor-made. Children's clothes and women's lingerie are on the same floor. The shoe department is so big it has its own zip code registered with the USPS. I saw a pair of gloves with a price tag that said $650.

For *gloves*.

Across the street from this temple of materialism is Rockefeller Center, the palace of the Messiah of American Capitalism himself, complete with a pornographer's idea of a Christmas tree and graven images of pagan gods. Chief among these idols is that of Atlas, the Titan who led a war against the gods, and when he lost was made to carry the world on his shoulders as punishment. The Titan's eyes are fixed in a stare looking directly across the street at Saint Patrick's Cathedral, which is one of the most elegant buildings in North America. It has heavenly spires, ornate stained glass, and many tons of polished, white marble. It's one of those landmarks that's so distinctive that you recognize it even if you don't know what it is. I think Saint Patty's stands out so much because it doesn't fucking belong there. If you visit New York and walk the streets, you'll understand what I mean. Regardless of what direction you approach it from, it sticks out. It's surrounded by towers full of financiers, huge advertisements with naked bodies selling luxury brands, and steam pouring out of manhole covers into lurid streetlights. Art deco and corner delis. And there, stretching toward Heaven, like a fallen angel grasping at the throne of God, is Saint Patrick's giant, white cathedral. Squatting stubbornly on an entire city block across from one of the holiest shrines to Greed ever built, constantly under the hateful gaze of the world-bearing Titan who wants nothing more than to kill

God. Like Jesus descending into Hell, or the white tree in
the city of Gondor, that cathedral doesn't belong there. And
right next to this conglomerate of spiritual paradoxes was
666 Fifth Avenue.

My office.

With me.

My freshly broken heart.

And a head full Goddamn Gandalf dreams.

I don't usually write this much exposition, but in this case,
I felt it was necessary because I wanted to be able to tell
you this next part without it sounding irredeemably insane.
Which on the face of it, I admit, it does. But now that I've
provided some context, hopefully you won't be shocked when
I tell you that demons had been sent to kill me. Which has
happened before on two occasions. Once as a boy, and again
in college, and although those were bad experiences, they
weren't too terrible. Except for the night in college when I
painted my copy of *Taxi Driver* with a rainbow of blood, I
was never in any serious danger.

But this was different.

This time I had fucked up good and proper. I had come
out from behind my hedge of protection and onto Satan's turf
uninvited, and without God's direction. The Old Serpent had
been trying to get at me for years, but I slipped up this time.
I'd lowered the guard around my heart. He'd cut me deep and
torn my mind. I wanted revenge so badly I'd rushed out after
the bastard like Custer at Little Bighorn. And now, just like
Custer when he saw the Lakota horde riding toward him, I

had the distinct and palpable sensation that I was about to get fucked.

And I knew it.

And Satan knew it.

And God knew it.

And Gandalf knew it.

And I will tell you in plain English that I didn't give a good Goddamn about the whole wicked business. I wanted blood and I didn't care whose it was. I'd had enough. It was time for a reckoning. So, instead of sleeping, I spent long hours praying in the spirit and standing on scripture. Preparing to do combat with demons on the streets of Manhattan. It was a suicide mission, and I was itching to burn.

* * *

Jerry Lee Lewis is one of the baddest motherfuckers of all time. Before Jerry Lee became the scalding hot cum exploding out of the hard cock of rock n' roll, he was a Pentecostal evangelist. But he couldn't hang either, so instead he famously burned his piano on stage while playing "Great Balls of Fire" and started a riot that turned Boston inside out. Even crashed his car into the gates of Graceland once.

They call him The Killer.

Once Johnny Cash and Jerry Lee were on an all-night drive to a gig together, and Jerry Lee said, "You know John, God's going to send us to Hell for playin' this music." To which Cash replied, "Maybe you're right Killer. Maybe you're right."

I always liked that story because instead of stopping the

car, they kept right on driving. Anyway, The Killer booked a show at B. B. King's club in Times Square, and I bought one ticket to go see the mean old man do a whole lotta shakin'. The show was set for a week before Christmas. Two days before the concert the woman I loved, who hadn't spoken to me in almost a year, reached out.

And K— and I had a painful conversation.

About how I no longer had any place in her life.

And never would.

About how I wanted what was best for her.

Even though I didn't fit into that picture.

She said she didn't like that, and I said I didn't either.

But it was better for her, and that was good enough for me.

She said she was sorry.

I said I was sorry too.

Neither of us felt any better about it.

And I swear to Almighty God, I wanted to fucking die.

I sat up all night in my living room looking out over New York City.

Praying loving-kindness on her and her new boyfriend.

Beseeching God for her safekeeping.

But she wasn't the one in danger.

The sun came, and I went to work.

Another day on the altar of Mammon.

The night before the concert, I spent hours walking through the city.

I took off my tie and climbed down a subway platform somewhere on the Upper West Side. My feet followed the tracks out into the tunnels.

Still praying.
Drenched with winter sweat.
Like Jesus at Gethsemane.
Asking God to get me out of this.
But it was no use.
The Balrog was coming.
And Gandalf was late.
I sat down.
And watched the trains go roaring by.
Singing Hank Williams songs
to the other rats.

* * *

I walked home past Rockefeller and Saint Patrick's in the wee indigo hours. The throngs of smart shoppers and savvy tourists were nestled in for a long winter's nap, and I was standing out in the middle of Fifth Avenue with all the other contradictions.

Just me and the Titan.

In a staring contest.

I made it home and took off my suit. I sat in the shower and let the hot water run over me until it turned cold. Then I shut it off and just laid there for a while. By the time I got out of the shower, it was six o'clock in the morning and time to go back to work.

It was a long day.

At seven o'clock that evening I left the office and went straight to the concert wearing a tailored, black suit and a vintage, black, skinny tie. That's how it started. It was a week before Christmas in New York City, and I'd been up for two days fasting and praying when I walked into B. B. King's, and the hostess took me to a table up front, and I saw a very sexy girl dancing by The Killer's piano with a huge red tattoo of an upside-down cross on the back of her neck, and I knew immediately that my seat would be next to hers.

It was Little Bighorn, and the demons had our table ready. It'd been a long Goddamn time since the last one. They weren't going to pull any punches. This wasn't your ordinary spiritual attack. This wasn't just tough times and temptation and the usual pitch about eating forbidden fruit. We were way past that Mickey Mouse bullshit. This was a murder raid. Pure and simple. And that was fine by me. There wasn't going to be any divine intervention, and my guardian angel wasn't going to rush in and stop the charging rottweiler. I'd come down this road all alone. I'd seen the warning signs and kept right on driving. Spiritually, I was ready for death. The time for prayer and fasting was over. The opening act was about to come on. I sat down at the table and, without opening the menu, told the waitress, "I want the biggest steak you have and I want it rare."

I'd just handed the menu back to the waitress when a man approached my table and spoke to me like he was expecting to see me.

"You're never gonna believe this, but I just met the drummer from Foghat in the bathroom. Oh, you're probably too young for Foghat aren't you? You know who Foghat is?" the man said as he sat down on the chair next to mine.

I nodded. "Yeah, 'Slow Ride,' 'Fool for The City,' sure."

He lit up. "That's right! Well I guess if you're at this show you're not too young to know anybody, right? But yeah, anyway, their drummer's in the bathroom. You hurry you can still catch him." He pointed toward the bathrooms.

"I'm alright, thanks." Maybe I was wrong. Maybe the girl with the neck tattoo wasn't going to be sitting with me.

"That drummer must be here to see Jerry Lee too. I knew there'd be a lot of guys here to see him. That's Jerry's family at the table behind us. Lots of other VIPs around here too, but I can't make out their faces. Everybody's so old now, and they all look different in person, you know what I mean? But man, everybody wants to see Jerry Lee when he comes to town."

"Yeah."

"I'm Jeffrey."

"John."

We shook.

Jeffrey was a bald white guy in his late sixties with an effeminate slant and short grey hair around his dome. He was wearing a black jacket, black shirt, black pants, black shoes, and thin-framed glasses. He had on a gold pinky ring, and was wearing too much cologne. "Nice to meet you, kid. We're in for one hell of a show tonight. The Killer always does a great show. You seen him before?"

"No."

"Ah, well then you're *really* in for something. Yeah, I guess I must have seen The Killer a couple dozen times by now. Course, I been around a while. Used to work in a studio when I was a kid. Been hooked on rock n' roll ever since. I was a law professor for a few decades, but now I'm retired and I live upstate. Just came into the city to catch the show. Nice bein' retired, you know. Come and go as I please. See all the best shows. Not a bad setup. You here by yourself too?"

I nodded.

"Ah well, this must be where they put all the single people then. I'm by myself too, and so is she." He pointed at the dancing neck tattoo. "I only met her briefly. She went up front to dance almost as soon as she came in. Said she wanted to touch his piano. One of those super-fan types, I guess. Little strange if you ask me, since there's no band up there yet. Seems like a nice girl though, if you don't mind all that shit in her face. 'Bout your age too," he said as he nudged my shoulder suggestively and raised his hand for the waitress. "I'm gonna get another drink, you want another drink?"

"No thanks, I don't drink," I said.

"You don't drink? What're ya sick or something?" He laughed. I didn't answer.

"Well just sit tight, kid, you'll be alright soon as The Killer comes out here."

The waitress came over and he ordered his drink, and I watched the tattoo walking back to the table. She smiled at me as she reached her seat. Jeffrey introduced us. "Danny Joe, seems we got ourselves a newcomer here. This handsome young man is John. John, Danny Joe."

I half-stood as I shook her hand. She had tattoos everywhere. It was dark, and I didn't want to stare, so I don't remember too many of them in detail, but there was a clear theme. The small upside-down cross between her eyes matched the one on the back of her neck. On her forehead, above the cross, in very fine print, was tattooed in black ink, "mystery." She did have "a lot of shit in her face," as Jeffrey put it. There was a ring in her nose, a stud in her tongue, a few in her eyebrows, and a medley of bars, studs, and rings in each ear. But the thing that struck me the most was her eyes. Her smile slowed time as she said my name and looked into me with those two vessels and their piercing glow. Strange fire beneath a veil of golden citrus.

The opening act came on, and the food came out. I listened and ate. Jeffery talked constantly. Danny Joe kept her surreal eyes on me. She wasn't staring—she was looking. Her seat was across the table from me, Jeffrey was to my right, and the band was to her left. Whenever she turned back to the table, her gaze would pass over me, and I would feel like I was standing too close to a heat lamp. She wore eyeliner, so maybe the make-up heightened the effect, but she had impossibly wide eyes with these insane, iridescent pupils. A moment ago, I could have sworn they were amber or ochre, but when I caught them from a different angle, they were almost emerald green, always with the same hypnotic flame. They looked to me like dragon's eyes. Focused and penetrating. She didn't glance around the room frantically looking at everything. When she wanted to look at something, she really looked at it. There was deliberate intent in it. Every time her eyes fell on me, I felt like I was being studied. Like she wasn't looking at my clothes or my face, but at what was behind them.

Ordinarily, I would have found this kind of ocular inspection disturbing, but everything about this woman was far from ordinary. To start with, she was sexy as hell. Which, as is commonly known, gives a person license to get away with things that other people simply cannot. She was light-skinned and wearing a bright shade of lipstick that was somewhere between red and orange. It set off her eyes and skin like fireworks. The result was radiant. No matter where I looked, I was always hungry for the rest of her. Consequently, whenever she was looking at the band, I was looking at her.

She was wearing a white blouse with a single, red rose over her breast and another larger one in the middle of her back and one of those post-war dancing skirts that came down to about the knee but didn't lift up too far when she spun her hips, which she did a lot. She had heels but danced barefoot. Her necklace was a black choker and her nail polish matched her lipstick. She listened politely to Jeffery's ramblings and gave off an air of modesty and poise all through dinner, even though she kept looking at me like she wanted dessert.

After the opening act, Jeffrey went to the bathroom again, leaving us alone at the table. I came out of the holster fast and shot from the hip. "Are you a big Jerry Lee Lewis fan?"

She smiled like she was embarrassed. "Oh yes, I love him. He's the greatest of all time."

"You think so?"

"Yeah, for sure. I mean I like Elvis a lot too, but Jerry Lee is just so wild. He brings such a unique energy to rock n' roll."

"How do you mean?" I could tell that she took this very seriously.

"Well I don't know exactly, but he always creates this

intensity and urgency about his music. He plays the piano like it's a crisis, and he sings like the cops are on their way."

"They usually are when he's around," I said. She laughed. I kept talking. "I can't believe I was able to get tickets to see him."

"I know. I've been watching for them for so long. He was going to come last year, and I had tickets for that, but they cancelled the show. I didn't think I was going to get to see him again."

"Oh wow." She really was a big fan of his. "Yeah, I just saw something online and bought them on a whim. You must really like his music."

"I'm obsessed," she said like she meant it.

"I saw you dancing when I came in. You're really good,"

"Aww, thank you. Yeah, I teach dance, I love it."

"What kind of dance?"

"Well I teach everything from ballroom to salsa, but my favorites are the mid-twentieth century pop steps. They're just so much fun, and I get to dance to my favorite music too, so it's perfect. I get totally lost in it. Like I'm in another world or something. I've been dancing since I was a little girl. It'll always be my first love."

"That's awesome. So, is that what you do? You're a dance instructor?"

"Mhm. Instructor, performer, and other things, you know how it is. This and that. The artist life."

"Yeah, I imagine it's quite a hustle."

"It is, but I love what I do, and it's a tight-knit commu-nity. You know, I'm part of a dance club for people who love this kind of music. You should come, we'd love to have you. Always need more handsome guys at dances," she said, leaving her eyes on mine.

I laughed it off. "I'd be happy to come, but I don't know how much good I'd be on the dance floor. I'm just here for the music."

"I can help you with that, and besides—" she leaned forward and lowered her voice to a sultry register, "—if you love *this* kind of music, you're already halfway there."

Her green fires flared up and the voltage surge charged the silence. Her face changed, and she suddenly said in a quick, flat hush, "I'm going to take your virginity tonight."

"What?"

An omnipresent voice blasted through the loudspeakers to begin Jerry Lee's introduction as Jeffrey came rushing back from the bathroom to take his seat. Danny Joe jumped up and grabbed my hand, and I followed her without hesitation.

Maybe that kind of a statement from a woman I had just met should have elicited a stronger response—but like I said, I had come for war. There was also something very attractive about a woman having the audacity to say that to me. It wasn't as though I looked like a virgin either. I mean I'm a mid-twenties, white-collar New Yorker—I look like I fuck—but she said it anyway. There was no question now that I was in danger. Something was up. I glanced back at the table and saw Jeffrey raise his glass at me. He winked.

Finally, The Killer came on stage, and hot damn what a show. Jerry Lee played a great set while Danny Joe and I danced. I watched her skirt twirl as she spun away from me and back again. She liked to slam her body into mine, and every now and then she'd reach down and squeeze my ass. I let her.

I had no idea what I was doing, so I just hung on tight and tried not to step on her feet. This also gave me a chance to get a closer look at her tattoos. The upside-down burning red cross on the back of her neck had an Enochian pentagram behind it. I don't read too many Enochian runes, but I know enough to get by. Her pentagram said "Leviathan." She had a large piece of excellent work on her left arm that must have cost her thousands. It showed the back of a naked woman kneeling with her torso and head turned around, so she was almost facing backwards. Her head was tilted up in pleasure and there was a tattoo on her ass that said 'Danny Joe.' Two huge snakes—one green, one red—were coiled around her legs, arms, breasts, and neck—and were penetrating her in both holes and sticking their tongues down her ears.

It was quite a little self-portrait.

When The Killer was finished, we went back to our seats and Jeffrey offered to split a dessert. The three of us shared a big slice of chocolate cake, and she made eye contact with me as she moved her tongue around the fork after each bite, savoring it longer than she had to. Jeffrey said good night and left Danny Joe and I to walk out together.

"So where are we heading now?" I asked as I helped her put on her coat.

She was pleased with the presumptuous question. "I know a little place on the Upper West Side if you don't mind a cab ride."

I pulled my own coat over my shoulders. "Sounds good to me."

She smiled as she wheeled around, and I followed her up the stairs. She rushed out onto the sidewalk and grabbed a cab. I opened the back door while she leaned in the front and said something to the driver. We climbed in and rolled off through the wet winter lights of Times Square.

"Where are we going?" I asked again.

Her nose crinkled in playful refusal. "You'll see."

I looked out at the neon streaks and passing shadows. We sat in silence for a moment, but this time it wasn't uncomfortable. She was sitting close and leaning on me. My mind wandered back to the concert.

"Mercy," I whispered.

"Mm?" she asked.

"Why do you think he always says 'Oh, Mercy'?"

"Who?"

"Jerry Lee Lewis—after every song he wipes his forehead and says, 'Oh, Mercy,' or something like that."

She shrugged. "I don't know. I think it's just something to say while he catches his breath."

"Yeah, I know, but what does it mean? Who's he asking for mercy?"

"What do you mean—who?"

"Well if he's up there every night asking for mercy, he must be asking somebody, right?"

"I don't know, I never thought about it before."

"Me neither, but it's an interesting question, isn't it?"

"Why?"

"I don't know. I just find it interesting." I didn't think it needed to be explained.

"Does it matter?"

"It matters to me," I said.

"Why? What difference does it make who he's talking to?"

"Well, it seems pretty obvious doesn't it?"

"What do you mean?" She squinted at me.

"He must be asking God for mercy," I said.

"What?" The statement offended her.

"Think about it—who else would it be? He must be asking God for mercy."

"Oh, please." She pushed me, half-serious.

"What? That doesn't make sense to you?"

"Jerry Lee Lewis?"

"Yeah, why not?"

She took my arm and pulled herself in close. "You think Jerry Lee gets up on stage every night to play rock n' roll so he can ask God for mercy?"

"I don't know. Maybe."

"You think after a lifetime of sex, drugs, and rock n' roll, Jerry Lee Lewis is still gonna be asking God for mercy?"

"Who else would he be talking to?"

"I can think of someone he'd be better off asking for mercy than God."

"Like who?"

Danny Joe gave me a look. She didn't say it, but she didn't have to.

Dragon eyes.

I turned away and watched Eighth Avenue go past the

window. A snowfall in New York City is more rapturous than almost anywhere else in the world. It's an outpouring of sacred beauty that comes dancing out of the heavens and seems to cover the city in a kind of grace. I've always loved seeing snow in New York, but after it falls it changes from a pristine marvel into a wretched, filthy, mess. The city corrupts each individual divine gift into a single, odious ruin—leaving the streets clogged for months with gray, icy slop.

"How long have you been practicing wicca?" I asked still looking at New York.

"Since I was six," she answered without hesitation.

"Gardnerian? Alexandrian? Gregorian? What?"

"I've studied all of them. I like Gardener the best of those. I'm pretty old-school."

"Santeria?"

"Mhm. From my Dad's side."

"I bet you have a tattoo of Diana, don't you?"

She looked impressed and opened her blouse a bit to reveal an image of Diana over her heart.

"Did I miss anything?"

"Yes," she said proudly, "I studied under a druidic priest for a summer in the desert mountains out west."

"Kinky."

"Mm."

"So, what do I call you? Do you have a title, or what?"

"I have a few."

"What I mean is are you, like, a priestess or, like, a—"

"A witch?" she said.

I looked into the dragon's eyes. She smiled. "Yes, I am a

witch. I actually prefer that term. Like I said, I'm old fash-ioned—keep things simple."

"I see. Sorry to be blunt, I just thought it was time we got started. Might as well get this over with, you know what I mean? It's getting kind of late," I said.

"Are you in a hurry?"

"I just don't see any point beating around the bush. We both know the score here."

She was a bit surprised, but she nodded her agreement. "I'm all in favor of that approach."

"Good. Then maybe we can come to an understanding about all of this."

"Oh, I think we understand each other just fine," she said.

"I doubt that." Nobody ever understands.

"What's stopping you?"

"Stopping me from what?"

"Becoming a warlock." She put her hand on my leg.

I looked down. "That's not for me."

"The hell it isn't. Don't bullshit me, John. Like you said, we both know what's going on here, so don't start lying to me now."

"I don't know what you're talking about."

"Yes, you fuckin' do. Your aura fills half the Goddamn block. You lit up that place like the fucking sun when you walked in the room tonight."

I twisted a pinky around my thumb. "I know," I said.

"So, then when are you gonna wake the fuck up and just accept your own power?"

"There is no power outside of Christ."

"Oh, fuck off, you don't believe that."

"It doesn't matter what I believe, it's the way it is."

"It doesn't have to be the way it is."

"Yes, it does."

"Oh, God. There it is. There's that old-time fuckin' Christian spiritual-brainwashing. Always kicks in when you need it most. You think you're talking to an intelligent person, pull back a few layers, and you run smack into Leviticus. God forbid you have an original thought, right?"

"Oh, that's really rich coming a Luciferian. When was the last time he had an original idea? I will ascend? I will exalt my throne above the stars of God? I will be like the Most High? That what you call original thinking? How's that been workin' out for you?"

"A lot better than living in hypocritical self-deception like you. Pretending you're some kind of holy man—some beacon of righteousness."

I laughed. "Don't worry, I haven't any such notion."

"What about K—? What about her?"

Her dagger sank into my broken armor. "Watch your fuckin' mouth."

"Ooo, touchy boy. Did you think the familiars wouldn't tell me about her? You think she's off limits?"

My hands were clamped.

"You were in love with her, John. And she was in love with you. I don't care what you say, I'm telling you that's Holy. And you wouldn't commit yourself to her. Why? Because of what? A few words written thousands of years ago by men who knew less about God than you know about them? You cling to your rules and say fornication is a sin, but you and I know damn well that she's the only thing in this universe that's ever offered you peace."

"That's a fucking lie."

"No, it's not, John. It's the truth, and you know it. That's why it hurts so much."

I bit my lip. "It wouldn't—it wouldn't have lasted. It wouldn't work. She was—"

"It doesn't matter, it was sin. Turning your back on her was a sin."

"I—" My lungs pulled, but no air came in. "—I did the best I could."

"You sinned, John. Badly. And not against God either—fuck God—you sinned against her, and you know it, and it's killing you because you rejected your destiny." Sweat formed on my brow. "That's why you quit your job and moved to New York. It's also why you bought a ticket to this show, and it's why you're sitting in this car with me right now. Because you resent God for keeping you away from her, and you hate yourself for hurting her, don't you?"

My toes clenched inside my shoes. New York rushed past the window. She touched my arm like a nurse with a patient. "It's alright. You don't have to hurt anymore. It's going to be alright from now on. I'm here to give you the peace and freedom you've never known."

I was shaking. "I tried so hard."

She squeezed my hand. "I know you did. It's okay. You don't have to carry that weight anymore." The hug was the only thing that staved off the panic attack. I wondered if either of us would survive the night. I prayed—not for any-thing specific—just a plea for mercy.

We got out of the cab and she led me into a dive. It was dark, and she walked fast toward the back. She turned a couple corners and went through a few doors until we were climbing a tall narrow staircase. The only light in the corridor came from a red neon sign hanging above the stairs that read Belial's Boudoir.

I reached the top and stepped through the door into an upper room. There was a long, black, leather couch against one wall that served as an oxygen bar. There were two tanks with masks on either end of the couch. Across from the couch was a short bar with a TV hanging from the ceiling. There was a small coffee table between the oxygen-bar couch and the bar, and two large windows in the back wall. On the ground beneath these windows, and next to the far end of the couch, was a small radiator. On the wall opposite this win-dowed wall there was the door we had entered by, and to the right of the entrance were two more black doors. The ceiling and the walls were all painted black.

Danny Joe took two steps forward into the center of the room and spun around to face me. I surveyed the empty room, and then my eyes rested on hers.

"Well?" she said.

"Well what?"

She put her hands on her hips. I closed the gap between us and stood close to her. She didn't flinch or look away.

"You don't ask a lot of questions, do you?" she whispered.

"I do when I need to."

"You don't have any questions for me at all?"

I thought for a moment then asked, "What's your favorite movie?"

"I'm serious."

"So am I."

"You're not the least bit curious who I am, or why I came to find you?"

"I know who you are."

"You know who I'm with, but you don't know why, and you certainly don't know who I am."

"Would it make any difference?"

She searched my face, then shook her head. "You really don't care, do you?"

I shrugged. "I know enough."

"And you're not afraid?"

I didn't blink.

She shook her head. "You aren't like other men."

"That's a little clichéd isn't it?"

"Maybe so, but I've been with a lot of initiates, and I've never seen one like you. You're not interested in anything that makes sense. You're so—what is it you're after, John? Why did you come here?"

I felt her warm breath on my lips.

"It is not good that man should be alone," I whispered.

The radiator clinked on, and we listened to the throbbing bassline of the bar noise below. Her fingers closed around mine. I took her in my arms and kissed her hard. Our clothes came off fast. I was down to my black boxer briefs when she pushed me onto the couch, and I jumped back to my feet, half expecting her to attack me. Instead she kicked off her skirt and said, "Make yourself comfortable, baby. I'll be right back."

She disappeared behind one of the black doors, and I collapsed onto the couch.

By this time, it was soon after midnight and I was deeply exhausted in every conceivable sense. My body was screaming at me to rest. The couch was deep and soft. I rolled my head to look out the windows again. My eyes dropped and I saw the oxygen mask. I'd never been to an oxygen bar before, but I felt like in my condition it would be a great help. I reached over with sluggish hands and lifted the mask to my nostrils. Nothing. My fingers found the tank and somehow had enough strength to turn the valve. The satisfying squeak of decompressing gas told me the passage was open. I took a deep breath and didn't even notice when the other black door opened. The sound of footsteps on hardwood moved across the room toward the other end of the couch. The leather stretched to announce another occupant had joined me in my repose. I sank deeper. It took me a while to find him with my eyes, but my ears told me right away who it was. I also recognized his cologne. Thinking back on it now, he definitely acted like he was on some kind of upper. Coke, or meth, or molly, or something—but at the time that didn't register with me. All I remember thinking was that Jeffrey talked too much.

"You know they say that the Internet is going to make the university system obsolete in a few years. They say that about almost everything these days. Information age. Artificial intelligence. Robotics. Elon Musk and his terraforming drones. It's a brave new world alright. One thing they can't counterfeit, though, is people. Oh, sure—they imitate us—little things like memory and motor skills, but no matter how far they take it there's always going to be something they can't recreate. That's the big joke waiting at the end of all technology. There's more to a man than the sum of his parts."

The ceiling was infinite. The leather felt good.

"It's like how a university is more than books, and classrooms, and final exams. It's an organism too, and it's made up of people trying to learn. Oh yes, they study certain subjects, sure, but they're really learning about themselves. What they like and don't like. Needs and passions. Exploring new feelings, new freedoms. Uninhibited. Boldly pursuing their truth wherever it leads them, liberated from petty taboos. That's why I stayed in academia. That community. The free pursuit of the truth of oneself."

I didn't want to hear any more of this, so I interrupted. "Look Jeff, I don't want to be rude—"

"No!" He sat up shouting and pointed at me. "Don't you dare call me that. You will not take me back to my family. It's Jeffery—you got it? My name is Jeffery."

I didn't answer, I just looked at him. I realized that he was the end result of a little gay kid with overbearing Christian parents searching for his place in a hostile world. Jeffrey made a lot more sense. He sipped a drink and kept talking.

"I've been studying craft since I was your age. At first it was just a gag, you know, the curiosity of it all, but then once I discovered the deeper power, I was hooked. I studied under one of Crowley's apostles when I was a visiting professor at

Oxford. That was a long time ago. Now that I'm older, I prefer to help others in their search. Danny Joe has been in my coven for years. She came to me young, but she's one of the most powerful witches I've ever known."

The windows were huge, but I couldn't see any stars.

"I've been teaching initiates so long I got to where I could tell about a person right away. Like you, for example. You're strong. Any novice could see it in you."

My wrists hurt. I couldn't tell if I was still wearing my underwear or not. Jeffery kept talking.

"I don't know who you are, but you've got the anointing. And it's time for you to carry a different kind of anointing now."

What the fuck was he saying to me? Was I on the floor? How did I get on the floor?

"No one forced you to come here. You came because you know your rightful place as well as I do. You belong with us. Soon you'll be one of the most powerful warlocks in the world, and then you can have anything you want. We'll begin with a few initiation ceremonies tonight—nothing too complicated—just need to sever all those chains on your soul and align you with the true God of this World."

What did he just say? I tried to stand up, but something was holding me to the floor.

"Whoa, whoa, now. Take it easy Johnny boy, don't start struggling now. You'll just hurt yourself. Relax and let the nitrous take effect."

Nitrous?

"Nitrous?!" I repeated out loud. My voice sounded funny.

He laughed. "That's right, nitrous. One of our coven's a

dental hygienist. What'd you think it was? Oxygen? This one's oxygen." He knocked his pinky ring against the steel tank on his end of the couch. "But you chose the nitrous all by yourself, didn't you?"

I stared at him. His smile revealed yellow teeth. "You made all your choices a long time ago, we all did. Ever since Eden there's only ever been one answer—one truth."

He put on the oxygen mask and took deep drags as he quoted scripture. "And ye shall become ... like Gods ... knowing good ... and evil."

His cock was out, and he was stroking himself. I don't know how I didn't notice that before. I realized I was laughing. My body was sweaty and red, flexing hard under the tension of full-body laughter spasms. I brushed off the mask with my arm and felt tears all over my face. My laughter drowned out the ringing in my ears. He was laughing too. He stood up and walked toward me with his hard cock sticking out in front of him. Still wearing his mask. I flipped over and saw that my hands were cuffed to the radiator. I don't know how that happened. He must have done it while he was talking. Now he was coming toward me as I lay naked on the floor. I had the distinct and palpable sensation that I was about to get fucked.

Reality tore through the dense fog surrounding my brain and something happened to me that had never happened before. I don't know how to describe it other than to say I experienced a psychotic breakdown. There were a lot of factors involved. The nitrous. The sleep deprivation. The concert. Making out with a sexy witch. The fear that I was about to be raped by a seventy-year-old satanic priest. The heartbreak over the girl I'd lost. The fact that I had read the Bible over a dozen times in my life. All the Johnny Cash music and Martin Scorsese movies I'd absorbed. All of it. In that moment, lying on the floor handcuffed to a radiator, in a state of extreme exhaustion and what I'd assume to be legal insanity, something cracked. Everyone has a point like that, I guess. The bedrock at the bottom of the self. Whatever is left working when the system is only running on emergency power. If you drill down far enough with anybody, eventually you'll hit it. I guess there's as many different versions of this as there are people in the world, but this was mine. It all came bursting out of me in a blast of shuddering insanity.

I put my feet against the wall and pulled like I was trying to tear my hands off. The cuffs dug in. Sharp pain. No use. Jeffery positioned himself behind me. Blurry shapes were all I could find through the tears. Still laughing. I pulled harder. The blood started. His fingers traced the notches of my spine running their way down my back. I spoke without thinking.

"Bless God, my strength!" I was laughing so hard I thought I was going to break a rib. "He teacheth my hands to war, so that a bow of steel is broken by mine arms!"

A horrific scream of scalding steam filled the room as I tore the whole radiator off the wall and the rotten plaster crumbled.

Jeffery shrieked, "Jesus Christ," and backed off.

I filled my lungs with the boiling air and felt the fire in my chest and belly—Hell on the inside as well as the out. "Thou hast given me the shield of thy salvation and thy gentleness hath made me great!"

I made it to my feet.

"Wait, stop John, wait—please stop!"

The radiator clunked and scraped the floor as I advanced on him. He stumbled and fell as he backed away. The words kept coming out of me. "Thou hast enlarged my steps under me, that my feet did not slip!" I pulled myself up, and with blind rage swung the radiator through the air.

He cowered, and the blow struck his back. "John, please, stop, wait!"

"I am returned unto Jerusalem with mercies and the Lord shall yet comfort Zion!"

Steel splintered wood.

"Will you wait a minute, please!?"

"Whoa be unto Ariel, to Ariel, the city where David dwelt!"

"I'll take off the cuffs, I promise. Please, stop!"

I hit him again. "Where are the gods of Hamath and Arpad? Where are the gods of Sepharvaim?"

"Don't kill me!"

I swung harder. "Ye shall not surely die! Ye shall become like gods!"

"Help!"

Slam.

"Let no one deceive you with empty words, for because of these things the wrath of God comes upon the sons of disobedience." He lifted his arms to protect himself, but I aimed carefully this time.

"Bow thy heavens, O Lord, and come down."

Another blow, this one to the head.

"Cast forth lightning and destroy them."

Crunching steel.

"He also will drink the wine of God's wrath, poured full strength into the cup of his anger." He was scrambling and pleading—badly hurt. "Get thee hence into the herd of swine! Get thee behind me, Satan!"

The cheap handcuffs finally broke and the radiator dropped hard. There were ugly dents in the wood floor. Jeffrey was wounded and my wrists were bleeding. One way or another, there was a good amount of blood. I was crying and laughing. The adrenaline was pumping so hard I felt invincible. I took in a huge breath. "And you shall know my name is the Lord, when I lay my vengeance upon you!"

I grabbed the collar of his black T-shirt. With tears flowing from blood-red eyes and what was left of my cracked and scratched voice, I shouted into his face, "I AM THE THIRD REVELATION! I AM THE VOICE OF ONE CRYING IN THE WILDERNESS! I AM THE GATHERING DARKNESS!"

His reply was whimpering sobs.

I threw him down and took a long breath.

The black door opened.

Danny Joe came out wearing a skin-tight black latex body-suit, heels, and a giant black strap-on dildo. She was holding the leashes of a man and woman who were crawling behind her completely naked except for black-leather hoods covering their heads and collars connected to the leashes. There was dark red liquid on Danny Joe's mouth and chin, and she was holding a chalice. She looked at Jeffrey and the radiator.

"Goddamn you, John."

"Likewise, I'm sure."

"Why do have to make everything so hard?"

"Fuck you."

"You don't understand what we could—you'd be a god, John. Do you understand what I'm saying to you? I can make you a fucking god."

"Well, why didn't you say so? Let's go down to the throne of Lucifer and drink the blood of fallen angels together. I can't wait."

"Don't blaspheme!"

"Fuck you, you infernal cunt. Fuck your religion. Fuck your lies. Fuck Azazel. Fuck Lucifer and all the fallen angels. You want to know why I came here tonight? Because you all have been attacking me my whole life, and I wanted to look you in the eye and tell you and all the rest of 'em to fuck off. I may wrestle with God too much, but as far as I'm concerned, you can all go fuck yourselves."

"You sure about that?"

"Goddamn right."

"Well in that case, there's someone here I think you should talk to."

"*John?*" I froze. Mind and body. *Her* voice was coming from behind the black door. "*John? Is that you?*"

Danny Joe was smiling like the cat who caught the biggest mouse. "Answer her, John."

Her voice came again. "John, please stop this. It doesn't have to be this way."

"Please—please stop," I begged.

"You're the only one who can stop it, John," Danny Joe taunted.

"Please, John let's just be together. We'll both be so happy. I promise," she said.

"Maybe you should listen to her." Danny Joe took a step forward.

"That's not her," I said.

"Yes, it is."

"It's not *really* her."

"You're right, it's not. But it could be. And you know it."

"John, please. Don't you want us to be together?" she said with tender intimacy.

The anxiety blast was frying my circuits. "Please make her stop," I asked again.

Danny Joe led the leashes out of the doorway and into the room. "It would be so easy. It would be easiest thing you've ever done."

"*John?*" The tone of her voice saying my name like that will never leave my memory. My armor was melting. I pleaded with Danny Joe.

"Please don't do this. Please stop."

"You know I can't do that, John." Danny Joe turned and looked back at the black door. It creaked and turned on its hinges opening wider and wider.

One of the most precious moments of my life was a late summer night I spent in bed with her. The window was open, and the air was rich with the familiar smell of Virginia leaves. She held me in her loving arms and joyful eyes, and I felt so at peace with the universe—so full of love—that I could have died with perfect contentment then and there. It was the closest to home I have ever been. But that was years ago, and I never expected to see her again. The whole world disappeared as she stepped across the room and stood before me.

K— emerged from behind the black door wearing the exact same camisole top and black lace panties she had been wearing that night in her bed back home in Virginia. As soon as I saw her, the tremors started. I couldn't speak. My knees locked. My heartbeat spiked. I gasped for breath. Total nervous arrest. "It breaks my heart seeing you like this, John. You're so lonely. You've been calling out for me, so I came. You're so afraid of being alone, but you don't have to be alone anymore," K— said, coming to me.

She stretched out her hand and the tips of her fingers shot ten-thousand bolts of cold lightning through my chest as they touched my bare skin. Full-throttle panic. "You're just a man, John. And as much as you want to save everyone, you can't. You're not responsible for all of them, but you can still save yourself. You've been so tired for so long. Will you please rest? Will you come home with me? Please?"

I couldn't look at her. She leaned in and breathed an invitation into my ear.

"All you have to do is nod your head and we'll be in my bedroom together again."

Jesus Christ. I thought I was going to die. I wanted to. I would have been grateful.

"Please? I love you, John," the being who looked like K— said.

Upon hearing those words, I snapped back out of the ceiling and looked her right in the eyes. I'd recognize K—'s eyes if I were blind, and that's not what I saw looking back at me.

She wasn't there. It wasn't her. It was the serpent. Kundalini. Leviathan. The fucking Dragon. I gritted my teeth with rage and hate.

"Okay, K—. I'll come with you—I'll do anything you ask, but before we go, I just have one question."

She smiled sweetly. "What's that?"

"I've been wondering about something for a long time, and I was hoping you could help me with it."

"Of course, John. What would you like to know?"

This time it was my dagger that sank in. "Did Jesus Christ really come in the flesh?" I said like it was the most casual thing in the world.

"What?" Her smile was gone and her voice faltered.

"Well you were there, right? Or one of you was, so it stands to reason that you ought to know."

She said nothing. I pushed the dagger deeper. "I want to hear you say that Jesus Christ—the Son of the God of Abraham, Isaac, and Jacob—came in the flesh, was crucified, and then rose again on the third day after taking back the keys to Hell, death, and the grave." She was changing. "And I want to know what exactly you plan to say at the judgement. If you can tell me that, I'll come with you."

She snarled and hissed.

"Also, K— never said 'I love you, John.' You were there, so you ought to fucking know that too."

"Fuck you!" A different voice came out of her this time.

"In the name of Jesus Christ, by the power of the Holy Spirit of the Living God, I rebuke you. Leave me, get out of my sight."

The spirit hissed again and was gone. Danny Joe shrieked and threw the chalice at me through the yellow mist.

"Goddamn you, John!"

"He probably will, but do me a favor would you please? If we ever see each other in Hell, let's just pretend we never met before."

Jeffrey was standing beside her and the two masked slaves were crouched at the ready.

Leviathan squinted.

"Oh, fuck."

She let slip the dogs of Hell, and I snatched up my clothes and shot through the door. I bounded down the stairs, through the bar, and out onto the street. I had no idea where I was, but I didn't have time to find out. One of the masked slaves was hard on my heels, so I just ran—naked and clutching my wad of clothes. I have no idea where I was or how long I was running. It could have been two blocks, could have been twenty. The cold air started to burn my lungs and I ran toward the brightest lights I could find. I burst through the front door of a quaint little sex shop and went straight for the back.

"Hey—hey, you stop! You can't come in here like that, hey!"

I threw all my stuff down on the floor and started getting dressed as fast as I could. Out front, I heard the owner yelling.

"What the hell you think this is?"

Another voice from inside the store answered, "Honey, it's a goddamn fuck shop not a holy shrine. Calm down."

"Well he can't just come running in here naked like that. What if the police are looking for him?"

"They probably are, and if they come in here, you're gonna

let me do all the talking or I'm gonna tell all my girls not to shop here anymore." The voice threatened.

"You can't—he can't just—"

"He can if I say he can, and I say he's alright. You leave that boy alone."

My pants were on, but I had more to go. Shirts have too many buttons.

"You hear that back there, papi? You take all the time you need, okay? I gotchu baby—you gonna be alright, sugar."

I didn't know what to say, so I said, "Thank you."

"No problem, papi."

The electronic doorbell rang and I heard a voice ask, "Did he come in here?"

"Ooo, hey sexy man, you wanna go in the back with me for a minute?"

"Did a naked guy just come in here?"

"I'll treat you right, papi. Twenty roses, no rush, best head you've ever had in your life."

"What?!"

"They got little rooms in the back. Come on, baby. Lighten up, have some fun. It's just twenty bucks."

"I'm looking for my friend."

"Well, what he look like?"

"I told you he was naked."

"Papi, I promise you if a sexy naked man had come in here, I'd be on my knees suckin' his dick right now—believe that shit, baby."

"What about you? Did you see him?" the voice asked the owner.

"Yeah, what about you? Did you see him come in here?" the stranger repeated.

There was a moment of awkward grumbling from behind the counter.

"Well what about it?"

"No! No, I see nothing. No," the owner said.

"You're sure?"

"See, he just told you, papi—ain't no naked men in here, but there should be."

The electronic doorbell rang again.

"If you find your friend, come back and we can all have some fun together, papi!"

The door closed and I heard her say, "It's okay, baby. He's gone. You can come out now—it's alright."

I walked back out to the front, fully dressed except for one thing. I'd forgotten my shoes. The woman who owned the voice that stood up for me noticed before I did.

"What's the matter baby, you ain't bring no shoes?"

"No, I—uh—"

I realized I had no idea how to explain this. She saw in my face that I didn't know what to say, "Shh, shh, don't worry, papi—you don't gotta say nothing, okay? I told you I got-chu. Believe me—it's okay. You're okay now. You're safe now. Nobody gonna hurt you."

I collapsed into her arms. By this point I was a complete wreck. Adrenaline had been the only thing keeping me going. Hearing her comforting words and the kindness she had shown me meant more to me than I could explain. Sure enough, a cop showed up a few minutes later. Sometime after

this, she told me that she'd called him herself, but at the time
I didn't know that. I thought I was about to spend the night
in a holding cell. She sat me down in the entryway of the sex
shop and talked to the cop outside. The owner didn't speak
to me. He just stared at me with his arms crossed and a judg-
mental look on his face. He was a fat Middle Eastern guy
with stupid eyebrows and a seventies mustache.

Jesus Christ, I was so fucking tired.

She came back inside. "It's okay, papi, he gonna take you
home now, okay? Wherever you wanna go—you just tell him,
and he gonna take you back home."

I looked outside at the waiting cop and then back at her.

"Really?"

"Mhm. Yeah, it's no problem, okay? You're alright, papi.
You're gonna be okay."

I had lost the capacity for thought, so I stammered and
asked, "W-Why? How?"

"You think I never been with an asshole like that before?
They get your pants off and right away they start getting rough.
I don't blame you for getting the hell out of there, honey. I
lost count all the times I had to run outta someplace naked,
okay? Believe me, papi. You're lucky you only left your shoes."

She put her arm around me and pointed out the glass door.

"That's my friend out there, okay. That's Officer Ortiz. I
been suckin' his dick a few times a week since he was in high
school, so you can trust him. He's a good man, okay? He ain't
gonna hurt you or nothing. He just gonna take you home
wherever you need to go, okay, papi?"

I looked at her closely for the first time. She had a long

blonde wig and five o'clock shadow. Her aging face was caked with makeup and there was a little scar over her Adam's apple. It was freezing outside, but she was wearing fishnet stockings under a short sequin skirt, high heels, and taking swigs from a brown paper bag.

She also had a tramp stamp of the Virgin Mary.

"Thank you," I said. "Thank you so, so much."

She opened her purse and took out a stack of mismatched business cards with her name and number handwritten on the backs.

Paulina.

"You call me if you need anything, okay? Get home safe, alright?"

I staggered outside and got into the passenger side of the waiting cop car.

"Where ya live?" the officer asked. I just stared. "Hello?"

"Huh?"

"Where'd ya wanna go, man?" he asked again.

There was only one place in the world I wanted to be at that moment. My shredded voice was barely a whisper.

"Take me to 666 Fifth Avenue."

* * *

I got out of the car and he drove away. The asphalt was rough and wet on my bare feet. I sat on the white marble steps between the titan and the cathedral to rest and try to think. I threw up and watched it freeze.

The last time there'd been a showdown like this was in college. I remember being in my bathroom with ringing in my ears as darkness seeped in from the edge of my field of vision. Watching the red pool on the white tile grow as the black circle closed around it. At six o'clock the next morning I was released from the hospital. A cop drove me home. He dropped me off at my apartment and I threw up walking back to my door. I knelt there for a moment and watched it freeze. I never thought I'd be that tired again. Demons are exhausting. When I finally made it into my apartment, I sat at my desk and thought about what had happened. My blood had spurted across the white bedroom wall in a long arch. A rainbow of blood. Right across my copy of *Taxi Driver*. Travis Bickle's bloody face was staring at me. I sat there asking him questions for over an hour before I had to go to class.

Who am I? Why am I here? What do you do about the loneliness?

Mohawk eyes.

The ER doctor who saw me said that most people who lose that much blood pass out and void their bowels. I'd almost died, alone in a dark puddle of wasted suffering on my cold bathroom floor.

But I didn't. Why?

Why?

It was useless. My mind was shot. A fat drop of blood fell out of my nose onto my white cotton shirt and brought me back to the cathedral steps. I'd been staring at my reflection, searching for answers in the gray ice water.

All I could think about was K—.

This may come as a shock, but I went to work the next day. I went home, showered, put on another suit, and reported for work on time. Even though I had practically lost all ability to function. I made a mistake that day that turned my boss's opinion of me, and by the end of the project, neither of us thought it was a good fit. In my exit interview, he said, "John, you're one of the smartest people who's ever worked for me, but you don't belong here."

I couldn't agree more.

As I was walking out of 666 Fifth Avenue for the last time on the day before Christmas Eve, Ian McKellen passed me on the street.

Gandalf.

The dreams.

I turned around and chased after him.

I had to make sure it was real.

"Sir Ian?"

He looked.

"Sir Ian, I just wanted to say that I admire your work very much. Thank you for everything you've done."

He smiled and said, "Oh, you dear boy, thank you very much. I look forward to seeing some of your work someday. Good evening."

"Good evening, Sir."

And I let him walk off.

This time it wasn't a dream.

I met Gandalf on Fifty-second Street.

And he was wearing a neon-green trench coat and a blue fedora.

* * *

Paulina and I kept in touch. She was a great storyteller, and she always wanted a meal after she climbed out of a K-hole, so I'd take her to diners now and then. She died about a year after we met. The funeral was held on a bleak Sunday morning in February way up in the Bronx. Afterwards, Officer Ortiz drove me home again and, just like last time, we didn't speak. We had nothing to say to each other. He drove. I looked out the window. I never told him where to take me though, so he took me to the same address I'd given him last time. A little stretch of Fifth Avenue that runs between Forty-ninth and Fifty-first streets in middle of Manhattan. The most damnably confounding place in the whole godless world.

This time the tourists were gone and the sales were over. Mr. Rockefeller had taken down his tree and Saks Fifth Avenue had packed up their music-and-light show. They were having mass at Saint Patrick's, and Atlas and I stood on the street and listened to the heavenly sound of the pipe organ and the congregation singing praises. Gandalf had stopped invading my dreams, but I didn't have any answers. I've thought about all this a lot since it happened, and I'm still not sure about anything.

Who am I? Why am I here? What do you do about the loneliness?

I shook my head and looked up at the sky as the music played on.

And—of all Goddamned things—it started to snow.

Behold, the Face of God

Now it came to pass in the thirtieth year, in the fourth month, in the
fifth day of the month, as I was among the captives by the river of
Chebar, that the heavens were opened, and I saw visions of God.
—Ezekiel 1:1 (KJV)

Diodorus Siculus relates the story of a broken and scattered god, a story which, like that of the scattered body of Osiris or the fall of Babel, invokes a universal recognition in the human heart that there is something infinite and holy that has been either lost or denied to us. The blessed Argentine epistolary Borges conjures this visage of "The True Portrait of the Holy Face of God" and yearns to behold "My Lord, Jesus Christ, true God" and the fashion of his semblance, while lamenting that—even if we were to find the paradise of this single true face of God in the labyrinths of our own dreams—we would not know it tomorrow. He postulates that perhaps the face lurks in every mirror or was willfully obliterated by the Christ himself so that God could be all of us. Wherefore it is said by the beloved apostle John that, "no man hath seen God at any time; the only begotten Son, which is in the bosom of the Father, he hath declared him."

Blood Covenant

The Church therefore functions as the means by which the Eucharist, of bread and wine, through the Mystery of Transubstantiation, may have its essence changed into that of the body and blood of Christ. Once received by the communicants, Holy Communion between God and Man through Jesus Christ, and only Jesus Christ, is made possible. As Simon Peter writes, "For Christ also suffered once for sins, the righteous for the unrighteous, to bring you to God."

In Remembrance of Me

In the days when Satan tested him, Job repeatedly cried out for someone to stand in the gap between himself and the throne of God to restore harmony. We have gained in Christ the mediator sought by Job, but the agony of this gift is that using a mediator requires that one be made acutely aware of their separation from God—seeing only shadows, as Paul, the least of the Apostles, writes in his Epistle to the Hebrews—but never beholding with waking eyes the true and complete face of God. For which reason men through time have sought to recover this lost knowledge of the true and perfect image of God denied to them since Adam's fall.

Raphael's fresco in the Vatican, "The Disputation of the Holy Sacrament," depicts a scene with the Holy Trinity and the heavenly host presiding over the Eucharist while those below on Earth debate the controversial sacrament. This debate has now raged from more than two millennia.

The Light-Bearer

Christ's position as God's mediator has made him the target of jealous attacks. Therefore, some of the more blasphemous heretical sects of occult and esoteric Christian Luciferian Gnosticism have portrayed Christ not as a savior and mediator, but as a tyrannical, selfish obstructionist. Those who take this view often find themselves seduced by the temptation to seek unnatural means through which to circumvent the mediation of Christ and gain direct audience with God the Father.

Total Cinema

This radical doctrine which seeks to supplant Christ has given rise to many bastard theurgical practices, but none of such great import as Andre Bazin's ancient, theoretical notion of *Total Cinema*. By which we mean to say the deliberate and permanent dissolution of the natural barrier dividing Life and Art—and by extension—the Artist and God, which would eliminate the need for Christ and Holy Communion through the Church and bring the Artist into oneness with God.

Art instead of Eucharist. Bread into Body. Wine into Blood. Lead into Gold. Art into Life. Man into God.

Although Bazin is known for formalizing the idea of Total Cinema, he is certainly not its originator. Therefore, in order to better understand the project of Total Cinema, it may be useful to investigate the origin of this idea. However, the invocation of precepts taken from Thomas Mann show that—when seeking any point of origin, such as the face of God—the origin is "unfathomable." The genesis of Total Cinema, the seventh and perfect Art of God, is no different. But the beginning and end of all literature is myth, so it may be that all forms of Art are part of an infinite cycle of metaphor and myth. Paradoxically, it may be said that *Don Quixote* marks the origin of the modern novel.

So let us begin there.

The Quixote

The authorship of Cervantes being a trivial matter of circumstance, the true power of *The Quixote* comes from a subtle understanding of the author's partial use of "magick." The author of *The Quixote* was inspired by the figure of a golden idol of Mohammed—the reproduction of whose likeness is wisely forbidden—which was cast in secret by craftsmen skilled in metallurgy who had been blinded before creating the figure and then killed in sacrifice immediately afterwards. The figure was stolen by Montalban and after many centuries was rediscovered somewhere in the vast geographies of Spain, "in the valley of the Moon, where the time wasted by dreams is contained." After seeing this golden figure, Cervantes wrote *The Quixote*.

The Quixote is a work of realism, not in the sense that it excludes the supernatural in order to show the marvelous in the everyday, as Conrad, James, and other nineteenth-century realists do, but rather in that it reveals reality through the juxtaposition of prosaic and imaginary worlds between which Don Quixote moves freely. *The Quixote* mingles the subjective and the objective, the natural and the supernatural. It blends the realities of the reader and the book into one. Cervantes achieves this supernatural feat through the ingenious method of writing a second part of *The Quixote* in which the characters themselves read Part One. Just as Don Quixote insists that the windmills be made into knights, Cervantes insists that his protagonists be made into his readers, and his readers be made into his protagonists. Thus, Cervantes has achieved alchemical transubstantiation.

Lead into Gold. Wine into Blood. Windmills into Men. Man into God.

Art into Life. Life into Art.

Virtual reality.

Total Cinema.

Magnum Opus

In the same manner, we see God's Shakespeare include within his *Hamlet* a staged tragedy almost identical to the tragedy of Hamlet himself, "wherein I'll [Hamlet] catch the conscience of the King." This tragedy within a tragedy is useful for understanding the goal of Total Cinema. Through the creation of Art wherein the Artist and God are One, the Artist attempts to glimpse the true face of God in himself.

This ambition is not limited to literature and theater but has also been attempted in film. Charlie Kaufman is a particularly zealous practitioner of this religion. *Adaptation* is a movie about a screenwriter writing the screenplay for the movie he is in and *Synecdoche, New York*, is a film about a director whose play is the size of the world itself. Total Cinema then becomes equal to The Magnum Opus or The Great Work of Alchemy. The Philosopher's Stone. Infinite Jest.

Therefore, we must fail to reject Thomas Carlyle's hypothesis of 1833 that the history of the universe is an infinite sacred book that all men read, write, and try to understand— and in which they are also written.

Or put more simply—

The Universe is *The Quixote*.

Philosophy and the Infinite

However, the Artist is not alone in seeking this synthetic apotheosis but is joined in his labors by the Philosopher.

Plato's solutions to Zeno's nine surviving paradoxes, including the famous infinite stack of tortoises, represent the earliest attempts to grapple with *reductio ad absurdum*, or "reduction to absurdity." Thinkers taking Plato's side against Zeno's skepticism have filled millennia with arguments arising from these paradoxes. However, Zeno has proven difficult to defeat.

Jacques Derrida, in his lecture at Johns Hopkins University, points out that the logocentrism of Western philosophy is flawed in that it misunderstands the linguistic lessons of Wittgenstein's *Tractatus Logico-Philosophicus*. Derrida seeks to deconstruct all meaning through observing the eternal deference inherent to all language and logical systems. In other words, because all ideas expressed in language or logic are only able to be understood in reference to other parts of the same arbitrary system, they invariably create a large network of circular reference that is self-defeating and provably meaningless.

In the context of this dissolution of meaning through philosophy, efforts at creating Total Cinema to circumvent Christ lead back to this same infinite loop of deferred meaning. In his first volume, *The World and The Individual*, Josiah Royce formulated the thought experiment of the creation of a perfect and complete map of England on a section of soil in England. This map would therefore contain a map of the map itself, and so on into infinity.

Therefore, even Carlyle's hypothesis, although impossible to reject, is useless. There is nothing in these metaphors. The infinite is meaningless because it cannot be comprehended by the finite.

Absurdity.

Therefore, let us approach it from a different perspective.

View From the East

In many Eastern traditions, the initiate is not taught that the image of God is lost, but rather that each individual is part of the image itself and therefore must simply be reminded of their oneness with all things and with God. If the initiate can clear the mirror of their mind, freeing themselves from all illusions, they may then behold the true and perfect face of the attribute-less primordial Buddha—which is to say, their own true self—which is to say, the perfect face of God.

The Dharma, the Tao, and others acknowledge no

separation from God by sin, but a forgetfulness of oneness brought about by life, which is seen as "a festival of disruption." Since there is no way to stop life without causing death, it is necessary to find a way to prevent illusions from causing forgetfulness of oneness. The only solution is to stand in the place of God and take control of life, which leads back to the myth of Total Cinema. We are left facing the same paradox. The Eastern metaphors link hands with those of the West and reinforce the inscrutable web of circular infinity with which God has imprisoned human consciousness.

The Universe as God's Prison

If by reading this you have become frustrated, confused, or exasperated—then you have done well and ought to be commended. The angst you feel is that created by assailing the enclosure of human agnostic consciousness designed by God to torment those who would seek to circumvent his Christ. We are locked inside the dimensional trap of the space-time universe by God, who exists outside of it. Consequently, trying to see Him or commune with Him becomes an absurd exercise in maddening futility, as addressed by Homer in *The Odyssey* and by Kubrick in *2001*.

We are without the sensory or intellectual faculties with which to comprehend God and therefore remain trapped in space-time and myth. The only means of escape is to either accept His Christ or wriggle out of the trap. So let us try again.

The Fearful Sphere

Six centuries before the Christian era, the rhapsodist Xenophanes of Colophon wearied of the Homeric verses that he traveled from city to city reciting. In an attack on the poets and their myths which attributed anthropomorphic traits to the gods, he offered to the Greeks a single God, a God who was an eternal sphere.

As history progressed, these gods Xenophanes had denounced were demoted to figments of poetic fiction. One of the gods, Hermes Trismegistus, dictated several books—forty-two, according to Clement of Alexandria. It is said that in these books are written all things. This divine library, the *Corpus Hermeticum*, tragically has been fragmented and dispersed by those seeking its knowledge, much like the scattered god of Diodorus Siculus.

Near the end of the twelfth century, the French theologian Insulis discovered the following lines written on a fragment of parchment attributed to this library and to Hermes Trismegistus himself: "God is an intelligible sphere whose center is everywhere and whose circumference is nowhere." This seems to play on the words of Solomon unto whom God appeared twice: "The heavens and heaven of heavens cannot contain thee."

Years later, the idea from Insulis's parchment would produce the heliocentric model in Nicolaus Copernicus's *De Revolutionibus Orbium Coelestium* (*On the Revolutions of the Heavenly Spheres*). This revelation was a liberation for Giordano Bruno, who said in *La Cena de le Ceneri* that the world is the infinite effect of an infinite cause, and that divinity is close by, "for it is within us even more than we ourselves are within ourselves."

However, in time, this liberation turned into a feeling of being lost.

The Labyrinth and the Abyss

If the future and the past are infinite, and if all beings are equidistant from the infinite and the infinitesimal, then it is impossible for a man to know when or where he is or the size of his own countenance, let alone that of God. Added to this came the notion that, as the gods of the poets had been demoted by the fearful sphere of the eternal and single God, so too had man been continually declining in all attributes since Adam's sin. The seventeenth-century clergyman Robert South said, "An Aristotle was but the rubbish of an Adam, and Athens but the rudiments of Paradise."

In other words, we were losing more of ourselves—more of God—over time.

Upon reaching the genius-Christian mind of Blaise Pascal, the idea that Xenophanes had conjured as a liberation from myth had become a labyrinth and an abyss. "What is Man? A Nothing. Compared to The Infinite," he lamented. Pascal abhorred the universe and sought to adore God, but all he encountered was the universe. He likened this experience to that of a castaway on a desert island. Pascal expressed his feelings by saying that, "nature is an infinite sphere, whose center is everywhere and whose circumference is nowhere." The arrival of the nineteenth century brought with it the holy saint Kierkegaard, who did not abhor this abyss, but rather implored man to look into it with radical faith. Extoling the virtue of silent inwardness, he described his beloved God as, "a sphere of infinite depth." But as Nietzsche was quick to point out, "if thou gaze long into an abyss, the abyss will also gaze into thee."

And so it may be possible that all of the history of philosophy, theology, and art may be understood as a series of slightly different attempts to articulate the same metaphors in an effort to sum up the futile efforts of human beings to see the true, infinite, and perfect face of God—which simultaneously and paradoxically exists within us but beyond the bounds of the prison of our universe and the limits of our own comprehension.

Visions of God

The final cruelty of all of this is, of course, that at times God has revealed himself to prophets.

Holy Moses saw part of God and gave Israel the law so that they might know a semblance of his likeness.

After his encounters with God, great King Solomon counted all things in the Earth as mere vanities and lost his soul in an effort to escape our prison and gain power and contact with the Divine.

The blessed prophet Ezekiel beheld visions of God and struggled in vain to describe what he beheld—saying he had seen "a wheel within a wheel."

Like a map within a map, or a play within a play, or a book within a book—on and on into deranged infinity.

Transcendentalists

Emerson and the American Transcendentalists suggested true being as that of an eye that is nothing but sees all and is part and particle with God. This may be a delusional self-idealization created by consciousness to reconcile itself with its own existence because this idea is prevalent, in some form, in nearly all philosophy and theology in both the East and the West.

Locke shows that we rely on observation and reflection to create theories, but Descartes and the skeptics show that we can't trust our senses. This leaves us with no way to reliably accept or reject any hypothesis taken up. So finally, one must take it on faith to believe whatever one chooses about the enigma of God and existence. The result is Kierkegaard and Abraham. Maybe we must all submit to God's plan of salvation by grace through faith in Christ manifested by acts.

Maybe that's all. Or maybe not. Maybe nothing. Maybe everything.

Be Thou My Vision

It may also be that Augustine and Aquinas's idea of the beatific vision applies to this infinity paradox of the face of God. Augustine, writing of his epiphany of God, says that God was, "more inward than my own inwardness," and, "eternally more intimate to me than I am to myself." He advises others who wish to see God to, "turn inward and look upward."

Thomas Aquinas's *Summa Theologiae* is still one of the most revered works about God ever produced. However, he left this great work unfinished after a vision he experienced during the feast of St. Nicholas in 1273. Aquinas said, "I can write no more. I have seen things that make my writings like straw." He died three months later.

Augustine and Aquinas seem to teach that the true and perfect face of God does not exist in the external world, but rather as internal experiential phenomena.

Therefore, if this labyrinth of metaphor and myth is the best approximation of the image of God that man is capable of conceiving, then through contemplation of it mankind may be able to peek through the prison bars of the universe at the infinite face of God. This is the darkness above the light.

The Transcendentalist film style of Bresson, Ozu, Dreyer, Schrader, and the Apostate Apostle of Cinema, Martin Scorsese, seeks to force the audience into an encounter with "The Wholly Other" of the spiritual realm outside of the universe. It is then up to each individual audience member to make sense of this phenomenon in their own way. This is the true definition of a "cinematic experience" or a "beatific vision".

But for God's sake, don't look too long, or you will go irretrievably insane.

Authorship

Originality is not only unfathomable, but also an illusion.

Xenophanes of Colophon denied teaching that God was an eternal sphere and named several others who taught the same thing.

The writings attributed to Hermes Trismegistus, Thoth,

and many other ancient gods are not exclusively their own work, but the product of many authors.

The Holy Bible was written by several people, many of whom are unknown, or simply guessed at.

The story of Christ is the sum of many witnesses.

Moses did not write all the law himself.

Plato's work is a collection of ideas from many thinkers.

Cervantes claimed to have bought the manuscript of *The Quixote* from an Arabian mystic and had it translated at great expense.

Shakespeare's plays were not entirely written by him—but are the products of many authors.

And I—John—have not written almost anything in this book. God alone is all things. When we reach the end of our space-time prison, we will leave it and, God willing, join God. The history of the universe is that of many, and of one, of one, and of many. And it is God's.

"Every man is born as many men and dies as a single one."—Heidegger

Everything and Nothing

One final myth, not of an age, but for all time. This one by Borges.

Upon finding himself in the presence of God, Shakespeare told Him, "I who have been so many men in vain want to be one and myself."

The voice of the Lord answered from a whirlwind: "Neither am I anyone; I have dreamt the world as you dreamt your work, my Shakespeare, and among the forms in my dreams are you, who like myself are many and no one."

Shakespeare, after speaking with God, sold his theater and wrote no more plays in this universe. He died on April 23, 1616.

Vanquished by reality, Don Quixote died in his native village in 1614. He was survived but a short time by Miguel de Cervantes.

Ezekiel last experienced an encounter with God in April, 570 BC. His time of death has not been recorded.

On Christmas Day 2016, Martin Scorsese released *Silence*.

Beside the lobby of the Hotel Chelsea on West 23rd Street in Manhattan is a Spanish restaurant that has been there since 1930.

The name of that restaurant,

is El Quijote.

It's closed for renovation.

Behold, the Face of God

here lies bob dylan
killed by a discarded Oedipus
who turned
around
to investigate a ghost
& discovered that
the ghost too
was more than one person
-bob dylan

Blasphemy

In October 1967, near the height of his fame, Johnny Cash crawled into the Nickajack Cave not far from his home in Memphis, Tennessee with nothing but a flashlight and a bag of amphetamines. That cave system stretches all the way to Alabama and has some chambers the size of three football stadiums. His intention was to crawl until the flashlight went out, and then take the drugs until he died alone in the dark.

After about three hours, his flashlight went out. Darkness gripped him. Cash later wrote, "The absolute lack of light was appropriate, for at that moment I was as far from God as I have ever been. My separation from Him, the deepest and most ravaging of the various kinds of loneliness I'd felt over the years, seemed finally complete."

Cash prayed to God to forgive him and lead him out. Miraculously, Johnny Cash crawled on bleeding elbows through the darkness to an exit he had never been to before and found his wife June and his mother waiting outside with food and blankets. Johnny records June as saying that they both just had a feeling that he needed their help. None of them could explain how they found him.

Cash said, "There in Nickajack Cave I became conscious of a very clear, simple idea: I was not in charge of my own destiny ... I was going to die at God's time, not mine."

Who am I? Why am I here? What do you do about the loneliness?

God knows.

Cash's story, of course, is not true. But, then again, of course it is. It is the impossible fantasy of a deranged mind, and it is also the ecstatic truth of all things revealed by the experience of an individual.

Cash said when God called him out of the cave he felt "a sensation of utter peace, clarity and sobriety."

I guess that's why I wrote this book. Articulate the ineffable. Finitize the infinite. Commune with the Holy. Comprehend paradox.

The main entrance to Rockefeller Plaza bears the words of Isaiah: "Wisdom and knowledge shall be the stability of thy times."

Above these words, the fingers of a pagan god form the masonic square and compass representing the Hermetic maxim, "As above, so below."

Crowley said, "Do what thou wilt shall be the whole of the law."

Augustine said, "Love, and do what thou wilt."

Hermes and Jehovah. The Church of Satan and the Church of Christ.

When John Lennon said that the Beatles were bigger than Jesus, it was blasphemy, and it was true.

In the chaos between these facts lies the eternal echo of Kierkegaard's laughter and a heartbroken man in a black suit standing alone in the middle of Fifth Avenue with the gods and devils of all ages making war in his soul.

Seeking Christ's light in Lucifer's darkness. Praying to God in a Satanic nation.

On the gravestone of Johnny Cash are written the words of King David: "Let the words of my mouth, and the meditation of my heart, be acceptable in thy sight, O LORD, my strength, and my redeemer." Psalms 19:14

* * *

The dawn is coming through my window now, and soon I will be lost in longing dreams of the grace in her eyes.

Such sweet nightmares.

I know I should love everyone the way I love her.

Like Jesus does.

But I don't.

I am not Jesus.

And I don't want to be.

Like Bob Dylan said,

all I can do is be me.

Whoever that is.

And so, I will wake in the morning.

And try to start lovin' again.

May the grace of our Lord Jesus Christ be with you all.

Amen.

Acknowledgments

My sincere thanks to Paul Cohen, Colin Rolfe, Dory Mayo, and everyone at Epigraph for their help in publishing this book.

To Alexandra DeSanctis for her friendship and gracious help in my struggle with language.

To Phoebe for reading this and telling me it was frustrating (sorry).

Alex Cook for being my dearest friend and for teaching me about literature.

Celeste for the Molto Holy Moments.

John Milus and Paul Schrader. Robert Zimmerman and Hank Williams. Elvis Presley, John Wayne, and the soul of Johnny Cash.

To all the women that I have loved and all the women who've loved me.

To my brothers and my parents.

And most of all,

to Marty.

With Love and resolution,
John

Author:

At ten years old, John Matthew Gillen was sent to a Christian summer camp. Campers were allowed one elective activity. Out of four hundred campers, John was the only one who chose Storytelling. The camp director asked him to choose another class so they wouldn't have to offer Storytelling that year.

John refused.

Since then, he has been fired for writing poetry at work, cussed out by the Chief Clerk of the United States Supreme Court, and has spent over $10,000 on tickets to Bob Dylan concerts.

In addition to writing and directing short films in New York, John's work has appeared in literary publications including *The Laurel Review*, *Storgy Magazine*, and *The New Guard Literary Review*. His favorite authors include Jorge Luis Borges and Hank Bukowski, and he harbors a deep reverence for Martin Scorsese. Manhattan is his home.

If you enjoyed this book, please leave a review. I read them all personally and appreciate your feedback. For updates on future projects, visit www.johnmatthewgillen.com